PURSUED

Books by Lisa Harris

SOUTHERN CRIMES

Dangerous Passage
Fatal Exchange
Hidden Agenda

THE NIKKI BOYD FILES

Vendetta
Missing
Pursued

THE NIKKI BOYD FILES, #3

PURSUED

LISA HARRIS

Revell

a division of Baker Publishing Group
Grand Rapids, Michigan

Published by Revell
a division of Baker Publishing Group
P.O. Box 6287, Grand Rapids, MI 49516-6287
www.revellbooks.com

Printed in the United States of America

Library of Congress Cataloging-in-Publication Data
Names: Harris, Lisa, 1969– author.
Title: Pursued / Lisa Harris.
Description: Grand Rapids, MI : Revell, a division of Baker Publishing Group,
   [2017] | Series: The Nikki Boyd files ; #3
Identifiers: LCCN 2016050408| ISBN 9780800724207 (pbk.) | ISBN 9780800728564
   (print on demand)
Subjects: LCSH: Women detectives—Fiction. | Missing persons—Investigation—
   Fiction. | Murder—Investigation—Fiction. | GSAFD: Christian fiction. | Mystery
   fiction. | Suspense fiction.
Classification: LCC PS3608.A78315 P87 2017 | DDC 813/.6—dc23
LC record available at https://lccn.loc.gov/2016050408

Published in association with Joyce Hart of Hartline Literary Agency, LLC.

18 19 20 21 22 23   7 6 5 4 3 2

To the Master Storyteller
who pursues us
and longs to bring us home.

For our light and momentary troubles are achieving for us an eternal glory that far outweighs them all.

2 Corinthians 4:17 NIV

1

Nikki Boyd grabbed the armrest of the aisle seat as the plane
hit another air pocket and the FASTEN SEAT BELT light flickered
on above row 29 on the Airbus. Her stomach lurched at the
sensation, rattling her nerves like it had throughout the past
hour of the flight.

"Ladies and gentlemen, the captain has just turned on the
seat belt sign again. We need all passengers to return to their
seats immediately and ensure that your seat belt is on."

Nikki frowned, not amused with the flight attendant's sing-
song voice making it sound as if they were on a ride at an amuse-
ment park instead of thirty thousand feet above the ground,
flying on the edges of a storm. She tugged on the end of her seat
belt, then glanced out the window, where rain slashed against
the pane and streaks of lightning flashed in the distance. Flying
on a commercial airline across the country should be a piece
of cake compared to her day job, where risking her life had
become routine. If one could ever call risking one's life routine.

Shooting up another prayer that they'd make it to Nashville safely, she let go of the armrest and slid out the photo of Tyler Grant tucked away in the pocket of the e-reader in her lap. She willed herself to relax. If she were honest, the constant turbulence over the past hour wasn't the only thing that had her stomach tied up in knots. Even more nerve-wracking than the bumpy flight was the fact that Tyler would be waiting for her once they touched down.

The plane dipped again, rattling her tray table. The twenty-something brunette sitting in the middle seat beside her snapped shut the book she'd had her nose buried in most of the trip and gripped both armrests. "I thought reading would distract me, but even that's not helping anymore."

"You okay?" Nikki asked as the other woman grabbed a couple pills from her purse and washed them down with a half-empty bottle of water.

"I will be once we land." She shoved the bottle back into the seat pocket. "The next time I have to make this trip, though, I'm going to drive."

"Hopefully we'll be through this turbulence soon," Nikki said, catching a flicker of fear in the woman's brown eyes. "But I'm sure we'll be fine. I've always heard flying is safer than driving."

"Maybe, but a lot can go wrong at thirty thousand feet." She clutched the book between her fingers until her knuckles turned white. "Sorry. It's just that I was nervous about this trip before I stepped on the plane. Add a turbulent flight and I feel like my heart's about to burst out of my chest."

Nikki nodded, wondering how the man sitting next to the window with the military haircut had managed to sleep through the entire nerve-wracking flight without noticing the light display across the darkening skyline outside his window. She flicked the edge of Tyler's photo with the edge of her fingernail, completely understanding the woman's unease. She wasn't the only one trying to get her nerves in check.

"Boyfriend? Husband?" the woman said, then shot her an apologetic look. "I know it's none of my business, but he's gorgeous."

Nikki chuckled at the description, but as far as she was concerned, the woman was right. She'd taken the photo of him three months ago, right before Tyler had left for Liberia. As former military, he still wore his hair short. Add to that a five-o'clock shadow and those familiar brown eyes that could always see straight through her, and yeah . . . he was definitely gorgeous.

"He's . . ." Nikki paused, trying to find a logical response to the question. "Honestly, I'm not sure what to call him. It's a long story, actually. And a bit complicated."

Nikki slipped the photo back into the e-reader. She never talked about her personal life with strangers. Or her job and certainly not her relationships. And talking about Tyler was definitely personal. Three months ago, he'd left for Liberia to work with the State Department in an effort to help improve regional stability. That and to figure out how to deal with life as a single dad and widower. But before he left, he'd asked her to wait for him. Something she was still half certain she'd dreamed up. Because not very long ago she would have laughed at the idea of falling in love with her best friend's husband. Then somehow over the past few months, everything had changed.

"I've got time for complicated." The other woman grinned. "Because by the look in your eyes, I'm thinking you're already smitten."

"You can tell that by my eyes?" No. Nikki wasn't ready to believe that she was actually that far gone.

"Definitely. I've always been told I'm perceptive. When it comes to other people's relationships anyway. My own perceptions of men usually leave something to be desired."

Nikki laughed, still not ready to admit the woman was right. "For now, he's just a friend. Well, maybe a bit more than a friend. He's been overseas the past three months, so we've never even been on an official date. I've been waiting for him to come back so we can figure things out."

Three months in Liberia had been the perfect combination of time away to figure out his new role in life, as well as giving him the extra experience he needed that would allow him a foothold into a new career path here in the US.

Nikki's finger ran along the edge of his photo. And time for him to decide if he was ready to start a new relationship after losing Katie. Something she knew she couldn't do for him. What she hoped, though, was that after being away for so long, he'd discovered there was a place for her—full time—in his life.

The woman beside her glanced down at the book she'd been reading. "Sounds far more romantic than this story. So no wedding plans yet?"

"Wedding plans?" Nikki felt a blush creep across her face at the personal question. No. They definitely weren't at that stage. Not that she hadn't thought about it. When that day did come, she knew her mother would try to talk her only daughter into a large, catered reception in some swanky Nashville hotel ballroom, but all she wanted was a small wedding and reception at her church with family and a few close friends.

She brushed away the thought. "No. A wedding—even if it does happen—won't be for a long, long time."

The plane hit another pocket of turbulence, rattling the carts in the galley behind them.

Nikki glanced out the window at the darkening sky, wondering if the bad weather was going to follow them all the way to Nashville. The problem was, talking about Tyler was not only personal, it was still new. Something she preferred to think about while she was by herself. And while her mother had a habit of trying to set her up with men she believed to be perfect marriage material, Nikki hadn't even told anyone in her family about her relationship with Tyler. Which was why saying it out loud made it feel real.

While he'd been in Liberia, they'd stayed connected via Skype and texts. And while they hadn't exactly skirted around the subject of their relationship, it wasn't the same as the two of them sitting down face-to-face and exploring their feelings. But she hadn't minded. Building a relationship that went beyond friendship was going to take time, something she was willing to take. Tyler had gone from being her best friend's husband, to a grieving widower, to the man who'd managed to completely steal her heart. Completely unplanned. Completely unexpected. And yet she knew for herself, anyway, there was no turning back to just the friendship they'd had for so many years.

She really had no idea what the future held. The only thing she did know was that whatever did happen, she wanted to spend that future with him. But getting to that point—for both of them—wasn't going to be easy.

If she closed her eyes for a moment, she could feel the lingering kiss he'd given her at the airport the day he'd told her goodbye. Their first kiss had left her breathless and promising she'd wait for him. But the waiting had been harder than she'd expected.

"Is he going to be there to pick you up?" The woman's question pulled her out of her thoughts.

Nikki glanced at her watch and nodded as another wave of anticipation fluttered through her. She'd been counting down the weeks to his return. Then the days. Then the hours. And now she could finally count the minutes. They'd land in twenty. In another ten or so she'd be at the baggage claim, where he'd promised to meet her. His scheduled return hadn't exactly meshed with hers. He arrived back in Nashville three days ago. Four days after she'd left for a week of required training in Houston. On the positive side, she knew it had given him time to connect again with his son, Liam, leaving her out of the mix. But that hadn't taken away her longing to be there with him. With both of them.

"What about you?" Nikki asked, ready to change the subject. "Going to visit family?"

"Now, that's a long story," she said with a laugh. "I lived in Nashville for a long time, then moved to Houston because of a guy. I'm coming back to see some old friends and take care of some business." She glanced at the man next to her, but he was still asleep and wasn't paying attention to either of them. "Your relationship sounds so romantic. Mine on the other hand . . . well . . . it's been pretty turbulent."

Nikki wasn't sure what to read into the statement. An abusive boyfriend? Cheating spouse?

"Relationships can be complicated sometimes," Nikki said. Tyler had told her their relationship didn't have to be complicated, but she still wasn't sure that was possible.

"Though I am looking forward to one thing while I'm there," the woman continued. "I'm a bit of a country music fan. I never miss a chance to go to at least a concert or two when I'm in town."

Nikki smiled, not minding the conversation, but glad the subject had finally shifted away from Tyler. "My brother's one of the hundreds of aspiring musicians, so I go listen to him play from time to time."

The plane dipped again, shuddering from side to side.

"I'm not sure how much more of this I can take." The woman's face paled as she turned to look out the window. "And on top of that, they booked me in a middle seat. I hate the middle seat." She leaned over to slide her book into her bag, then groaned as her watch snagged on her red cardigan and dropped into her lap. "Can you believe I just had the clasp fixed?"

Nikki looked at the beautiful detail on the watch. "It's lovely."

"Thanks—it was my mother's, and—"

A deafening explosion rocked the back of the plane before the woman could finish. Nikki's stomach heaved as the plane dropped several hundred feet. She glanced out the window and caught a glimpse of the forested ground below. This wasn't normal turbulence. Something was very wrong.

"This is the pilot speaking. I need everyone to stay calm and brace for impact. We're expecting a rough landing."

A coffeepot smashed to the floor as the plane made a sharp descent. Someone screamed behind her. Nikki glanced at her seatmate's terrified expression as she leaned forward and braced herself on the seat in front of her. The man at the end of the row was now wide awake as the plane plummeted toward the ground. Her mind spun, unable to focus. So this was what it was like to die? To watch her life flash before her during these final seconds? Her parents, her sister, Tyler . . .

Her body strained against the seat belt. Funny how she'd accepted years ago that the possibility of dying in the line of duty was high, but this way—a plane crash—this was never what she'd imagined.

And why was it that all of a sudden she felt like so many things had been left undone? So many things she wanted to tell her family. Instead, all that was left was a fleeting kaleidoscope of memories of people she loved. Random thoughts of things she wanted to say to her family and friends.

Like how her parents had already lost her sister. How were they going to survive the loss of another child?

And then there was Tyler—

I'm not ready to die, God. Not yet.

Nikki held her breath as the ground rose up to meet them. Instead of panicked screams, the passengers around her seemed lost in a state of confusion. As if the reality of what was happening had yet to fully sink in. The feeling of weightlessness washed over her as gravity seemed to disappear completely, and the landscape appeared beside them in the window. Then for a few brief seconds after impact there was only silence.

2

Nikki's shoulder slammed against the seat in front of her as the plane skidded for several more seconds before finally jerking to a stop. Baggage tumbled from the overhead bins. Someone whimpered in the seat behind her.

Ignoring the pain shooting down her arm, Nikki glanced out the window toward an open field, wondering where they'd landed. While the pilot had clearly missed the runway, it didn't look like they'd hit any buildings. But there was no way to see where they really were until they disembarked.

An eerie silence swept through the plane. Nikki glanced around the cabin. The air smelled like smoke and burning plastic. Passengers started moving as she unbuckled her seat belt. She'd heard about the ninety-second rule somewhere. That the first ninety seconds after a crash were the most important. That your odds of survival were much greater if you simply stayed calm and got off the plane as quickly as possible. Because if the plane caught on fire . . .

Nikki pushed away the thought. Years of crisis training helped stave the panic, but still everything seemed to move in slow motion. She ran her hands across her legs and then her arms and forehead. As far as she could tell there were no signs of blood. No signs of broken bones. All she could feel was a dull ache from the impact of her shoulder that would probably feel sore for the next few days. But shock could cover up pain.

One of the flight attendants spoke loudly, informing everyone to stay calm and to file off the plane in an orderly fashion as quickly as possible, and that emergency personnel were already arriving at the scene. Nikki pressed her hand against her chest. Funny how calm the woman's voice was while her own heart was racing out of control. She was used to dealing with crises happening on a daily basis. But they usually occurred to someone else, and she managed to stay neutral and keep her emotions uninvolved. That's what she did. But this . . . this was different.

Sunlight filtered through the cracks seven or eight rows in front of them where the plane looked as if it had ripped in two like a child's toy. Her own seat was tilted at a sharp angle with her seatmates slightly above her. Someone opened the emergency door behind them. A flash of lightning from the stormy sky briefly lit up the inside of the plane.

The woman in the middle seat clutched Nikki's forearm as she started to stand up.

"I think he's dead." She was staring at the man beside her, her voice laced with panic. "The man next to me. He's dead."

"You never told me your name." Nikki leaned over to check on the man. Had he even moved since they'd landed? She didn't think so.

"It's Erika," the woman said above the noise of the passengers.

"Erika, I need you to take a deep breath and try to relax. We'll be off the plane before you know it."

Their seatmate was leaning against the window, his hands

limp at his sides. His neck twisted at an odd angle. She noticed the air marshal badge clipped to his belt. He couldn't be dead. Could he?

Nikki touched the man's shoulder. "Sir . . . sir, we need to get off the plane. I can help you if you're hurt."

There was no response.

Balancing with one knee on her seat while reaching around Erika, Nikki turned the man's shoulder slightly, then felt her breath catch. He was staring straight ahead; his glassy eyes were vacant. Surely he hadn't died in the crash. She grabbed his hand and felt for his pulse.

Nothing. No pulse. No breathing.

The man was dead.

Erika's fingers dug into Nikki's forearm. "I need to get off this plane."

Nikki pulled her arm away gently. "It's going to be okay. Just try and take a deep breath. Everyone's going to get off."

"No . . . No. You don't understand. I've got to get out of here now."

Erika's hands were shaking. Blood trickled down her forehead and across her cheek from a cut above her eye. Nikki fumbled for a napkin from the seat pocket and handed it to her.

"Press this against the cut on your head."

Erika nodded, then shoved past her toward the congested aisle. Someone sobbed in the background. The smell of smoke hung in the air. A flight attendant was giving directions for the passengers to leave suitcases behind and make their way toward the emergency exit at the back of the plane as quickly as possible.

Instinct kicked in. She'd have to deal with the emotional impact of the crash later, but for now, her own fear of what could have happened vanished, replaced by what she'd been trained to do in a crisis.

Nikki took one last look at the man who'd sat two seats from her, knowing there was nothing she could do to help him now. She grabbed her small bag containing her badge and wallet, secured it across her shoulder, then paused. She picked up the silver diamond-studded watch from the seat where Erika must have dropped it during the crash. She looked toward the back exit where the emergency slide had been deployed, but there was no sign of Erika's red sweater in the crowded aisle. She shoved the watch into her pocket. Once she got off the plane, she'd find Erika to make sure she was okay and give her back her watch.

A man stood in the middle of the aisle, gripping an oversized carry-on tightly against his chest, blocking traffic.

One of the flight attendants, with a small gash above her eye, made her way through the crowd in front of him. "Sir . . . I need you to put your luggage down and walk to the exit."

He stared at her for a few seconds as if in a daze, then set the bag in an empty seat and started moving. There was no screaming or shouting from the packed aisle. Just a few quiet sobs as the passengers started again toward the exit.

Nikki grabbed the attention of the flight attendant as she passed and lowered her voice. "This man who was sitting in my row . . . he didn't make it."

The flight attendant pressed her hand against her mouth, clearly fighting to keep her emotions in check. She knew as well as Nikki that the last thing they needed was panic to erupt over a dead passenger.

Nikki touched the young woman's shoulder. "I'm a police officer. If there's anything I can do . . ."

A look of relief flooded her pale face. "There is something, actually. One of the carts has wedged against the other exit up front. I was just on my way to unblock it but found a woman two rows behind you who's trapped in her seat belt. I need to find something to cut off her belt."

Nikki didn't miss the fear mingled with determination in the young woman's eyes. She couldn't be more than twenty-five, trained to be able to open the door of an airplane in her sleep, while hoping to never experience something like this.

Nikki looped the strap of her small bag over her head and across her chest while the smell of smoke filled her nostrils. They were running out of time. "Go unblock the exit, then try and find a knife. We'll get her off the plane."

"Thank you."

Nikki found the woman sitting in the aisle seat, frantically jerking on her seat belt. A little boy sat on the floor, crying.

"I can't get my seat belt off," the woman said, her voice breaking.

"Let me help, okay?" Nikki reached out and grasped the young woman's hand, pulling it gently away from the seat belt before trying to unbuckle it herself. The attendant had been right. The metal clasp wouldn't budge. "What's your name?"

The woman hesitated. "Paula."

"Paula, my name's Nikki. I'm going to help you get off the plane. I just need you to try and calm down."

"I've been trying, but it's stuck." The young woman was still frantically pulling on the buckle. "And my son . . . I never should have brought him with me."

She was crying harder now, her chest heaving with every breath.

"Paula, I need you to calm down. I'm going to help get you out of here, but it might take a minute. I'm going to make sure your son's okay. Can you tell me his name?"

"Caden."

Nikki glanced at the young boy clutching one of the airline pillows. He looked to be about three or four years old. There were no outward signs of bruising or injuries from what she could see, but at this point there was no way to be sure.

"Caden . . ." Nikki reached across the mother's lap to try to coax him out of the corner. "How are you doing, bud? I know this is scary, but do you think you could get up?"

He shook his head.

Nikki looked back to where the aisle had now cleared of passengers. The smell of smoke was intensifying in the cabin. "Can you tell me if anything hurts?"

He stopped crying briefly and shook his head.

"I know this has been scary, but you and your mommy are going to be fine."

His lower lip quivered as he nodded.

Nikki turned to the flight attendant, who'd finally returned with a utility knife.

"Caden . . . I'm going to get your mommy out now."

Glancing out the window, Nikki caught sight of a fire-rescue truck. Foam was hitting the wing in front of them. If a jet-fuel blaze got out of control . . .

Nikki began using the knife to saw against the seat belt. Caden was crying again. Her own head pounded from the smoke and acid smell filling the plane.

"What can I do?" the flight attendant asked.

"I've almost got it." Glancing at the exit, Nikki didn't need to have anyone tell her how urgent it was to get off the plane.

A second later, the knife snapped through the last threads of the seat belt. "I've got it off, Paula. I want you to stand up carefully now. We're going to get you and your son off the plane."

Paula was crying again as she scooped up her son. "Thank you."

Nikki rushed toward the exit with them, trying not to let the emotions of being the victim of a crisis—instead of the responder—overcome her as she quickly checked the rows of the aircraft, ensuring all the passengers were able to disembark.

Outside the plane, rescue crews were setting up beneath

dark clouds closing in on them. Lightning struck in the distance. A helicopter hovered over the lineup of ambulances working together to evacuate injured victims. The fuselage was torn open in front of the wings. A row of seats had broken away from the airplane, and a glance at the cockpit confirmed the slim possibility that the pilots could have survived the impact.

How in the world had this happened? Weather related? Mechanical failure? No one would know for sure until the investigation was completed.

God, there are so many injured. So many scared and confused, and there's still the impact to come as families of the passengers begin to show up.

A covered triage station was already being set up, where colored mats were laid down away from the crash and passengers were being directed to them. Nikki searched each mat she passed for Erika, but couldn't find her.

More off-site emergency services drove up. The noise around her pounded against her head like a hammer. Someone was standing off to the side and videotaping the scene with a cell phone as Nikki stumbled over a piece of wreckage.

A woman wearing a raincoat and a badge approached her. "Ma'am, if you'll come with me—"

"It's okay." Nikki held up her hand. "I'm fine." She didn't care about the rain. Nor did she want any medical attention. She just wanted to find Tyler and go home.

"I'm sorry, ma'am, we have to interview each passenger to ensure that everyone is okay before they leave."

Nikki pressed her lips together. The woman might just be doing her job, but all she wanted to do was leave. She forced herself to focus and answer questions while the woman logged her responses into the database. She glanced down at the triage tag the woman gave her and read through the list. "Oriented

. . . disoriented . . . unconscious . . . deceased." She couldn't think about how this might have ended.

Someone else escorted her toward the terminal, where yet another woman in uniform took her into one of the VIP lounges that had been set up for the passengers. Rows of comfortable chairs were lined up behind her, next to snacks set out on a long bar. There were flight monitors, a television screen with footage of the crash, newspapers, and an internet workstation, but her mind didn't want to focus on what was going on around her. She was waiting. Everyone seemed to be waiting. Waiting for family to be escorted in. Waiting for a connecting flight. Waiting for this nightmare to be over.

She glanced around the room for Erika, wondering how she'd managed to vanish in the middle of a hundred and fifty rattled passengers. Her gaze stopped at the flat-screen TV blaring out the latest news from the crash. A reporter stood frowning at the camera, holding up an umbrella to block the rain.

Nikki turned away from the screen, trying to ignore the knot in the pit of her stomach as they replayed the footage. She started digging through her purse until she found her phone. She needed to call her family. Needed to let Tyler know she was okay. She pushed the power button. Nothing. She shook off the frustration of a dead battery on top of everything else. She needed to make a plan. She'd find Erika, make sure she was okay, then find Tyler and use his phone to call her family and let them know she was okay.

Which meant first she needed to find someone in charge. A woman with a ponytail and cat-eye glasses and a uniform was walking through the room.

"Excuse me." Nikki grabbed her badge from her bag and held it up. She shouldn't get involved, but neither could she stop the nagging feeling that something was wrong with Erika.

"I'm Special Agent Nikki Boyd with the Tennessee Bureau

of Investigation. I'm trying to find a woman who was on this flight."

The airline representative frowned, tugging on the end of her ponytail. "Is there a problem?"

"I was a passenger on the flight, actually. And I'm just . . . worried about her. I haven't seen her since the crash, and she was pretty upset."

The woman hesitated, then glanced down at her tablet. "Okay. What was her name?"

"Erika. I don't know her last name, but she sat beside me in row 29—29B."

"Just give me a second . . . Everyone who's been accounted for after the crash has been logged into our system. We're checking those names against the flight list now. You said her name was Erika?"

"Yes."

"I'm sorry, but no one by that name has been logged into our database yet." She looked up at Nikki. "Are you sure you have the correct name?"

"That's the name she gave me. Could you please check again? She was sitting next to me on the flight. Seat number 29B."

"Let me check the flight manifest . . ."

Nikki fidgeted with the strap of her bag while the woman scanned through the list.

"Actually, it doesn't look as if there was anyone by that name on the flight manifest."

"That's not possible. She sat next to me." Nikki frowned, the pounding in her temples increasing. "Maybe she gave me a nickname, or her middle name. Please . . . if you could check again."

"I really am sorry, but you must be mistaken." The woman shook her head and caught Nikki's gaze. "According to the flight manifest, that seat was empty."

23

3

According to the flight manifest, that seat was empty.

The agent's words replayed through Nikki's mind. No. It hadn't been empty. That simply wasn't possible.

Nikki stopped herself from grabbing the woman's tablet out of her hands. Instead she worked to push back the panic. Her head throbbed. She felt lightheaded . . . confused. No. Not confused. She knew what she'd seen. She'd spoken to Erika *and* watched her walk off that plane.

"Can I look at the manifest?" Nikki asked.

"I'm not sure I'm supposed to—"

Nikki nodded at her badge, then took the tablet from the young woman's hands. Airline . . . flight number . . . date . . . airport codes . . . time. Then the list of names. She scanned through the list of passenger names.

Nikki Boyd 29C
Patrick Hughes 29A

24

The middle seat was empty.

Why wasn't Erika on the flight manifest?

"There's a mistake here—"

"That's not possible, ma'am. Since 9/11, security is extremely tight."

"You're telling me that it isn't possible for you—for someone—to have made a mistake?"

"Flight manifests are checked and rechecked throughout the boarding process, and to miss something like this . . ." The woman's gaze narrowed as she took the tablet back and pulled it against her chest. "Listen, you've just been through a traumatic situation. A plane crashed. People died." She let out a sharp breath. "You have to understand that it's going to take time to sort through the passenger list and ensure we've accounted for everyone, but it's quite possible that she simply hasn't checked in here on the ground and that 29B wasn't her assigned seat. If she was actually on the plane—"

"She was where she was supposed to be. She mentioned how she hated middle seats."

No. There was no question in Nikki's mind that Erika had been on that flight and in her seat. There had to be a simple explanation, because Erika wasn't a figment of her imagination. She knew that much was true.

"Is there someone else I could speak to?" Nikki asked. "A supervisor perhaps?"

"Yes, but maybe I could make a suggestion?" The woman hugged her tablet tighter against her chest. "From my limited medical training, I know that even a mild concussion can cause memory loss, and on top of that, there are often symptoms that show up later that could need to be treated. You've been through a frightening ordeal—along with everyone in this room—and we've been encouraged to make sure that everyone gets checked out if they have the slightest concern."

Nikki frowned. So the woman didn't believe her. "I don't have any medical concerns, and your manifest is wrong. She was on that flight."

"Nikki!"

She turned around at the sound of her name. Tyler walked toward her in a black-collared shirt, a pair of jeans, and a lightweight military-type jacket. She took in his short haircut and those familiar brown eyes that took her breath away. A wave of relief washed through her.

"I'm sorry." She turned back to the representative, shoving her worries of Erika aside for the moment. "I've got to go."

The chaotic scene around her faded as Nikki ran toward Tyler.

"Please tell me you're okay," he said, pulling her into his arms.

"I am now," she said, leaning back to study Tyler's face. His gaze intensified with traces of worry as he looked down at her. There was a hint of a shadow across his jawline, and worry lines marked his forehead; but still he exuded that ever-present strength she'd come to rely on.

She leaned into him and felt his breath against her hair as she inhaled the familiar scent of his cologne and felt the warmth of his arms around her shoulders. For a moment, it was as if he'd never left. No long months apart. No worries over the direction of their relationship once he returned. And for a brief moment, no final moments of panic from the plane crash. Because all she wanted to do was push away the last few weeks and minutes and be completely in this moment where she felt safe and protected.

"You're shaking," he said, pulling her tighter against his chest.

She hadn't realized she was still trembling. Or, for that matter, stopped to realize how close she'd come to dying today.

He reached down and cupped her face with his hands, then searched her gaze as if he were trying to make sure she was really standing in front of him. "You're sure you're okay?"

She touched her shoulder. "Just a couple scratches and a bruise or two."

"I'm so sorry you were on that flight."

She managed a laugh, feeling the need to lighten the moment between them. "It's funny, in a way. Here I've worried about you for the last few months while you were in Liberia, and I'm the one on the flight that crashed. But really . . . I'm okay."

"I just . . ." Tyler rubbed his fingers down his chin. "I watched the video someone took of the crash, Nikki. I can't even imagine how terrifying that had to have been."

She closed her eyes for a moment as flashes of the crash replayed through her mind. The sound of the explosion and the smell of smoke. The terror of free-falling, and then the lingering silence before the crash.

"And on top of that, you're wet." He grabbed a strand of her blonde hair and tugged on it gently.

"It was drizzling when I got off the plane."

He took a step back, took off his jacket, and slipped it around her shoulders. "I don't think I've ever been so scared. I'd checked to see if you were going to be on time and saw your flight was delayed. I didn't think anything about it until I heard them talking about the crash on the news, and when I checked my phone to see what had happened . . . They kept playing the video over and over, and then I realized they were talking about your flight."

Nikki shook her head, hating feeling flustered and vulnerable, but she could still feel the panic threatening to suffocate her. Instead of giving in to the fear, she focused on Tyler. Because with him was where she'd dreamed about being these past three months.

"This isn't the way I imagined your homecoming," she said, pulling his coat closer around her.

She'd imagined it for weeks. Dinner with him and Liam at their house playing with the Wii or watching a movie. Really, she hadn't cared what they'd do as long as they were together. His three months away had seemed like forever.

"None of that matters," he said. "All I care about is the fact that you're alive. Because if I'd lost you now . . ."

"You didn't lose me, Tyler. I'm here." She forced a smile as she looked up at him. "And I'm going to be fine."

"But you're still shaking."

He grabbed her hand, led her over to one of the few empty chairs in the busy lounge, and told her to sit down while he went to grab her some coffee.

"I really am fine, Tyler," she said as he came back and handed her the drink.

At least she hoped she was. Maybe the agent's implications had been right. Maybe Erika had been nothing more than a figment of her imagination, and she was losing it. Maybe she should just let it go. Erika—if she really had been on that plane—had been understandably upset. She'd probably managed to avoid the emergency personnel and took a taxi out of there.

"I'll take you home in a few minutes," Tyler said, "but humor me for now. I want to make sure you're okay and warmed up a bit before we leave."

She took an obligatory sip of the coffee and felt the warm liquid flow through her. Maybe he was right. She'd felt okay during the aftermath of the crash. Adrenaline had kicked in during those first few minutes, giving her the focus she needed to help get people off the plane. But now that there was no one else to save and the shock was beginning to wear off, she couldn't stop shaking.

"What about you?" she asked, taking another sip. "You've just finished a tough few months and that long trip home."

He sat down on the edge of the seat next to her. "I'm still suffering a bit from jet lag. My body's completely swapped day and night."

She stared at the black liquid swirling in her cup. The coffee was bitter and not hot enough, but her hands were already feeling steadier from the shot of caffeine. "I wanted to be there when you landed, but when I got called to go to this training in Houston . . ." She looked up at him. "I hated missing your homecoming."

"I missed you too, but Liam and my mom were there with a bouquet of balloons and a stuffed bear."

She smiled, catching his gaze again. "I helped him pick out the bear. He was so excited for you to get back."

"I'm convinced he grew at least an inch while I was gone. But it makes me wonder—"

"Stop." She brushed her hand against his arm, at the regret she saw in his eyes. She knew exactly what he was thinking. "He missed you, but I honestly think he understands—as much as a six-year-old can understand—how important this job was for you. And how much you love him. He's going to be okay, Tyler. I have no doubt of that."

"I hope so. All I want right now is to be the best father for him I can. And I'm back and ready to be exactly that."

She understood why he was questioning his decision. She had struggled at first to understand his determination to take the job in Liberia. He'd told her that not only would it give him a foothold into another job here in the US, it would also help him figure out who he was on his own without Katie so he could move on. It was something he'd needed to do for himself in order to be a better father for Liam. And in the end, she knew he was right.

"What about your parents?" he asked, standing up to toss her empty cup into the trash can beside them. "Have you been able to get ahold of them?"

"Not yet. The battery on my phone is dead."

"I tried to call them, but didn't get through." He pulled his phone from his back pocket. "Try again with mine. They'll worry if they see this on the news."

His voice was soothing as he handed her his phone, helping to keep her focused. She dialed her father's number, wishing her fingers would stop trembling. He'd be working at the family restaurant like he did every day with her mom, hopefully so busy with customers that he wouldn't have had time to look at the news. But if her brothers watched the news or one of their friends who knew she'd been gone had called to ask . . .

The call went straight to voice mail. She tried again, then wrote a text, adding her brothers and sister-in-law Jamie to the message in hopes that would help them not to worry until she could stop by and see them herself.

"We'll keep trying until I can get you there," he said.

She dropped the phone back into his hand and nodded. "This isn't exactly the reunion I expected."

He laced his fingers through hers. His touch was warm. Protective. It was what she needed. His presence and strength. Even when she'd tried to be there for him, he was always her rock.

He squeezed her hand. "We can stop by your parents' and let them know you're okay, then I'll take you home."

A flash of red caught her eye as they started for the door. A woman with brunette hair, wearing a red sweater, was talking to someone in uniform on the other side of the room.

Nikki paused midstep and let go of Tyler's hand. The woman turned around, looking past Nikki at a man who'd just walked into the room. Nikki let out a sharp breath. It wasn't Erika.

"Nikki, what is it? You seem . . . distracted."

"It's nothing. I just thought I saw someone."

She glanced around the rest of the crowded room. There were reunions taking place all around them. Paula, the woman from the plane, stood in the corner of the room with her son and a man who was holding her tight around the waist as they spoke.

Commentary from the flat-screen TV, where one of the passengers was being interviewed, played in the background. Nikki glanced at one of the airline staff, wondering why they didn't turn off the news feed. Most of the people in this room had been on that plane. The last thing she wanted to do was relive the scenario by watching what had happened.

Everyone she could see had been tagged green. They'd been the lucky ones who might leave emotionally traumatized from the experience, but physically they were okay. She didn't want to think about what it was going to be like for families of those who'd been taken to the local hospitals with injuries. Or those who hadn't made it.

Like the man two seats over.

"Nikki?"

She looked back up at Tyler. "I'm sorry. There's something I need to do before I leave here."

His brow furrowed. "What's that?"

"I need to speak to someone in charge. There was this woman in the seat next to me."

She knew she shouldn't worry about her. A complete stranger she'd only spoken to briefly on the plane. And yet she had to be here somewhere. "You're going to think I'm nuts, but I checked with one of the agents earlier, and according to the manifest, she wasn't on the plane. Except I know she was. And she was really upset when she got off the plane."

"I don't know, Nikki. Things seem fairly organized, but a mix-up doesn't seem that unusual at this point. And besides that, between passengers, family members, and the emergency crews, there are hundreds of people here. Just because you haven't seen her doesn't mean she isn't here."

He was right. She was overreacting. But she couldn't shake the nagging feeling that something was wrong.

"I just . . . I need to at least try to find her. She was so nervous flying. I told her it was safer to fly than to drive. And then . . . and then we crashed." She rubbed the back of her neck, willing the knots to disappear along with the worry. "The agent told me to see a doctor. That I might have a concussion and basically had imagined the woman sitting beside me."

"Nikki, if there's even the slightest chance of a concussion . . ." Tyler cupped his hand around her elbow. "I know you don't want to hear this, but she's right, Nikki—"

"I don't need to see a doctor." Nikki pressed her lips together, trying to tone down the frustration in her voice. "I'm sorry. But I'm fine. And I didn't imagine her. She was on that plane."

"I believe you, but it's still not a bad idea. I heard someone say when I got here that there are a couple doctors here to see passengers who have concerns but don't need to go to the hospital. It probably wouldn't take that long."

Nikki squeezed her eyes shut, trying to push away the growing fog settling in the corners of her mind and, for a moment, doubting herself. What if the woman was right? What if the manifest was correct and there hadn't been anyone sitting next to her? What if Erika had somehow been nothing more than a figment of her imagination? Some kind of coping mechanism in the middle of a crisis.

Except she could see the woman's face as clearly as she could see Tyler's right now.

"What do you think?" Tyler asked.

"That the whole thing sounds crazy. I know she was sitting beside me. We talked about the book she was reading. The turbulence. How she didn't like the middle seat. And you. We talked about you. But according to the manifest she wasn't on the plane. Why isn't she on the manifest?"

"I don't know, but right now my concern is you and making sure you're okay. If there's any chance that you hit your head, it's better to be safe than sorry."

Nikki blew out another breath. Maybe he was right. Not about Erika, but maybe she should make sure she didn't have a concussion. And besides, if she didn't see a doctor, her mother would bug her until she did. What did it matter, really? It would only take a few minutes.

"Fine. I'll see one of the doctors, then you can take me home."

She'd make sure he and her family didn't worry. But she wasn't crazy. Erika had been on that flight. And she was going to find her.

4

Ten minutes later Nikki sat in the middle of the makeshift consulting area with a doctor who didn't look old enough to have graduated from med school. He waved a light in her eyes, his expression solemn. "Any unusual symptoms? Headache? Nausea? Ringing in the ears?"

"Headache, yes, and I'm still a bit shaky. But other than that, I'm fine."

She shifted in her chair, trying to relax. Trying not to replay those last moments of the crash. And trying not to wonder about what had happened to Erika. Because more than likely, Erika had simply managed to step off that plane and leave the airport grounds without talking to anyone.

Like Nikki should have done.

"It's always better to be safe than sorry in cases like this," the doctor said, switching to her other eye. "Because here's the thing with concussions. They can be particularly challenging. Every patient reacts differently, not always following the same symptoms. What about any memory loss, pressure in the head, slurred speech, or confusion?"

"None of those."

"Good." The doctor took a step back, then ran his fingers through his spiked blond hair. "My advice to you is to go home and get some rest, but make sure you schedule a follow-up visit with your own doctor if you end up having any of the symptoms we discussed, or if you notice anything that feels off. Pay attention to any feelings of panic, any sleep disturbances, and any depression over the next few days."

Nikki frowned, wanting to tell him that feeling panicky and not being able to sleep were normal consequences of surviving a plane crash. Instead, she stood up and thanked him, then stepped back into the crowded lounge and searched for Tyler.

She found him standing near the coffee machine next to Jack Spencer and Gwen McKenna, her partners who worked with her on the task force. She let out a sharp sigh, grateful for more familiar faces.

"You don't know how glad I am to see you," Gwen said, pulling Nikki into a tight hug.

"Sorry I haven't called yet. My phone died."

"All that matters right now is that you're okay," Jack said. "What did the doctor say?"

"The doctor just cleared me," she said, glancing back across the room. "No concussion. Just a bit shaky."

"Anything we can do?" Gwen asked.

"I don't think so." Nikki shook her head as the four of them headed toward the exit and onto the patterned carpet. "I've been encouraged to go home and rest this afternoon."

"At a minimum," Gwen said. "I spoke briefly with Carter on the way here. The boss flies back from Boston in the morning, but he's already told us to make sure you know you have no business coming back to work for the next few days."

Except she wasn't sure resting at home was what she really wanted. In order to forget what had just happened, she needed to stay busy. Someone on the overhead speaker welcomed them to Music City. Lines of passengers were glued to the monitors covering the crash. An older woman stood in front of one of the screens, no doubt saying a prayer of thanks she hadn't been on flight 1545.

Nikki slowed down as a couple of FBI agents hurried past them, one of them engrossed in a phone conversation. The FBI wouldn't be involved as consultants with the National Transportation Safety Board unless there was believed to be the possibility of a criminal act behind the crash. Nikki wondered if they knew yet that an air marshal had died in the crash. And she couldn't help but wonder as well if there was a connection between Erika and the marshal. She hadn't seen any interaction between the two of them beyond a few bits of casual conversation, but the man's death had clearly upset Erika.

Just like it had upset herself.

No. She was letting her imagination get the best of her. Looking for a conspiracy theory in every corner.

"Something wrong?" Gwen asked as they passed a boutique selling sweatshirts and luggage.

"It's nothing . . ." Nikki hesitated, not sure if she wanted to get Gwen and Jack involved, but still unable to shake the nagging. "At least I don't think it's anything. There was this woman on the flight who sat next to me. I haven't been able to find her."

"That doesn't surprise me," Jack said. "This was a major commercial crash with a couple hundred passengers involved. Finding one woman—"

"It's more than that." Nikki stopped in front of a newsstand, knowing what tomorrow's headline would read, and glanced at Tyler before continuing. "When she got off, she was extremely upset—which, granted, is perfectly normal—but when I talked to one of the agents, there was no record of her on the flight manifest."

"She could have changed seats—"

"She was in her seat," Nikki countered. "And on top of that, there was an air marshal sitting next to her. Maybe it's all just a coincidence—"

"But you don't think so," Jack said, finishing her thought.

"No," she said, scooting aside to let a family with a double stroller pass.

"You're right that it doesn't make sense," Jack said. "With all the current security measures in airports, they have to keep accurate records that are checked and double-checked."

Jack was normally good for a round of comic relief, but today Nikki caught the hint of skepticism in his voice. "Which is what the agent said. Implying I imagined the woman."

"No one believes you imagined her." Tyler moved in front of her and put his hands on her shoulders. "But you were just in a plane crash and saw the man beside you die. That alone is enough to unsettle any rational person."

"Maybe," she said, taking a step away from him and walking again down the crowded concourse. Normally she loved people-watching at the airport, but today . . . today the crowd was closing in around her. "But I'm trained to be able to cope with a crisis, and I'm supposed to be able to handle something like this."

"Training can't stop you from feeling, or even going into shock," Jack said. "None of us are immune."

"I know, but—"

"He's right," Gwen said. "Everything you're feeling is normal. You've been through a huge trauma, and it's going to take awhile to put it behind you. I know it would for me. I'm not sure I'm ever going to want to fly again, and I wasn't even on that flight."

"Everything might be normal that I'm feeling, but something

just doesn't add up." She was overanalyzing the situation again. One that wasn't any of her business, and yet for some odd reason, the image of Erika's face wouldn't disappear.

She shoved her hands into her front pockets, then stopped again.

Erika's watch. She had Erika's watch.

"Wait a minute. She was wearing this." Nikki dug the silver watch out of her pocket, trying not to sound frantic. But even if she couldn't prove it to them, she needed to prove it to herself. She needed to know she hadn't made up the entire conversation in her mind as some kind of coping device.

"Where did you get this?" Jack asked.

"I picked it up off her seat on the plane as I was leaving. She'd shown it to me right before the plane went down. The clasp was loose and it had fallen off."

"Listen, Nikki. I'm convinced that there's a perfectly logical explanation to all of this," Gwen said. "But let me handle this. I've got a few contacts in the TSA. I'll see what I can find. I bet it won't take long for me to find out who she was."

"Okay." Nikki nodded, shoving the watch back in her pocket. At least it was a start and would help put her mind at ease. "Her name was Erika—I don't have a last name—but she was in seat 29B, next to me. And find out who the air marshal was sitting beside her in the window seat as well. If there's a connection between the two of them—"

"We'll find her," Jack said, "because Gwen's right. There's got to be a logical explanation. As hard as the airlines try to avoid them, mistakes happen."

"We're parked this direction," Gwen said, stopping at one of the exit doors. "Take her home, Tyler. We'll research Erika and call you as soon as we find out something."

Nikki nodded as they left, thankful for their help but still feeling the need to find out for herself.

"Do you feel better now?" Tyler asked, taking her hand again. "You know Gwen. She'll find the woman. She's almost as good as you are at tracking down people."

Nikki shot him a half smile at the compliment, grateful for how he'd become the calm in the middle of her storm. Something she needed right now. Knowing he was here with her, his hand wrapped firmly around hers . . . She drew in a slow breath, almost able to believe everything was right in the world again. She just needed a day or two to clear her mind, then she'd feel back on track again.

A second set of men in FBI coats and badges caught her eye as they passed them in the middle of the concourse. Nikki slowed down, her mind firing in a dozen different directions.

"You're not going to let this go, are you?" Tyler said.

"I know I should just let Gwen handle it, but if I spoke to the FBI—"

"Nikki—"

"Humor me." She stopped to look up at him. "Okay?"

"I'm just thinking about you and what you need." Tyler frowned, not looking convinced. "Not only did Gwen promise to try to find the woman for you, your parents are waiting to see you, and you need to rest—"

"And I will. All of those things. I promise. But first I want to speak to someone who might be able to give me answers."

He let out a sharp sigh. "As long as you promise me you'll get some rest when you're done here."

Nikki turned around and started jogging the other direction in order to catch up with the men.

"Excuse me," she said, stepping up in front of one of them and holding up her badge, hoping it would get her the information she was looking for. "I'm Special Agent Nikki Boyd with the Tennessee Bureau of Investigation."

"TBI?" The taller of the two glanced at her badge before

pushing his wire-rimmed glasses up the bridge of his nose. "I'm Agent Sam Brinkley, and my partner here is FBI Agent Mark Wells. And you're here because . . ."

"I work with the state's missing persons division."

"I'm not sure I understand." Agent Wells, shorter and pudgier than his partner, shook his head. "We're working with TBI on this investigation, but missing persons?"

She nodded, knowing she only had a few seconds to get to the point. "I was on the flight, and there was a woman sitting beside me who I haven't been able to find, but who also isn't on the flight manifest. I was hoping the FBI might have more information than the airline representative I spoke to."

Brinkley glanced at his partner. "With regulations as tight as they are after 9/11, manifests are checked and double-checked to ensure an accurate count before any plane leaves the terminal. Mistakes by the airline are rare."

"So I've already been told." Nikki dug the watch she'd found on the plane out of her pocket. "But I have evidence she was on the plane. She was wearing this. She sat next to me. She was reading *Love's Fury*, a romance she thought was dull—"

Agent Brinkley held up his hand. "Okay. I believe you, but I'm really not sure how we can help you. If you already looked at the flight manifest, it's the exact same record I have right here. But even if there is an issue, it's going to take us days to sort through all the data and information regarding this crash. We don't even know why the plane went down at this point, let alone have accurate details on the passengers. But we will."

"Then one more question," Nikki said, knowing she was going to have to back off. "Did you know there was an air marshal on the flight?"

"Yes, but as far as I remember, Agent Boyd, TBI's missing persons division doesn't have jurisdiction in a commercial plane crash. So my suggestion to you would be for you to forget about the woman you supposedly spoke to on the plane, and let us do our job—"

"Was he on the flight with a passenger?" she pressed.

"Like I just said, your division doesn't have jurisdiction in this situation."

"Nikki." Tyler pressed his fingers around her elbow. "I think you should let them go."

Agent Brinkley shot her a tight-lipped smile. "It was nice to meet you, Agent Boyd."

Nikki waited until they walked away, then turned to follow Tyler to his car.

"I wasn't trying to interfere," he said as they stepped outside into the late summer heat, "but they weren't going to give you any information, even if they knew something."

"I know." She pressed her thumbs against her temples, trying to ease her headache. She knew how to handle trauma. Knew what was real and what wasn't. But after everything that had happened today . . . "You think I should walk away and forget this."

"Yes," he said as they started across the crosswalk. "Though I know you well enough to realize you're not going to do that. This is who you are."

Tyler's phone rang inside the short-term parking garage a few cars down from his pickup. He answered it, then handed it to her. "It's your mom."

"Nikki?"

A wave of relief flooded through Nikki at the sound of her mom's voice. "Hey, Mom. I'm here and I'm okay."

"Nikki. You don't know how good it is to hear your voice. I saw the video of the crash on television—"

"I'm fine, Mom. Really. I've tried to get through to you, but my phone's dead, and then when I tried to call on Tyler's phone, it went to voice mail."

"Don't worry about it." She could hear the relief in her mother's voice. "We got your message, but you can't imagine how many times I've tried to call. We're stuck in traffic right now, and I'm not sure how soon we're going to be able to get to the airport."

"Why don't you go back to the restaurant, then. I'm here with Tyler, and he's promised to bring me by."

"If you're sure you're okay . . ." There was a long pause on the line. "It's just that the news is reporting there were fatalities, Nikki. I watched the video they keep playing over and over."

Nikki stared at an oil spot on the parking garage floor, wishing they weren't having this conversation. "I know there was at least one man who died in the crash, but I'm really fine, Mom. I was even checked out by a doctor. I've got a couple bruises, but that's all."

"Nikki . . ." She could hear the quiet sobs of her mother. "After losing Sarah . . . You know what it's been like. If anything would have happened to you . . ."

Her mother didn't have to say anything else for Nikki to know what she was thinking. Sarah had vanished ten years ago, and with her disappearance had come the heartache of never knowing what had happened to her younger sister. And that lack of resolution had brought with it its own never-ending grief.

"Nikki?"

"I'm still here, Mama."

"I know this accident didn't have anything to do with your job, but you don't know how many times I wish you'd stuck with teaching. I just . . . I worry about you, Nikki. You've had too many close calls lately."

Nikki squeezed her eyes shut, wishing she could somehow magically take away her mom's worry. Like all choices, her decision to become a cop came with a price tag. And her family had to pay part of the price.

"I know, Mom. And I'm sorry."

"I don't want you to be sorry. I just want you to be careful. I'll tell your father to head back to the restaurant now, but promise you'll get here as soon as you can. And in the meantime, I'll let your brothers and Jamie know you're okay."

Nikki said goodbye before hanging up and giving the phone back to Tyler.

"Is she okay?"

"She will be. I know this is hard for her."

He drew her into his arms, temporarily drowning out the noises of the busy garage surrounding them. And all of the worry that had settled inside her heart. They might still have things to talk about—the details that had to be figured out to make a relationship work—but when his arms were around her, that moment became the one moment when she knew everything was going to be okay.

"Agent Boyd?"

A man's voice pulled her back to the present.

Nikki stepped out of Tyler's embrace and turned around. It was the FBI agent she'd spoken with a few minutes ago. Brinkley. He'd stopped half a dozen feet away from her, a frown on his face. His jaw tense.

She glanced at Tyler, then back at the agent. "What's wrong?"

"I'm going to need you to come with me."

5

Nikki followed two agents down a long hallway inside a secured section of the airport, wondering why Tyler hadn't been allowed to come with them. And more importantly, why they wanted to talk with her.

"I need to know what's going on," she said, hurrying to keep up with them. Her nerves were already on edge. An interrogation by the FBI wasn't exactly going to help.

Agent Brinkley glanced at his partner but didn't slow down. "We'll explain everything in a minute, but we're going to need some privacy."

She followed them inside an air-conditioned conference room set way too cold, containing nothing more than a long executive table, eight rolling chairs, a mini-fridge, and a handful of vintage airline photos lining the wall.

Agent Brinkley pulled out one of the chairs, offering her a seat, then leaned back against the edge of the table. Wells took the chair across from her.

Brinkley's jaw tensed as if he didn't like what he was about to say. "I'll get right to the point. We need your help."

"You need my help?" Nikki pulled Tyler's jacket closer around her as she looked from Brinkley to Wells, then back to Brinkley again. She was missing something. A request for help was the last thing she'd expected. The FBI had more resources than the TBI. Why in the world would they need her?

"Is this about Erika? Because so far everyone has nicely implied I need to go home and rest, because the woman wasn't on that plane and in fact no one at all was sitting in 29B. She was nothing more than a figment of my imagination. Isn't that what the two of you are thinking?"

Brinkley splayed his hands on the table on either side of him and leaned forward. "We happen to know for a fact that Erika Hamilton was on the plane. And that she sat next to you."

Nikki's mouth dropped open at the news. "Then why wasn't she on the flight manifest?"

"We were keeping close tabs on the flight and managed to step in and remove her name from the database immediately after the crash," Wells said. "We knew there would be an investigation, and knew we needed to keep her safe. Because you were right about another thing. Patrick Hughes, the man who sat next to her on the flight, was an air marshal, with the task of getting her to Nashville in one piece. Obviously he didn't do a very good job, because she's now missing."

"Maybe that's because he's dead." Nikki worked to wrap her head around the limited facts she'd been given so far. "So why was she being escorted by an air marshal?"

"Erika Hamilton is a material witness for an upcoming grand jury trial. Our only witness, in fact, or at least the only person we've found willing to testify. That's why she was on her way here."

Nikki shook her head. The fact that Erika was a witness

might explain some of her nervousness on the flight. Testifying in a high-profile case often came with its own set of risks, depending on who the defendant was.

But why did they want to involve her?

"While I'm thankful for the reassurance that I'm not losing it," she said, "I still don't understand why you need my help."

"We have reason to believe there was a leak in Erika's security. We've been prepping her for Thursday's grand jury as our key witness," Brinkley said. "And now with her missing . . ."

"What kind of information was leaked?"

Brinkley walked over to the mini-fridge, pulled out a couple of bottled waters, and offered one to her.

"Thanks."

He handed her the bottle, then screwed off the lid of the second one and took a sip before continuing. "We're still looking into the situation, but clearly someone—whoever was after her—took advantage of the chaos at the crash scene. We're checking airport surveillance, hoping to get some information, but as of now she's vanished. And if she's not in court tomorrow—"

"You lose your one witness, not to mention the fact that her life is clearly in danger." Nikki's gaze shifted to the photo on the wall across from her of Charles Lindbergh standing next to the *Spirit of St. Louis*, and shivered. So her gut instincts had been correct all along.

"A week ago, someone broke into the safe house where we were debriefing her," Brinkley said. "The agents on duty were able to intervene and protect her, but this time we're afraid she might not have been as lucky."

"You don't think she simply decided to run?" Nikki asked. "It seems like a logical option. She's scared to testify, having second thoughts, and when the plane goes down, she realizes that the air marshal guarding her is dead, and she panics and bolts. I know I'd have been tempted to get out of there."

"We hope not. From everything we could tell, Erika was intent on testifying."

"Okay, so once again, what does this have to do with me?"

Wells tapped his fingers against the manila folder he'd set in front of him. "We called in a couple favors and did a quick background check on you, your history with TBI, and your involvement with the Missing Persons Task Force."

"And . . ." Nikki grabbed a couple painkillers from her handbag and washed them down with the water he'd given her, still cautious about where he was going with the conversation.

Brinkley leaned forward and caught her gaze. "We know about your sister."

Nikki's hand went automatically to the necklace she always wore that held Sarah's photo. "You've done your homework," she said, suddenly feeling vulnerable.

Brinkley pulled out a chair next to her and sat down. "Erika's past shows tendencies of falling for the wrong men. A pattern of . . . destructive behavior, you might say. And as I just said, we believe she's still determined to testify, but there's a chance she'll go back to the man she's supposed to be testifying against. And in order to find her quickly, we need to know where to look."

"We need someone outside the agency," Wells said. "Someone who has no ties to the case. Someone Erika will trust. And someone who has her own motivation to get the job done. Because if Erika is out there and they find her, we believe they will kill her."

"So you want me to find her first," Nikki said.

"Your job is finding missing persons." Brinkley took another sip of his water. "And with a possible leak somewhere within our team, we need this done quietly and quickly."

Nikki wasn't going to deny she was interested, but before she decided on anything, she needed more information. "Tell me about the case and who Erika was planning to testify against."

Brinkley sat back in his chair, arms folded across his chest. "Do you recognize the name Felicia Abbott?"

Nikki's brow rose at the familiar name. While she might not have found her sister's abductor, the information she'd gathered over the years from both police reports and news articles had become invaluable in a number of recent cases. "Felicia Abbott was a victim connected to the Simon Crowley murders," she said.

Brinkley's smile widened. "I was told you were good. I guess they weren't exaggerating."

"What I don't know is the connection between our missing person and Felicia Abbott. Unless . . ." Nikki's mind began to spin. "Erika is Felicia Abbott."

"Exactly."

Nikki leaned back in her chair, digging through her memory for the facts of the case. Six years ago, Simon Crowley had been arrested for the deaths of four women who'd all been brutally murdered on hiking trails outside of Memphis over a period of seven years. He was eventually convicted of killing two of them. One of those murdered was Felicia Abbott's sister, who police believed was killed in a case of mistaken identity. Felicia had met Simon during her last year of college. He was charming and handsome, and she fell for him.

"I remember reading about how Felicia started noticing inconsistencies in Crowley's behavior," Nikki said. "She originally thought he was having an affair, because while he'd always been completely charming, he was beginning to lose his temper more frequently. One day she decided to confront him about where he'd been earlier that week, and he exploded."

"She was afraid he was going to hurt her," Brinkley continued, "so she managed to get in her car and drive away. But later that night Crowley returned to her house. Her sister was visiting. It was dark inside the house—"

"And Crowley mistakenly killed her sister." Nikki shuddered.

"You'd think she'd have learned on the first go-around," Wells said.

"She's not the first woman to fall for the wrong man," Nikki said.

"But twice?" Wells asked.

"There's a common pattern for women who fall for men like Crowley," Nikki said. "She's smart but vulnerable, and men like him are both charming and dangerous at the same time. They know how to play to her weaknesses." She wasn't completely ready to defend the woman, but she'd seen enough over the years to know how hard it was for some women to walk away. "So who's the man this time?"

Wells pushed the folder in front of him across the table toward her. "Brian Russell. He's a wealthy philanthropist, mainly through family money. But we believe he's using the nonprofits he's involved in to raise, launder, and transfer funds for a man named Dimitry Petran."

"Who's Dimitry Petran?"

"Petran's a high-value target involved in a little of everything, including narco trafficking, gun smuggling, and piracy," Brinkley said.

"Erika came to us a couple of weeks ago," Wells continued. "She told us she had evidence we could use against Russell and then agreed to testify against him."

"So she had the evidence?"

"That was the reason she was on her way to Nashville. She was supposed to hand it over to us today, then we were going to finish prepping her to testify in front of a grand jury. We were hoping Russell would be indicted."

Nikki opened up the file, where they'd added the photo of the thirtysomething mogul dressed in a designer suit and tie. "What made her turn on Russell?"

"Like Crowley . . ." Brinkley hesitated a moment. "I suppose she found out that her knight in shining armor wasn't quite the man she thought he was."

"Does Russell know she was planning to testify?" Nikki asked.

"We don't know, but if he does, I have no doubt both he and Petran want her to disappear. If he does realize what she's planning to do, and he finds her before we do—"

"He'll kill her," Nikki said.

Brinkley nodded. "Since you first talked to us about Erika, we double-checked with the doctor who saw you. He gave you a clean bill of health. And your boss has already okayed the assignment."

Nikki glanced out the window at the line of runways. "How much time do we have?"

"She's scheduled to testify in forty-eight hours, and after two continuances, I don't see the judge allowing a third. We need this to happen. Without Erika, we don't have any solid evidence that can put Russell where we want him . . . and get us closer to Petran."

"So forty-eight hours," Nikki repeated.

"Or less. Because if she doesn't show up, then like I said, our case is going to crumble."

She wanted to find Erika, but she also wanted a bit of normal. A long nap this afternoon, Chinese takeout and a movie tonight . . . And most importantly, time to reconnect with Tyler.

"I'd need my team in on this with me," she said, knowing there was no way she was simply going to walk away.

Brinkley glanced at Wells. "We figured you'd ask for that. I suppose we could use the extra manpower. But you'll work together and report directly to me. No one else needs to know what you're doing. We want this kept under the radar."

"Where would you want us to work?" she asked.

"You can treat this like any other missing persons case at your precinct," Brinkley said.

"And what about airport video surveillance from the time of the crash?" she asked. "We'd need access to that along with Erika's file."

"That's not a problem. There is surveillance in place that allows us to monitor the video feed over the internet from both on-site and off-site locations, including your precinct. And we'll get you a copy of Erika's file as well."

So they had it all worked out.

"What do you say?" Brinkley asked.

She'd have to put off Tyler again. Why was it that after three months another couple of days seemed like an eternity?

"I know we've got a short window of time. I'll need a phone to call and brief my team while you get set up to transfer the information we'll need." Nikki glanced toward the door. "But first, I need to tell someone goodbye."

She found Tyler waiting outside the string of offices in the concourse. "Hey. I'm sorry you had to wait so long."

"That's okay. What's going on?"

She looked up at him, still not completely able to soak up the reality that he was back. "I'm going to need you to take me straight to the station. They want me to work with them on a case. That's all I can say right now."

"The FBI? Is it related to the missing woman?"

"Yes."

He grabbed her hands and shot her a smile. "I just get you back and you have to leave? Can't say I'm too thrilled about that."

"The timing sucks, but I'm hoping no more than twenty-four hours. Forty-eight, tops."

"And you can guarantee that?" he asked.

She let out a soft chuckle. There were no guarantees in her work. That was one of the easy things about being single. She didn't have to report to anyone, could make her own hours, and no one except her cat missed her when she didn't come home for dinner. But that was also the reason she wanted this relationship. She wanted someone to come home to. Which meant they were just going to have to find a way to balance things.

"No guarantees," she said, barely noticing the crowds of people walking past them. "But I've got some pretty strong motivation to solve the case. I've got you waiting for me."

"I know it sounds selfish, but there are so many things I want to talk to you about, and as grateful as I've been for Skype and texting, it's not the same. I've missed you, Nikki."

Her breath caught at his nearness. And at the unexpected depth of her own feelings. "Me too."

"When I asked you to wait for me, I had no idea what that meant. Just that I knew I didn't want to go back to how things were. I was so afraid that you still saw me as Katie's husband. A good friend. I knew I couldn't walk away without telling you how I felt."

"And now?"

"Nothing has changed. I'm in love with you, Nikki Boyd. Three months away has made that even clearer."

"You're making this very hard."

"It was my plan to make this hard." He laughed. "Because I can guarantee that the FBI doesn't need you near as much as I do."

He pulled her into his arms. She nuzzled her face in his chest. Breathed in the smell of his cologne. She'd waited so long for this moment. But this job was just temporary. A couple days at the most, and then she was going to take some of her unused vacation time.

"I know I'm being selfish." He ran his thumb across the back of her hand. "There are just so many things I've been looking forward to in person. I've been offered a job. A full-time job, but I . . . I wanted to talk to you about it first."

"Forty-eight hours, tops," she said.

He nodded before pulling away. "I'll let your parents know what's going on, and I'll be waiting."

6

Nikki stood in front of the sketchy timeline she'd put together at the precinct with photos of Russell and Erika from the FBI's file. She glanced at the clock hanging on the wall. It had already been two and a half hours since the crash. In a missing persons case, every minute—every second—counted, and this one was no exception. She'd spent the past thirty minutes going over the file the FBI had given her, convinced Erika's life was in danger. And if Brian Russell had already found her—

"Couple things. I just got off the phone with our FBI liaison," Jack said, stepping up beside her. "Brinkley said they still haven't been able to locate Russell for questioning, though they believe he's still in Texas. They've got a BOLO out on him with local and state police in the hope they'll find him. I also managed to pull up Erika's phone records and have been going through her calls."

"Can you trace the actual phone?" Nikki asked. "Get us a location?"

"There is no GPS signal, so it looks as if she might have taken out the battery and ditched the phone."

"Which would mean she's scared." Nikki frowned. "And running from something."

"What about the case file the FBI gave us?" he asked. "Anything that might help there?"

"It's pretty bare bones," Nikki said, dropping the file she'd been going through onto the desk. "Erika met Brian Russell five years ago at a fundraiser when she was working for his wife. They ended up having an on-again, off-again affair. He kept promising Erika he was going to marry her, but never has, though divorce proceedings with his wife have been recently finalized."

"So maybe he finally decided he was going to marry her?" Jack asked.

"Maybe, but it looks like she changed her mind about wanting to marry him. According to the transcript of her conversation with the FBI, she recently stumbled across some information that made her believe there was a possibility Russell was involved with more than just a string of nonprofits, and she began to question their relationship and wonder if he was involved in something illegal. By this time, the divorce proceedings with his wife were going ahead, but she wasn't sure she could trust him to follow through with marrying her."

"And she was being escorted here to give that evidence to the grand jury," Jack said.

"The preliminary hearing is scheduled for Thursday. According to the transcripts I have between Erika and the FBI, she's been working with them for a couple weeks now and had agreed to testify against him if they could guarantee her safety."

"Except the plane crashed," Jack said. "Something spooks her, and she runs. Convinced, for whatever reason, she can't trust the FBI anymore."

"Maybe because someone broke into the safe house," Gwen said, glancing up from the computer where she'd been searching through the airport surveillance system. "That would cause me to think twice about putting my life into their hands."

"What about you, Gwen? We need to know how she left the airport."

"I've got her walking across the tarmac after the crash, but that was the easy part."

"And after that?" Nikki asked.

"I don't know yet. I'm still trying to find out when—and if—she left the airport," Gwen said, still glued to the screen. "I have to say, though, I've worked with some pretty sophisticated software, but this system's amazing. Not only will it stream the live video, but I can connect to all archived footage. On top of that it's got facial recognition to help identify terrorist threats and individuals on watch lists, and there's even software that will aid in detecting specific activities."

"Like?" Nikki asked, stepping up behind her.

"Objects left behind, congestion, passengers or cars loitering for too much time . . ."

Jack faked a yawn. "Sounds like a bunch of geek talk if you ask me."

Gwen looked up for a second and caught Jack's eye. "Says the guy who just got back from a *Star Trek* convention."

"A *Star Trek* convention?" Nikki's brow rose. "So that's where you took Holly this past weekend. Things must be getting serious."

Jack sat back down at his desk with Erika's telephone records and frowned.

"Should I ask if you dressed up?" Nikki asked, grateful for the brief comic relief that image conjured up.

"Now, I'd pay to see that." Gwen laughed, back to searching the video feed. "I heard they have a costume parade."

"And how would you know that?" Jack asked, bracing his arms against his desk.

"Hold that thought—or rather don't. You might mock my geek skills, but I just found our girl leaving the airport." Gwen rolled her chair back from the computer screen a few inches so Nikki and Jack could see over her shoulder. "First, if we look at the time stamp a couple minutes after the plane crashed, airport security video caught Erika running across the tarmac toward the main terminal. In the aftermath of the crash, apparently no one tried to stop her."

Gwen froze the video, let it pause long enough for them to recognize Erika.

Nikki studied the image. There was no doubt it was Erika, but where was she going?

"Give me another second." Gwen fast-forwarded the tape. "Okay . . . here we go. About sixteen minutes after that, footage picks her up again in front of the airport, picking up a cab."

"Okay. Do we know where she was going?" Nikki asked.

"I'll put in a call to the cab service right now," Gwen said, freezing the tape again as Erika slid into the backseat.

Nikki studied the image on the screen while Gwen made the call. Another passenger, a twentysomething woman, was getting into a cab in front of her. Behind them, an older man was walking toward Erika's cab. White shirt, dark ball cap, talking on a cell phone.

She'd seen him before.

"The cab company's going to call me right back," Gwen said, setting down her phone.

"Can you run the tape back to where she was on the tarmac?" Nikki asked.

"Sure."

Nikki leaned forward as Gwen queued up the video to just after Erika got off the plane. She kept looking back toward the plane as she ran. Even with the graininess of the footage, it was clear from her expression she was scared. And Nikki was convinced her fear hadn't come solely from the crash. The air marshal's death in the seat beside her had clearly spooked her, but that wasn't surprising. What did surprise her was why Erika hadn't headed straight toward the authorities who were working the scene.

She had to have seen something else that unnerved her.

"Stop," she said.

Gwen froze the video again.

"Right there." Nikki pointed to the screen. "There's a man in a white shirt and ball cap. The same man who was behind her when she got into the taxi."

"You're right." Jack folded his arms across his chest and turned to Nikki. "Which means she was being followed."

"Are you able to track her movements inside the airport?" Nikki asked Gwen.

"Given some time, I think so."

"What about her phone records, Jack? Did she talk to anyone after the crash?"

"Yeah." Jack grabbed his notes off the desk. "She made four calls. Three to an unregistered 931 area code and one to a . . . Kim Parks."

"Do we know who she is?" Nikki asked.

"I've got her number and address," Jack said. "The call lasted a minute and fifteen seconds."

"That was the taxi service," Gwen said, holding up the note she'd just scribbled on a pad of paper. "I've got the address where the driver dropped Erika."

"Wait a minute," Jack said, taking the pad of paper from Gwen. "That's Kim Parks's address."

"Let me have her number," Nikki said.

She pulled her cell phone off the charger, punched in the

number Jack gave her, then let it ring a half-dozen times before hanging up. "There's no answer."

Nikki looked at Gwen. "Keep searching the footage and see if you can find out more about her. In the meantime, Jack and I need to pay her friend a visit."

Nikki hurried out to the precinct parking lot with Jack, wishing she had time to change clothes. The weatherman she'd watched the night before had predicted the temperatures would rise to at least eighty-five after the morning storms dissipated. She'd shed Tyler's jacket at the airport after feeling sticky from the humidity.

Her phone rang a couple cars down from where Jack's red Impala was parked. She checked the caller ID, debating for a moment whether she should take the call from her doctor's office or let it go directly to voice mail. Then she figured that putting off the inevitable wasn't going to change the facts and would more than likely make her worry.

"I'll just be a second, but I need to take this call," she said, making her decision.

"Nikki? This is Debbie from Dr. Mallard's office."

"Debbie . . . hi. I didn't expect to hear from you so soon," Nikki said, fiddling with her necklace. Debbie worked as a nurse at her doctor's office but was also a friend from church.

"I know your schedule's busy, but Dr. Mallard would like you to make an appointment to come in as soon as you can to discuss your test results."

To discuss your test results?

Nikki felt the familiar knot in her stomach return. Why was it that everything always tended to hit all at once? She took in a deep breath and sent up a short prayer. She hadn't told anyone about the symptoms she'd been experiencing over the past few months. Figured they would eventually just go away. When they hadn't, she'd finally convinced herself that knowing what was wrong was better than worrying about what might be wrong. But now she wasn't so sure.

"So there is a problem?" she asked, turning away from Jack so he wouldn't hear what she was saying.

There was a pause before her friend continued. "Dr. Mallard will go over everything with you, but the blood work we did all points to ovarian failure."

Nikki needed answers, but she didn't have time to talk right now. Not that there was ever going to be a good time for this kind of news. "The doctor mentioned infertility during my last appointment."

"Nikki, I can't give you a bottom line at this point, and I know this initially seems overwhelming, but the doctor will be able to explain in more detail both the treatment and a number of options."

She blew out a sharp breath. Her brother and his wife had struggled with infertility, but she'd never imagined herself having to look at life without the possibility of having her own children one day.

"Listen," she said. "I'm in the middle of a case right now, but I'll call back in a day or two and make another appointment."

Nikki hung up the phone, then slipped into Jack's car, her head pounding again. The chance that she might not be able to have children was something she hadn't mentioned to anyone, let alone Tyler. He'd talked about wanting more children. What if their life together didn't include more than Liam?

God, I know you've got this, but from where I'm looking at things, it's a bit overwhelming.

"Is everything okay?" Jack asked as he pulled out of the parking lot.

"Yeah," she said, shoving aside any concerns from the doctor's call to deal with later. "Did you get ahold of Kim yet?"

"Still no answer."

Which had her worried. If Erika had gone to Kim's house and someone had followed her . . .

———————

Twenty minutes later, Jack parked outside Kim Parks's one-story house in one of Nashville's older neighborhoods. A couple of towering trees stood in the front, shading the lawn that was still damp from the morning's rain.

Nikki walked next to Jack up the empty driveway beside a row of colorful flowers and shrubs. Either Kim had a green thumb, or she paid a local business to keep up her yard.

She glanced into the window of the garage as they walked toward the front door. There wasn't a car in the driveway or in the garage. She'd called Kim's number three more times since leaving the station, but there was still no answer. A sense of urgency engulfed her. If Erika had come here, where were they now?

Jack banged on the front door, next to the yellow and orange fall wreath, then waited for an answer.

Nothing.

"Doesn't look like anyone's home," she said, glancing down at the doorframe. There was a muddy footprint on the bottom of the door, like someone had tried to kick it open. She tried the handle. "The door's unlocked, Jack."

Nikki stepped into the house behind Jack, her gun raised, feeling her stomach knot. On the long wall of the living room, the news was playing on a flat-screen television. Video of the crash was running in the right-hand corner while a reporter was interviewing one of the passengers.

But something wasn't right.

The place was simply furnished, with an assortment of mismatched furniture, including a desk, a couple cushioned chairs, and a couch with a handful of pillows. A number of stunning scenic photos lined the fireplace mantel and covered the walls. The Smoky Mountains, Cades Cove, the Tennessee River, and at least half a dozen old barns.

If the outside of the house was any indication of Kim's personality, she was neat and tidy. But this space had been trashed. Desk drawers gone through, couch cushions piled up on the floor, and papers strewn across the tan carpet.

"I'll take the bedrooms," she said.

Jack moved past her toward the kitchen, while she turned down the hallway lined with three doors and many more photos. She slowly opened the door to a bedroom, and a cat brushed past her. Ignoring the pet for now, she went on to the next room. This was a newly remodeled bathroom with more photos, this time of seashells and ocean scenes.

And a pile of clothes on the floor, including a red sweater with gold buttons.

She stepped into the master bedroom, that had at one time, she could tell, been a quiet, tranquil place. There were candles next to the bed with its brown comforter and orange accent pillows, along with three stunning photos of the Smoky Mountains in fall. White curtains billowed in the breeze from the open window leading out to the backyard.

But today there were signs of a struggle. Everything from the top of the dresser had been knocked onto the floor. The comforter and pillows lay in disarray at the bottom of the bed.

Nikki skirted the edge of the queen-sized bed, then froze. A young woman lay on her back, a trail of blood starting from the base of her head and running onto the carpet. Her eyes were open wide, as if she'd been caught by surprise.

Nikki reached down and felt for a pulse. Rigor mortis hadn't set in yet, but the woman's skin was tight and gray. She was thirtysomething with dark brown hair, but it wasn't Erika. And she'd been dead only a short time.

It had to be Kim.

Nikki's mind ran through the timeline. Erika had left the airport around noon and the taxi had dropped her off here about thirty minutes later. Had Kim been killed because of Erika? And if so, where was Erika?

"Jack?" she called out, grabbing her phone to call for backup. "We've got a body."

7

"The rest of the house is clear." Jack appeared in the doorway. "What have you got?"

"A dead female . . . midthirties. It's not Erika, so I'm going to assume it's our home owner, Kim Parks." Nikki pulled on a pair of latex gloves, then crouched back down beside the body. "I've just called for backup."

"So much for keeping the investigation quiet." Jack folded his arms. "Can you tell how she was killed?"

"There's a gunshot wound to the side of her head."

A leather purse lay beside the body, its contents dumped across the floor near the nightstand and under the bed. Nikki moved back the edge of the ruffled bed skirt, uncovering the edge of a compact Glock 19 handgun.

She felt a shiver go through her as she crouched down next to the weapon. "Looks like she was trying to get to her gun when the attacker came in."

"I searched the rest of the house. Whoever did this is gone," Jack said. "So what do you think happened? They show up looking for Erika, discover she's gone, so they try to get answers from Kim and end up killing her?"

"It makes sense," she said, pulling out a driver's license from the wallet on the floor next to the purse.

"It's a Tennessee license issued to Kim Parks. Thirty-two years old, living at this address, and the photo matches our body." Nikki held up the driver's license so Jack could see it. "I'll call Gwen and see if she was able to come up with any more information on our victim."

Jack nodded. "Stay here with the body, then. I'll go set up a perimeter and wait for homicide to get here."

Nikki reached for her cell phone again. Sirens were already beginning to blare in the background when Gwen picked up.

"Did you find Erika?"

"No, but we found our home owner." Nikki took a step back from the body. "She's dead."

There was a pause on the line, but Gwen didn't have to speak for Nikki to know what she was thinking. Their job wasn't to deal with murder scenes. It was to find people *before* something happened to them.

But this time they'd been too late.

"What about Erika?" Gwen asked. "Any sign of her?"

"The clothes she was wearing on the plane are in the bathroom—but she's gone." Nikki moved to look out the front window, avoiding Kim's lifeless body on the beige carpet. The morning storms had passed, leaving behind a sticky, high humidity. "Were you able to come up with anything on Kim Parks?"

"Just a few basics at this point. There is no marriage certificate on file for her, and she lived at that address for almost three years. She worked as an executive secretary for a law firm downtown."

"And her connection with Erika?"

"You'll have to give me a bit more time to figure that one out."

"We'll talk to the neighbors. See if anyone saw anything. And see what they might know about Kim and her relationship with Erika." Nikki glanced toward the door at the sound of voices coming down the hall. "Call me if you come up with anything else. I've got to go."

"I understand there's no sign of Erika?" Brinkley asked, striding into the room and stopping at the end of the bed.

"No, just a dead body." Nikki shook her head, wondering how the FBI had gotten to the scene so quickly. "We're assuming at this point, Erika came here for a change of clothes and to borrow Kim's car."

"So Erika was followed here, and whoever came after her tried to stop her," Brinkley said.

"Your guess is as good as mine at this point." Nikki glanced at the body, then back to Brinkley. There were questions she needed to ask the agent before official backup arrived, though Brinkley wasn't going to like them. "I read through the files you sent over."

"And?"

"There are three logical options at play at this point. Either Erika was able to get away in Kim's car before the intruder showed up, she was taken by the intruder after Kim was killed, or Erika isn't who you think she is."

"What do you mean Erika isn't who I think she is?"

Nikki drew in a deep breath. If they were going to find Erika, she needed to either shoot down or verify the theory. "I need to know how well you knew Erika. Because I need to know if it's a possibility she was playing you?"

"Playing me. You can't be serious."

"I'm very serious," Nikki said. "Erika had nothing to lose. In the transcripts I read through, you threatened her with jail time if she didn't cooperate. What if she found a way to pacify your agents *and* the man she loved at the same time."

"That's not what happened. We put a bit of pressure on her when she got scared," Brinkley said, keeping his voice down, "but she was scared of Russell, not us. Besides that, her flipping on us doesn't add up. She came to us."

Nikki frowned. No matter what Brinkley said, it all sounded too convenient. Too wrapped up in a package and delivered to the FBI's doorstep. And now two people, including the air marshal and Kim Parks—both people Erika had contact with—were dead.

"You think she's going to change her testimony when she gets up in front of the jurors?" Brinkley asked.

"I'm just looking at all the possibilities."

"Well, you're wrong. She wasn't playing us. Wells and I clocked countless hours interviewing her."

"Love can be a powerful motivator," Nikki said.

"So can doing the right thing," Brinkley said. "She was determined to do what she believed was right."

"Special Agent Boyd."

Nikki glanced up as Sergeant Dillard from homicide stepped into the room in front of Jack. The sergeant, whom she'd worked with in the past, stood a couple inches shorter than Jack's six foot two and was wider around the middle.

"I'm going to start worrying about you and your partner trying to take over my homicide cases if you keep showing up at my crime scenes," Dillard said, shooting her a grin.

"Trust me, as soon as we brief you, this one is all yours," Nikki said. A briefing that was clearly going to be limited, due to the FBI's involvement.

She glanced at Brinkley, who nodded at her, then quickly brought the sergeant up to speed, leaving out the part—for now at least—that Erika had been a key witness for the FBI.

"Thanks for the update," the sergeant said. "I was told you would need to be kept in the loop on this one. I'll personally ensure everything we learn is sent your way as long as you keep me up-to-date as well."

"No problem, sergeant," Nikki said. "And in the meantime, I'd like to see if I can find a couple of neighbors who might have known Kim."

"What about you, Agent Brinkley? Is there something I need to know about the FBI's involvement in this one?" Sergeant Dillard asked.

"There's a possible link with the victim to an ongoing investigation I'm working on."

"Then let me know if you have any other questions."

Nikki followed Brinkley and Jack out of the bedroom and into the living room. The television was still on, playing a seemingly never-ending loop of the crash in the background while a young blonde journalist reported on every angle. At the moment, they were showing photos of the four people who had died in the crash. The next of kin must have been notified. Either that, or someone leaked the flight manifest to the media after doing their own digging.

"They've confirmed Patrick Hughes as one of the men who was killed in the crash," Brinkley said, nodding at the television.

Four dead.

Seventeen injured.

The numbers might change over the next few hours, but one thing wouldn't change. The lives of every person who'd been on that plane had been altered forever.

A photo of Patrick Hughes was shown as they reported on the fatalities.

"Wait a minute." Nikki took a step closer to the television and shook her head.

"What's wrong?" Jack asked.

"What do you know about the dead air marshal?" Nikki asked, turning to Brinkley.

"Our team handpicked him to do the job. Why?"

She stared again at the man on the screen. "That's not the man who was on the plane."

"What do you mean?" Brinkley moved next to her in front of the television.

"I mean, that's not him."

"Of course that's Patrick. Like I told you, I handpicked him myself and have worked with him a dozen or more times."

"You told me the flight manifest didn't lie, but I'm telling you that isn't the man who sat next to Erika and me on that flight. So if that really is Patrick Hughes—"

"Then where is he?" Jack asked. "And who was the man in seat 29A?"

8

Nikki caught the panic on Brinkley's face as he grabbed his phone and punched in a number.

"You're positive that isn't the man who was sitting next to Erika on that flight?" Brinkley asked, waiting for the call to go through.

Nikki glanced back at the television. "Positive. Granted, there's a close resemblance, but the guy on the plane was a few years older, military-type haircut, and grayer."

"Close enough to pass for the marshal with the right credentials?" Brinkley asked.

"Obviously, yes," she said.

"So much for an accurate flight manifest," Jack said, with a hint of defensiveness in his voice as Brinkley stepped away to talk on his cell.

"I still feel like the FBI isn't telling us the entire story," she said, "but Brinkley looked genuinely surprised. He thought Patrick Hughes was on that flight."

Nikki felt a wave of fatigue wash over her. She watched Brinkley's animated gestures while he spoke on the phone, and wondered—not for the first time today—if she should have walked away from the case when it was offered her. She might have been the last person they knew of who spoke to Erika, but they didn't really need her. And besides that, she was feeling the tug of her personal life. Tyler, the doctor's call . . .

Her gaze settled back on the television, where a reporter was interviewing a spokesman from the airline. If Nikki had learned anything over the past few years with her job, it was that life went on, even in the middle of a case. And that tough cases at work didn't keep her immune from difficult situations in her personal life. It was a constant fight to compartmentalize work and that private side. Some days were simply harder than others.

Brinkley hung up the call a minute later, his jaw tensed. "Sorry about that."

"Who else knew that she was coming by plane?" Nikki asked.

"Just Wells, Hughes, the officer who dropped her off at the airport, a couple of higher-ups. We've kept the list as short as possible."

"You mentioned a leak in your team—"

"Yes, but it still doesn't make sense. I trust Wells and the others working this case with my life. Just like Erika was supposed to trust us with hers."

"That's all good and noble in theory," Jack said, "but you've still got a missing witness and now a missing air marshal on top of that."

"What about Russell?" Nikki asked. "Any sign of him? If he's the one after Erika—"

"No, but I'll let you know as soon as we find him."

"Okay, then what do you want us to do now?" Nikki asked, her hands resting on her hips.

"I'll work on finding our air marshal," Brinkley said, "while you keep looking for Erika."

Nikki nodded. "Gwen's still working back at the precinct, trying to trace who else Erika communicated with after the crash, but since we don't know where she went from here, the best next step at this point is talking with the neighbors."

"Agreed," Brinkley said, already heading for the door. "Call me as soon as you find something."

Nikki stepped outside the house with Jack behind Brinkley. A woman was standing on the sidewalk in front of the house next door. She pulled her earphones out of her ears, frowning as she glanced across the yard into Kim's cordoned-off property.

Nikki approached one of the officers working the scene. "Has anyone spoken to the woman next door?"

"She's been asked a few initial questions, but she hasn't yet been informed that the victim was murdered. She was getting ready to go running, but she knew the woman and agreed to stick around if there were further questions."

"Have you interviewed anyone else?" Jack asked.

"Not many people home this time of day, but Sergeant Dillard has a couple officers canvassing the neighborhood."

Nikki nodded. "Let me know if you find anyone else who knew Kim or might have seen what happened."

"Will do."

Nikki and Jack crossed the strip of grass between the two houses. Kim's next-door neighbor looked to be in her late twenties, with dark-brown hair pulled up in a ponytail. She wore Nike shorts and a hot-pink short-sleeved T-shirt.

"Ma'am," Nikki began, holding up her badge and introducing herself and Jack. "We were told you live here?"

"Yes."

"And your name?"

"It's Riley . . . Riley Silva." She was still staring across at Kim's house. Distracted. "I already spoke with one officer, but no one will tell me what happened. Is Kim okay?"

"Were the two of you friends?" Jack asked without answering her question.

"Yeah. But what's going on?" She pulled on her earphone cord and caught Nikki's gaze. "Please. You're scaring me."

Nikki took in a slow breath. Nothing she could do would ever prepare her for this moment. Because she knew what it was like on both sides.

"I'm so sorry to have to tell you this," Jack began, "but we found Kim murdered in her home this afternoon."

"Murdered? Kim? No . . . no, that's not possible." Riley stumbled back a few steps and sat down on the bottom porch stair, looking around like she was waiting for someone to tell her this was nothing more than some horrible joke.

Jack signaled for Nikki to take over. Dealing with weepy women wasn't one of his fortes.

"Riley . . ." Nikki took a step forward and knelt down in front of the woman. "Can I call someone for you?"

"No . . . I . . . I'll call my husband in a few minutes." Her hands gripped her thighs, and she was struggling to breathe. "She can't be dead. It's just not possible. I mean, everyone . . . everyone loved Kim. She took in stray cats, for goodness' sake. Worked Thanksgiving at the homeless shelter, and always remembered my birthday."

"I really am sorry, Riley," Nikki said, sitting down beside her. "What happened?"

"We're not sure at this point. It looks like someone might have broken into the house. We're doing everything we can to find out exactly who did this and make sure they're arrested."

"Someone broke in." Riley shook her head, tears streaming down her cheeks. "In the middle of the day? This neighborhood has always seemed so safe. I've never worried. Even when my husband travels on business."

"Can I ask you a few more questions?" Nikki asked. "We want to make sure we find whoever did this to Kim."

Riley pressed her lips together and nodded.

"Have you been gone all day?" Nikki asked.

"I had an early morning meeting at work, then came home to run. I'm training for a marathon." Riley stared at the sidewalk, her voice barely above a whisper.

"So you didn't hear or see anything unusual."

"No. Nothing."

"When's the last time you saw Kim?"

"Last night. She brought me a plate of brownies. She's a bit of a foodie. Always trying out new recipes. Her love for desserts only managed to wreak havoc with my running regime and diet, but now . . . a few extra unwanted calories don't seem to matter at all."

She was crying again. Quietly sobbing. Nikki gave her a moment to compose herself before continuing.

"How long had you known her?"

"My husband and I moved into this neighborhood about three years ago. She moved in a couple months after we did. Said she hated apartments and wanted a bit of land. She was nice. We hit it off right away. We're about the same age, working far too many hours away from home."

"Does Kim have any family?"

"Nobody close by. I guess that's why we were good friends. Most of my family's in New York. Her father passed away a few years ago, but her mother . . . I think she lives in Shreveport, and she's also got a sister who lives out in California. She usually goes to visit one of them for the holidays."

Nikki pulled out her phone and held up a photo of Erika. "Did you know Erika Hamilton?"

"Erika? Yes . . . She was one of Kim's friends. We used to hang out together sometimes. Wait a minute. Is she involved in this somehow? Is she okay?"

"We hope so. She's missing."

"Missing. I don't understand all of this." Riley pressed her fingers against her temples and started rubbing. "And you think that this . . . that Kim's death and Erika's disappearance are somehow related?"

"Yes, we do."

"This is crazy. I mean, you read about horrible things happening to people you don't know, but when they happen in your own neighborhood . . . to people you know . . ."

"Can you tell me about Erika?"

Riley sniffed. "She, uh . . . the three of us hung out sometimes. Went to the gym. Or more often than not, Kim and Erika talked about how they should be at the gym. I never could get them interested in running. Erika came around every few months. She had this really obsessive boyfriend, and from what she said, he didn't really like her to have other friends."

"Did you ever meet him?" Nikki asked, showing her a photo of Russell.

"Yeah, that's him. I just met him once. He seemed decent enough, I guess. Just too jealous and clingy for my taste."

"Do you know how they met?"

"I think she worked for his wife at one point, but they were getting a divorce. Or at least he kept telling Erika he was going to divorce her. You know how men can be. Full of promises they never intend to keep."

"What about friends, family?" Nikki pressed. "Anyone she spent time with?"

"I know Erika has a brother. I think his name is Justin. He came around here a few times with her. Nice guy, though I heard he ended up going to prison a few months ago. Not sure what he did. Erika wouldn't talk about it. I think it embarrassed her, though they seemed close."

"I'll see what Gwen found out about Erika's brother from the FBI notes," Jack said, stepping away from the porch steps.

Riley looked up at Nikki and caught her gaze. "Why all the questions about Erika? You don't think she's dead too, do you?"

"All we know right now is that she's missing," Nikki said. "Tell me more about her boyfriend. You said he was obsessed and jealous."

"Those are my words, not hers, but Kim and I talked about their relationship a few times, and we were worried about her. Kim even tried to talk to her a couple times about it, but I don't think she listened. She'd been seeing him for several years. Took her to all kinds of fancy parties and fundraisers. Gave her an allowance." Riley picked at a sliver of wood on the edge of the step. "He is a bit of a sugar daddy, though I think she really does love him. She came by one night wearing this black, open-back sheath dress. She told us it had cost over two thousand dollars. For a cocktail dress with barely a yard of material." Riley shook her head. "He'd also given her some diamond-stud earrings. Crazy, isn't it?"

"Was she afraid of him?" Nikki asked, as Jack stepped up beside her.

"She never said she was, but I wouldn't be surprised. There were a few times when she hinted there was a problem, but like I said, she never came out and said so. At least she didn't to me. She was closer to Kim, and I do know that he didn't like her coming to see Kim. I actually got the impression he didn't like her having friends at all. I mean, Kim was a hard worker, but she made a living as a secretary. He had this fancy house in an upscale neighborhood in Houston where Erika spent a lot of her time. Neither of us were exactly the kind of people he wanted her hanging out with."

"And yet she still came by?"

"Erika was loyal to her friends, though she always seemed torn. She loved the attention and the clothes." Riley took a tissue from her shorts pocket and blew her nose. "I'm sorry . . . I just can't believe Kim's gone."

"Riley, I'm going to give you my card. If you can think of anything else that might help us find her, or if Erika tries to contact you, please give me a call."

Riley took the card. "Okay."

Jack's phone rang as they headed toward his car. He took Gwen's call and put it on speaker.

"Did you find anything on Erika's brother?" Jack asked, stopping at the end of the drive.

"The woman you were interviewing was right. Erika's brother, Justin Peters, was convicted of embezzling from his boss and is currently serving a three-year prison sentence."

"Do you have any way to know when Erika last spoke with him?"

"Erika wouldn't have been able to call her brother in prison, but they do have a new system set up where friends and family members can leave a message. Messages are then passed on to the prisoner. I called in a favor and found out that Erika left a message for Justin shortly after the plane crashed, asking him to call her as soon as he could. I listened to the message. She sounded upset."

"We'll head back to the precinct now," Nikki said. "If you could arrange for us to talk to her brother, she might try to contact him again."

"And what about Russell's ex-wife," Jack asked. "She might be able to help us track down Russell. I'm convinced that if we find him, we'll be able to find Erika."

"It might take longer to get you both in to talk with Justin,"

Gwen said, "but I can have Russell's ex-wife brought in to the precinct in the meantime."

"Do you really think Erika might be behind Kim's murder?" Jack asked, ending the call.

"I don't know, but we've got two people dead and one common denominator," Nikki said, matching his stride as they headed for the car. They needed to tie the facts together if they were going to find Erika, but she wasn't convinced they had pieces from only one puzzle. "Which seems to mean that either Erika's having a string of very bad luck, or like I told Agent Brinkley, she's playing him."

Jack unlocked his car. "I definitely agree it's a possibility we can't ignore."

"Agent Boyd . . . Agent Spencer!" Brinkley jogged down the sidewalk toward the car. "Hold up, will you?"

"I thought you'd left," Nikki said, slamming the door shut and stepping back onto the curb. "What's going on?"

"I was just getting ready to leave the scene, but I received a phone call from a contact with the Houston PD."

"And . . ." Nikki said.

"A store employee found a body in a Dumpster this morning, about six miles from Hobby International Airport, and called 911." Brinkley's fists balled at his sides. "The authorities just identified the man as our marshal . . . Patrick Hughes."

9

6:03 p.m.
Kim Parks's front yard

"I just can't figure out how this happened," Brinkley said, stepping off the curb in front of Nikki and Jack, then shoving his fists into his pockets. The veins in his thick neck pulsed as he spoke. "Hughes called me on his cell phone when he was pulling into the airport short-term parking garage. He was there."

"What about the officer who was supposed to hand Erika off to him?" Nikki asked, feeling her own frustration growing. "Have you spoken to him?"

"He says he checked the man's credentials and everything seemed fine. They met next to security as arranged, and a minute later he left."

"What time was that?" Nikki asked.

"About forty-five minutes before the flight was supposed to leave," Brinkley said.

"Then there had to have been a second man," Jack said. "Someone had to have taken out Hughes right before Erika was handed off to our fake marshal."

"And he probably planned to 'escort' her right to Brian Russell when they got to Nashville," Nikki said, leaning against Jack's car.

"Agreed," Jack said, "but there was something they couldn't have figured into their plan—"

"The crash," Brinkley said, finishing his sentence for him.

"But the plane does crash," Nikki said, "and when Erika realizes her 'bodyguard' is dead, she gets off the plane, only to recognize one of Russell's men, so she panics and runs."

She looked back up at Kim Parks's house, where the sun was beginning to drop beneath the roofline. The coroner was rolling the young woman's body toward the ME's van. Most of what they knew was nothing more than speculation. Nikki longed for real evidence, something concrete to build out from.

Her cell phone went off as she started for the passenger door.

"Gwen?"

"Just wanted to let you know that Russell's ex-wife is on her way to the precinct. She goes by Claire Gordon now, and according to her, the next hour's the only time she could possibly even consider taking time out of her busy schedule."

"I'm going to assume she's not happy about coming in?" Nikki asked.

"Not at all."

Nikki watched Claire Gordon rush into the precinct thirty minutes later like a tornado, in her short tweed skirt, three-inch heels, and an oversized black purse slung across her shoulder. A young woman who didn't look a day over eighteen walked half a dozen steps behind her, lugging a leather briefcase.

"Ms. Gordon." Nikki thanked the officer who'd escorted the

woman into the station, then introduced herself and Jack, all the while taking in the bleached-blonde hair and heavy makeup. "We appreciate your coming down and speaking to us about your ex-husband."

"Please, call me Claire," she said. "I hope this won't take long. I have a dinner I can't miss at eight."

Nikki flashed the woman a smile. "Then the sooner we get started, the sooner we can finish."

A phone went off and Claire fished it out of her bag. "Would you mind excusing me for just a moment. I need to take this call."

"We really need to—"

She held up her hand, then stepped away.

"I'm sorry." Her assistant fiddled with the padded shoulder strap on the briefcase and shrugged an apology. "She has a huge art show starting this weekend and is a bit distracted with all the details. She won't even let me handle most of them, and I'm supposed to be her assistant."

"How long have you worked for her?" Nikki asked.

"Three months. She can be a challenge to work for, but I'm learning a lot. And she pays well."

Claire ended her call, then pressed her hand against her chest before walking back to them. "That was the caterer for this weekend's new art show. My regular caterer came down with the flu, which meant I had to find someone else at the last minute, but now the man calls me every hour with a new question." She caught Nikki's gaze. "Then on top of that, I now have to deal with Brian and some kind of federal investigation. He always did have bad timing."

Nikki opened her mouth to speak, but Claire wasn't finished with her tirade.

"Trying to come up with a new menu for the hors d'oeuvres is enough by itself to push me over the edge today, and now—"

"Ms. Gordon . . . Claire," Nikki interrupted. "I understand

81

that you're a very busy woman, and I'm sorry about the problems with your caterer, but if you wouldn't mind putting down your phone for a few minutes and stepping into the conference room with me, this won't take long at all. I promise."

"Fine." Claire frowned and turned to her assistant. "If he calls back with any more questions, tell him to call George. He might be sick, but he owes me that at the very least." She handed the girl her phone. "Make sure he got my message about adding those raspberry truffles so we have another gluten-free option for those with dietary restrictions."

"Yes, ma'am."

"And if—"

"The sooner we get started, the sooner we can finish," Nikki said through a forced smile.

"I'll wait here and handle the caterer," the young woman said, taking the phone from her boss. "And the show will end up being perfect, like it always does."

"Fine."

"Then if you'll come with me," Nikki said. "We just have a few questions we need to ask you about your husband and his businesses."

"I don't know why you people keep calling me in." Claire followed Nikki down the narrow hallway where Jack waited for them, her heels clicking against the tile flooring. "I'm sure it's in your records somewhere that I have already spoken to the FBI several times, and each time I told them that I don't know anything about Brian's business ventures outside the ones we share together. And yet they keep calling. And on top of that, they've never been able to prove any of their accusations against him, which are all circumstantial. Surely they know it's simply a waste of time and that the judge will throw out the case against him if it ends up going to trial."

Not if they have their witness.

"And," Claire continued, "my lawyer assured me that I was in no way connected in the upcoming trial." She paused. "Should I have called my lawyer? Because—"

"Claire . . ." Nikki said, stopping in front of Jack and interrupting the woman's tirade. "This is my partner, Special Agent Jack Spencer. He'll be joining us in the conference room."

Claire sat down on the edge of the offered seat in the precinct's simply furnished conference room, finally quiet.

"Like I've already mentioned," Nikki said, "we're only interested in finding your ex-husband."

"He was in Texas last time I talked to him, though I hardly keep tabs on him anymore unless I need to discuss business with him," Claire said.

"I understand that, but it is crucial we get ahold of him, which means speaking to those closest to him. Can you tell me when you last saw your ex-husband?"

Claire fiddled with one of her fake fingernails. "I spoke with him briefly on the phone five . . . maybe six days ago. He seemed fine."

"What is your current relationship with your ex-husband?" Jack asked.

Claire leaned forward, elbows on the table, long, manicured nails now clicking the tabletop. "Our divorce finally went through a couple months ago, but while we're definitely no longer a couple, our divorce was amicable, and we decided to remain business partners. It made sense financially."

"Tell me about the business ventures you have with him," Nikki said. "You run an art gallery. Does your ex-husband have anything to do with it?"

"We're co-owners. We work primarily with local artists both here and in Houston but also represent a few on an international level. Edgar Grimes, for example. We run one of his galleries in downtown Nashville."

"And some of the profits made through the galleries are then donated to various charities?" Jack asked.

"Brian's always been a bit of a philanthropist. He has family money and uses my gallery for fundraisers for various non-profits." Claire leaned forward and tapped her nails against the table. "But like I've said, the FBI has already asked me countless questions, which I answered to the best of my ability. I thought this was about finding Brian."

"It is. We have just a couple more questions, and then we'll let you get back to work." Nikki flipped over the folder in front of her and pulled out Kim Parks's photo. "Do you recognize this woman?"

"Should I?"

"Take another look," Nikki said.

Claire frowned. "I can't be certain, but I don't think I've ever seen her. You have to understand that not only do I own a number of businesses but I'm always hiring staff, both full-time and part-time, from gallery managers to the caterers."

"What about this woman?" Nikki asked, pulling out a photo of Erika.

A flicker of recognition crossed the woman's face. "I believe she worked at the gallery a few years ago. We have a number of interns in the summer, particularly who are enrolled in local art programs. They mostly answer phones and greet clients. I can't remember her name."

"Erika Hamilton."

"Yes, that was it."

"So she doesn't work for you anymore?"

"She's been working at our Houston gallery the past few months, I believe."

Jack leaned forward and caught the woman's gaze. "Did you know that Erika was having an affair with your now ex-husband while you were married?"

Claire shoved the photo back across the desk. "What happened when we were married doesn't matter anymore. And so what if they were? The key word in our relationship is 'ex.' He has the right to do what he wants and so do I, because trust me, any spark died out in our marriage long before the actual divorce went through."

"Was she the reason for the divorce?" Nikki asked.

"Not at all. It was a mutual separation that had nothing to do with anyone else." Claire sat back and folded her arms across her chest. "But what does she or any of this, for that matter, have to do with me?"

"That's what we're trying to find out," Nikki said. "Erika Hamilton is missing, and the other woman in the first photo I showed you—a friend of hers—was found murdered this morning."

"Murdered?" Claire's jawline tensed. "I don't understand."

"We are still trying to find out what happened, but apparently someone wants Erika dead," Nikki said.

"Someone like you who must have been upset . . . resentful even, when you found your husband had been unfaithful," Jack said.

"I—wait a minute . . . of course I was resentful, angry even, but it wasn't like she was the reason our marriage fell apart. She wasn't the first one, and she certainly won't be the last. Brian's weakness is beautiful women. And unfortunately, I wasn't enough for him. But none of this has anything to do with me."

"I think it does," Jack said, sitting down next to Nikki. "If your ex-husband is convicted of money laundering and other crimes, the government is going to scrutinize everyone he's in business with, including you."

"You're not actually implying that I had something to do with this?" Claire's eyes widened as if she'd never heard the same implications from the FBI before. "I have no idea where Brian is, so if you need to know anything beyond that, then you can contact my lawyer. I'm done here."

"That's fine," Nikki said, standing up. "I need you to wait here for just a couple more minutes and then you may leave."

Nikki signaled Jack to step outside with her before Claire could protest.

"Even if she does know where he is, she's clearly not going to tell us," she said once they were in the hallway.

"You think she's protecting him?" Jack asked.

"Maybe, but even more likely, I think she's protecting herself." Nikki glanced down the hallway. "I want to talk to her assistant. Maybe I'll get more out of her."

"I'll find a way to keep Claire here for a couple more minutes," Jack said, then stepped back into the conference room.

Nikki walked down the short hall to where the young woman sat on a long bench with the briefcase on the floor between her legs. Black-and-white polka-dot skirt, maroon sweater. Nikki grabbed a bottled water from the fridge in the break room, then headed back to where the young woman was sitting.

"Hey." Nikki handed her the bottle of water. "Sorry to keep you waiting. We shouldn't take much longer, but I thought you might be thirsty in the meantime."

"Thanks," the girl said, taking the offered drink.

"I didn't catch your name earlier," Nikki said, sitting down beside her. "I'm Special Agent Nikki Boyd."

The girl pushed her large-framed black glasses up the bridge of her nose. "Maggie Kemp."

"Maggie . . . You said you worked for Ms. Gordon."

"Yes, ma'am." Maggie shuffled the water bottle between her hands.

"How long have you known her?"

"She's my mother's cousin, actually. They were best friends

in high school. So when I graduated from college in the spring and needed a job, Aunt Claire hired me."

She spoke as if it were an opportunity she should be grateful for but wasn't.

"And what exactly is your job?" Nikki asked.

"I'm her personal assistant. Which really means I do whatever she asks me to do. Everything from scheduling, to keeping up with her agenda, to dealing with unhappy clients." Maggie glanced up and winced. "Not that there a lot of unhappy clients, but you know . . ."

"Sounds as if she's very lucky to have you," Nikki said.

Maggie shrugged. "My mother says I should be grateful to have a job, but it's temporary. I'd like to be an illustrator one day."

"Sounds fascinating," Nikki said. "I understand she owns an art gallery downtown?"

"The Moreau Gallery, but she also owns several other local businesses, so I have to stay on top of those as well."

"You must stay pretty busy."

"It's not exactly a nine-to-five job, if that's what you mean. I end up working a lot of overtime."

"I was wondering," Nikki said, pulling out the photo of Erika. "Do you recognize this woman? We're trying to find her."

Maggie set her water beside her on the bench and took the photo. "Erika? Yeah, she's a friend of Uncle Brian's."

"And by friend, you mean . . ." Nikki waited for Maggie to answer.

"I guess it doesn't matter if I tell you. Everyone knew they were having an affair, even my aunt. But I haven't seen her for a while." Maggie unscrewed the lid to her water bottle. "Is she okay? She was always nice to me."

Nikki took back the photo. "She's missing."

"And you think my uncle's involved?"

"I don't know, but I'd like to ask him," Nikki continued, not wanting to scare the girl away. "Do you have any idea where your uncle is?"

"I . . ." Maggie stared at the water and frowned. "No. I don't really see him all that much."

"But you've heard from him lately?" Nikki asked, taking a chance that Maggie knew more than she wanted to say.

"No . . . It's just that every now and then he calls me and asks me to do things for him."

Nikki caught the guilt in her eyes. She was lying about something. "What kind of things?"

"Sometimes he would have me set up dates with other women. You know, dinner reservations, or tickets to shows when he was in town. He made me swear I wouldn't tell anyone. Especially Aunt Claire. And especially before their divorce went through."

"So she didn't know he was seeing other women?"

"Oh, she knew. She always told me they had an open relationship and she was okay with it, but I know she really wasn't. Especially when she tried to butt into my own relationships. She's pretty protective of me, even though I'm an adult now."

"Maybe she doesn't want you to learn the hard way like she did."

Maggie finally took a sip of her water. "Maybe."

"We need to find him, Maggie. Anything you can tell me is very important."

Maggie shifted on the bench. "He's always been nice to me. I don't want to get him into trouble. He's promised to pay for me to go to art school, though my mother thinks that a second degree would be completely frivolous."

"Maggie, I need you to tell me the truth. When's the last time you heard from him?"

Maggie's gaze dropped and she drew in a sharp breath. "He called me yesterday and asked me to arrange a flight from Houston to here for him."

"A commercial flight?"

"No. He owns his own plane. I just had to make sure the pilot was available on short notice to arrange the details of the flight." Maggie glanced down the hallway. "He . . . he arrived here last night. Told me not to tell anyone, especially Aunt Claire. But I haven't heard from him since. In fact, I tried to call him this afternoon. Usually he has me make hotel and dinner reservations for him too, but he didn't this time. I'm not even sure where he's staying."

Nikki gnawed on the information Maggie had just given her. So Brian Russell was right here in Nashville. Helping to ensure Erika never made it back into the feds' custody?

"Will you promise me something, Maggie?" Nikki pulled out one of her business cards. "I won't tell your aunt about our conversation, but if you hear from your uncle, I need you to call me. Please."

Maggie nodded, but the guilt in her eyes had shifted to fear.

10

Nikki lengthened her steps in order to keep up with the prison warden who'd arranged for her and Jack to speak with Erika's brother. She'd met their escort once before. Michael Weldon was close to fifty, with thick salt-and-pepper hair, and thin as a rail. Though it wasn't the first time she'd visited the prison, there was something about the thought of continual confinement that always managed to rattle her nerves. She'd much rather be rappelling off the side of a cliff than spending time in the enclosed corridors of a prison.

Trying to shift her mind from their surroundings, she turned back to Weldon. She had her own file on Erika's brother that Gwen had put together for her, but she wanted to hear from someone who worked in the prison system and knew the man.

"Tell me what you know about Justin Peters," she said as they made their way down the dreary gray hallway and matching tiled floors.

"He's in for embezzling a large chunk of money from his boss."

"Behavior wise?" Jack asked.

"For the most part he keeps to himself and stays out of trouble. He's up for parole, so barring any complications, he could be out soon."

"Any family members come to see him?" Nikki asked.

"He's got a sister who comes by every month or so, I'd guess. I'd recognize her but don't remember her name."

"Erika Hamilton," Nikki said.

"Sounds familiar."

"Any other family or visitors?" Jack asked. They needed to know where Erika would go when she was in trouble, and so far their list was way too short.

"Not that I've noticed, though I can get you a copy of his visitors log to verify."

"I'd appreciate that," Nikki said.

Weldon stopped in front of an oversized metal door and pulled out his keys. "Take as long as you need. I'll have a guard waiting to escort you out when you're done."

Nikki nodded her thanks, then stepped into the eight-by-ten room in front of Jack. Beyond a table that was bolted to the floor and a couple of chairs, the room was empty of any furnishings.

A uniformed guard stood near the door while Justin Peters sat on the far side of the table. He had short hair and a hint of a beard, but was clearly more alert than his mug shot taken when he was arrested. When he looked up, Nikki caught the resemblance to Erika in his eyes. And the hint of cold indifference.

Weldon nodded for the guard to step out with him, then shut the door behind them.

Nikki slid into the seat next to Jack. "I'm Special Agent Nikki Boyd and this is my partner, Special Agent Jack Spencer."

Worry lines appeared across Justin's forehead as he leaned forward. "They wouldn't tell me what this is about. If there's a problem with my parole . . ."

"This isn't about your upcoming parole hearing." Nikki softened her voice. They needed him on their side if they were going to get the information they wanted. "We need to ask you a few questions about your sister."

"My sister? Wait a minute." He ran his fingers across the stubble on his jawline, the color seeping from his face. "Please tell me she's okay."

"We don't have a lot of information at this point," Jack said, "but we do need to tell you that she's missing, and we have reason to believe her life is in danger."

"What?" Justin slammed his fists against the table. "No . . . No, I told her something terrible was going to happen to her, but she wouldn't listen to me."

"Wait a minute." Nikki leaned forward. "Why did you think something bad was going to happen to her?"

"There's this man she's involved with. I don't trust him at all. His name's Brian Russell." The coldness was back in his eyes. "I've told her over and over to break things off with him, and if she didn't, she was going to end up getting hurt."

"We're aware that your sister was seeing Russell," Jack said.

Justin splayed his hands against the table and leaned forward. "Then tell me you're questioning him, because I promise you, if something's happened to her, he's responsible."

"We're in the process of bringing him in—"

"In the process?" Justin's voice rose a notch. "So you don't know where he is."

Nikki glanced at Jack. "No."

"And I'm assuming since you're here speaking with me and you believe her life is in danger, you don't think they just ran off together."

"No, but we are doing everything we can to find them both," Nikki said. "Which is why we wanted to see you. We need to know where she might have gone if she thought he was after her. Any friends or family she'd go to if she was in trouble?"

"We don't really have any family. We've got a stepfather who lives in Idaho. Haven't seen him for years. A few distant cousins scattered across the country, but Erika and I were pretty much on our own by the time I was seventeen."

"When's the last time you saw her?"

Justin shrugged. "She visits when she can. And we talk on the phone a couple times a month. I guess the last time I saw her was about three, maybe four weeks ago."

"And friends? Any she might go to if she were in trouble?"

"She's got a few friends here in Nashville. There's this one woman . . . Kim . . . Kim Parks, I think her name is. They're close. I met her once."

"Anyone else?" Nikki kept her expression neutral. There was no use in his finding out Kim was dead. "Any place where she might have gone if she was scared?"

"She's got friends at work, I'm sure, but I've been sitting here for the past two years, so it's been awhile since I hung out with my sister." His frown deepened. "But wouldn't your time be better served out there looking for her?"

She caught the anger in his voice as he spoke and couldn't blame him for feeling helpless. He was locked inside a prison, with no tangible way to help his sister. "We have people looking for both Erika and Russell right now. But the more information we have, the sooner we should be able to find her. And Russell as well."

"What do you know about Brian Russell?" Jack asked. "We understand you used to work with him."

Justin leaned back against the seat, his fingers tapping against the table in front of him. "We were actually once friends, believe it or not. Graduated together from Harvard. I was there on scholarship, he came from family money, and when we both finished school, he ended up helping me get my first job with his family business."

"So what ended your friendship?" Nikki asked.

"Brian was one of those students who claimed he was going to change the world but in reality only cared about his world. I guess I finally wised up." Justin's frown deepened. "I've seen the articles on him in *Time* magazine, but there's another side to him that most people don't know about."

"What side is that?" Jack asked.

"Brian has always struggled with addictive behaviors. He started gambling in college. He didn't need the money but craved the rush of winning. His mother tried to send him to counseling, but he refused to go. Eventually, when his mother's health began to fail, she had him take over running the business and the dozens of charities they were involved in, thinking it would make the addictive behavior go away."

"But it didn't?"

"No. On the outside he remained the poster boy for non-profits. But he was still gambling and drinking. Then I heard rumors he'd gotten involved with someone in the Russian Mafia."

"Dimitry Petran," Nikki murmured, processing Justin's answers. "And were those rumors true?"

"When I asked him, he didn't deny it. That's when I decided I wanted out."

Nikki frowned. "Why didn't you go to the authorities with what you knew?"

"Because I didn't *know* anything. I didn't have any proof. Like I said, Brian's smart. He knows how to cover his trail. He's been doing it for years. And if I went to the feds, it would be his word against mine, and a string of even more powerful people behind him, making sure I stayed silent. I'm sure you can figure out who a jury would believe."

"Where did he and Erika meet?" Nikki asked. If they knew more about who Brian Russell was, they might be able to determine what his next move was going to be.

"Believe it or not, I was the one who introduced Erika to him, something I've regretted ever since. But at the time, she was looking for a job, and he was hiring. I never thought he'd break her heart. Or put her in a situation where her life was in danger."

"How long ago was this?"

"Five . . . six years ago. At first she worked for his wife at one of her art galleries here in Nashville, so they didn't really have a lot of interaction. Then at some employee party, he noticed her and eventually offered her a job in his Houston office. It's not the first time he's done something like this. Brian's a womanizer who goes through women the way most men go through disposable razors. Though I have to say their relationship was unique. He was always coming back to her. Even after he moved to Texas."

"What can you tell me about him and their relationship?" Nikki asked, scribbling notes on the pad in front of her.

"Like I just said, to the world he's charming and good looking and knows exactly what to say. It's his job. His public persona for the family business. He's on the board of half a dozen charities, so he speaks at fundraisers, and you see his face on their brochures and videos. She'd been working at one of his wife's art galleries for about two months when he asked her out. They've been seeing each other off and on ever since, even while Brian was still married. She thought she'd found her Prince Charming, but while Russell might be charming, he's definitely no prince. I think she's finally beginning to realize that."

"What changed for her?" Nikki asked.

"Besides the fact she finally realized he won't stay faithful to one woman? About three months ago, she stumbled across something in his house that put up some red flag, and she started doing some digging. She called me but wouldn't give me any specifics. All I could do was tell her to be careful and hope she was finally seeing the truth for herself. But if Brian knew what she was doing—"

"That she'd gone to the FBI?" Nikki asked.

Justin nodded. "I called her back yesterday. Said she was on her way here for some . . . deposition or something like that . . . against him for the FBI. She told me I was right, and that she had found evidence he was involved in some seriously illegal stuff."

"Was she upset when she talked with you yesterday?" Nikki asked.

"It was more like she was scared. But I tell you, whatever he's into, my sister isn't involved. She might not have good taste in men, but she would never get involved in something illegal."

"Love can make people do crazy things," Nikki said.

Justin's jaw tensed. "Not Erika."

"Did she ever talk to you about the specific evidence she had?" Jack asked, changing the subject.

"She wouldn't tell me anything. She was afraid it would put my life in danger. Brian, he's got connections everywhere. Even here in prison. She was afraid if I knew, then he'd come after me as well."

"If she's afraid of him, why do you think she agreed to testify against him?"

Justin frowned. "I assumed you knew. Erika and Brian have a daughter."

"A daughter?" Nikki glanced at Jack, wondering why in the world Brinkley would have left that out of Erika's file.

"Lily turns four this month and is the cutest kid you'll ever see. Erika brings me pictures of her. And when I get out . . ." Justin's voice broke.

Clearly he had a soft spot for the young girl, but a child caught up in the middle of a missing persons investigation could change everything.

"Erika's afraid for her daughter," Nikki said.

Justin nodded. "After Erika had Lily, I think she expected her relationship with Brian to change."

"She expected a marriage proposal?" she asked.

"Yes, but Brian has kept her hanging since Lily was born, and I don't think he ever had intentions of marrying her. But neither does he want her to leave him. If she does, he says he'll fight for complete custody. And she's convinced he could get it. He's rich and well connected. She works for not much more than minimum wage and has a drug conviction on her record. Who do you think the judge is going to choose in a custody battle?"

"So she's trapped," Jack said.

Justin nodded.

"But if Brian were to get convicted and go to prison, she could end up with sole custody of Lily," Nikki said.

The picture of what they might be facing was slowly taking shape.

"Where is Lily now?" Nikki asked.

"She wouldn't tell me. Only that she had her somewhere safe until all of this is over."

"Friends? Family?" Nikki prodded. If they could find Lily, they might be able to find Erika as well.

"I don't know. Like I said, Brian has connections that have a long reach. She didn't want to take a chance that he'd find her until all of this is over."

"Is there anything else you can tell us that might help us find your sister?" Jack asked.

"Maybe." Justin was tapping on the table again. "When I talked with Erika about three weeks ago, she told me she was convinced she was being followed."

"Why did she think that?"

"She said she'd seen some man on two occasions. I don't have a description, but all I can think of is that Brian might have hired someone to keep track of her. I told her about a friend of mine who could sweep her house. He discovered that the house was bugged."

Nikki frowned. There had to be a connection. Erika was being bugged and possibly followed. The FBI believed there was a mole. Who else had Brian Russell paid off?

"What can I do to help?" Justin begged. "Please? There has to be something."

Nikki pushed a yellow notepad in front of him along with a pen. "I need a list of names. Anyone you can think of that Erika might have trusted Lily with."

"I can't even think right now." Justin tapped the pen against the pad. "It would have to be someone outside of Brian's influence that she would have trusted." He started writing a list of names. "I hope it's enough," he said, pushing it back across the table at her a couple minutes later.

Nikki glanced over the list. "It's a start."

"My sister, she had this thing for falling for the wrong men. Like she thought she could change them or something. Brian wasn't the first one."

Nikki tapped her fingers against the file, studied his face, and caught the flicker of pain in his eyes. "Like Simon Crowley."

He blew out a huff of air. "You know about Crowley?"

"I know Erika was in love with him and he ended up being convicted of killing four women, including your other sister."

Justin rubbed the back of his neck. "Which is why I need

you to promise me you'll find her. Erika and Lily . . . they're all I have in this world. If anything happens to them . . ."

"I will promise you one thing," Nikki said, picking up the file along with the list of names and standing up before catching his gaze. "We're going to do everything in our power to find them before it's too late."

11

Nikki followed Jack and the guard out of the interview room, wrangling with more questions than she'd had when they'd first arrived. There were too many holes in the files the FBI had given her. Like why hadn't they told her Erika had a baby? Or that she'd believed someone had been following her? And if everything Justin just told them was actually true, where was Lily?

"What are you thinking?" Jack asked as they made their way toward the entrance of the prison.

Nikki's mind churned through the facts they did have. "That the FBI continues to keep us in the dark over this case. I'm not even sure why they need us at this point. Because, do you honestly think that the FBI didn't know about Lily?"

"No, but if they were hiding that fact, I can't help but wonder what else they're hiding."

"And if Erika hadn't told them about Lily, then why? Wouldn't she want protection for her child?"

"Maybe she didn't trust them," Jack said as they continued

toward the exit. "And considering the fact that someone already managed to get to her while she was in the safe house, I'd say she had good reason for not trusting them. Lily gives both Erika *and* Russell motivation we didn't know about before. And if what we know about Russell is true, he'll use Lily as leverage to get to Erika if he finds her first."

Nikki nodded, ready to get out of the claustrophobic feel of the prison, already knowing at least part of the answer to the question of why the FBI didn't tell them about Lily. Clearly the stakes were far higher than a custody case. And whatever Erika had discovered was worth killing for.

"Nikki?"

Nikki turned around at the sound of her name, then smiled at the familiar face. Aiden Lambert worked as a deputy commissioner for the Department of Corrections and had called in a few favors for her the past few months regarding a recent lead on the disappearance of her sister.

"Aiden . . . hey. It's been a while."

Three months ago, she'd met him at a local restaurant, where he'd given her the name of the Coyote. And that name had become the only solid lead they had on her sister's abductor, even after a decade of combing through every piece of evidence. Robert Wilcox, aka the Angel Abductor, had terrorized East Tennessee in the early 2000s by kidnapping and murdering young girls.

Her sister, Sarah, had been one of his last victims.

But knowing his name had done little to move forward her sister's investigation and instead had proved to be another dead end. Robert Wilcox had escaped during a prison transport ten months ago, and no one knew his whereabouts. The leads they had might have all run cold, but she knew he was out there. And that not only did Robert Wilcox hold the key to her sister's disappearance, but he had the capacity of striking again if they didn't find him.

She shivered despite the warmth of the hallway.

"Do you have a minute?" Aiden asked.

His voice pulled her back to the present.

"Yeah, sure." She turned to Jack. "Give me a second, will you? I'll catch up with you at the entrance."

Jack nodded, then left with their escort as Nikki walked back to where Aiden stood, feeling the familiar ache churning in her gut. If he'd found another lead on the Angel Abductor . . .

"I've been planning to call you." Aiden shoved his hands into the pockets of his pants. "Been wondering how you're doing."

"Wondering if I've been following your advice?" She stopped in front of him. He'd told her she should walk away from her sister's case. That after ten years of searching it was time to let the past go. She might not have agreed with his advice, but he was only telling her because he knew the endless hunt for Sarah had put her through an emotional roller coaster. He was worried about her chasing ghosts. And getting hurt in the process.

Except Robert Wilcox wasn't a ghost. And while she might not be any closer to tracking him down than the day Sarah disappeared, she wasn't ready to give up. Because being on the victim side of a case was completely different from her day job.

He shot her a smile. "I knew you had no plans of taking my advice, but that doesn't mean I'm not concerned. The not knowing can be just as tough as finding out the truth."

"And you think I still need to walk away from my sister's case?" she asked, already knowing his answer.

"I just know the odds of finding out the truth after so much time has passed. But you know that as well as I do." His expression softened. "Did you follow up on any of the leads I gave you the last time we met?"

Nikki fiddled with the heart necklace where she kept Sarah's photo. No matter what Aiden or anyone else thought, she was far from being ready to stop searching for Sarah. "I spoke to the sister of Wilcox's girlfriend. She hadn't heard from Wilcox in years." It had been another dead end.

"What about Wilcox's attorney?"

"She doesn't know anything more than what you or I know. Or if she does, she won't tell me. Which means unless we can actually track down Wilcox . . ." She didn't finish her sentence, but ten years of dead ends took a toll on a person. Her mother. Her father. Her entire family. Ten years of not knowing if Sarah was dead or alive, or what she'd gone through in those moments during and after her abduction.

"I know that putting this case to rest isn't going to be easy, but I still think it's the right thing," Aiden said. "I've seen too many people struggle for too many years trying to find a resolution that isn't going to happen. It's tough when there isn't any closure, but sometimes there's nothing more you can do."

"Meaning Sarah's dead and we'll never find her?" Nikki tried to bite back the anger in her tone, but no matter how many years had gone by, no matter how small the chances were of Sarah being alive, there wasn't a day that passed that she didn't pray her sister would still walk through their door.

Flashbacks and nightmares came less frequently than they used to, but they still occurred. And sometimes it felt as if those moments had just happened yesterday. The day Sarah disappeared. The moment she'd realized Sarah wasn't coming home. When the police told them they were no longer going to actively search for Sarah.

That day, the officer had shifted on the worn leather couch across from her mother, while Nikki sat quietly beside her. "Mrs. Boyd, I understand that you're frustrated, but for the past eighteen months my department has been doing everything in our power to find your daughter. You know that. But in the last few weeks every lead we have has dried up. And unless we come across some new information . . ."

"So what are you saying? That you're done looking for my daughter—"

"Of course not." He leaned forward, hands on his knees, ready to bolt.

"But that is what you're saying. Except my daughter's out there somewhere. Some man has done something unspeakable to her, and you're going to walk away."

"Mom—" Nikki laid her hand on her mom's arm.

"Don't try to justify what you're doing. Your job is to find her. To dig up new information. Whatever it takes."

"Ma'am, I understand your frustration, but sometimes there's nothing else we can do. Though that doesn't mean that we won't get a break in the case at some point. But right now—"

"Do you have any children?" her mother asked.

"No." He was squirming again.

"Then don't sit in the middle of my living room and tell me you know what it's like to lose your baby. It's been eighteen months and you haven't found anything. No solid leads to where she might be. You can't even tell me if my little girl is dead or alive."

Her parents hadn't been the only ones searching for new information. After Sarah's abduction, Nikki turned in her resignation to her principal, applied to the police department, and entered the police academy training program.

"Nikki . . ."

She glanced up at Aiden, regretting the snap in her voice. Regretting that ten years later she still hadn't found Sarah. "I'm sorry. I didn't mean it that way. It's not an excuse, but it's been a tough day."

"Forget it. I really do understand."

She caught something in his eyes. Something she'd never noticed before. "All this is personal, isn't it?"

Aiden's gaze shifted. "I don't talk about it very much. My

mom was killed by a drunk driver when I was seven. They never found the guy in the other car."

She felt a shot of guilt slice through her. So he did understand. "I'm so sorry."

"My dad eventually remarried a wonderful woman when I was nine. But I wish I had more than a few photos and fuzzy memories."

Photos and memories were all she had left of Sarah. "Do you think it would make a difference if you found the person who killed her?" she asked.

"My dad has accepted and completely moved on with his life. But I always struggled to forgive and resented growing up without a mother. Anyway . . ." Aiden seemed to shrug off the question. "In the end, you have your motivation for taking your job. I have mine. Though I know your situation is different. At least we were able to have a funeral for my mother."

Nikki bit the edge of her lip, wishing she didn't feel so emotional. She forced the memories of Sarah back into their own compartment to deal with later. "I know that the odds of finding Sarah alive are almost nil, but that doesn't mean I'm ready to go there. I'm not sure I'll ever be ready to go there."

On the other hand, if Sarah was alive . . . But that was another tough reality. She'd followed the cases of the women who'd been held hostage for months and even years, like Elizabeth Smart, and like the three women who'd been kept for over a decade in Ohio. Studied their psychological profiles and the struggles they faced when coming back into society. Life would never be the same for them.

"What I need is closure for my family," Nikki said. "Even if that means finding Sarah's body or listening to a confession by the person who took her."

Nikki studied Aiden's darkening expression. He looked like he was trying to decide if he should tell her something.

"There's something else, isn't there?" she asked, trying not to get her hopes up. But even the smallest of leads allowed her to keep holding on to that thinning thread of hope that one day they'd find out the truth.

He glanced down at the tiled floor. "You always were good at reading people."

"It's my job."

"I've started to pick up the phone to call you a dozen times over the past couple days, but I didn't know what to say."

"What do you mean? What happened?" Nikki felt her stomach drop. "There's nothing you can tell me that could hurt me more than what I've already gone through."

Because on top of the loss of Sarah was the guilt that she could have stopped what happened to her sister if she simply would have been on time to pick her up that day.

"Even if it changes everything?" he asked.

She nodded, bracing herself for what he was about to say.

"The authorities found Wilcox."

"Wait a minute . . . They found him?"

"He's dead, Nikki. They found his body in a back alley in Memphis."

Nikki leaned against the cold cement wall, her heart pounding. If Wilcox was dead, she had just lost the only connection to the truth of what happened to her sister. "How did he die?"

"It looks as if he was murdered," Aiden said. "But the coroner hasn't finished his report yet. I'm sorry. I know this isn't what you wanted to hear."

"I'd like to see the coroner's report as soon as it's released." It probably wouldn't make a difference, but neither was she ready to let go. They needed to find out who killed Wilcox. See if there was a chance that he'd given someone details of what he'd done.

"Of course." Aiden nodded. "I'm sure that won't be a problem. And Nikki . . . I really am sorry."

"I know."

She fought back the swirl of emotions swelling inside her. After ten years of searching for the truth, was this how it was all going to end?

A couple uniformed guards rushed pass them, shouting something into their radios and pulling Nikki out of the past.

"What's going on?" she asked.

"I don't know. Probably just some routine drill."

Nikki couldn't help but let out a low laugh. Nothing had been routine about today. But an eerie feeling settled in her gut. She'd seen the look on one of the guard's faces. There was nothing routine about this.

A second later, Aiden's phone rang. He took the call, a shadow crossing his face as he turned back to her.

"Aiden, what is it?"

"I need to get you out of here," he said, grabbing her elbow. "I don't have any details, but there's been an attack. One of the inmates and a guard are down."

"Who?"

"I wasn't given any specifics," he said, quickening his pace.

He led her down a narrow hallway. She could hear their footsteps echoing as they walked past the gray walls. Doors were shut tightly on either side. The narrow hallway started to close in on her. Her pulse pounded in her temples. It was like being in a dark tunnel where she couldn't find her way out. Like being in a plane that was hurling toward earth at a couple hundred miles an hour and there was nothing she could do to stop it.

God, I feel so out of control today. Like everything is spinning in the wrong direction and I can't stop it.

Her job. Her personal life. Her health.

She tried to shove away the feeling of panic. She was the

one who conducted the investigations. Who stayed in control of every detail of her cases. But today everything had changed.

Her heart pounded, even though she knew they were safe. She glanced behind her. The upped security they had to go through just to speak with Justin should have been enough to assure her of that.

Aiden rushed her around another corner. She looked up and caught the worry lines around his eyes.

This was definitely not routine.

"If my wife finds out about this, she's going to make me quit." His jaw tensed. "We've got a baby on the way. Number two."

"Congratulations."

"Thanks, but kids somehow manage to change everything. Beth's getting tired of worrying if I'm going to come home in one piece. Recent budget cuts mean less security. The last six months have been rough."

"I'm sorry. That's got to be tough on both of you."

And she understood. Because what Beth had was what she wanted. That someone to come home to every night. She knew Tyler worried about her. A couple close calls in the past few months might have made them both realize they had feelings for each other, but today had made her reevaluate again how quickly everything can change. And the price she sometimes had to pay to ensure justice was served.

A noise behind her pulled her from her thoughts. She turned around as two inmates in orange ran toward them. Her mind scrambled to process what they were doing out of their cell-blocks.

A guard was down . . . one of the prisoners hit . . .

Nikki's heart jumped in her chest. Aiden moved in front of her, but before either of them could fully react, the shorter man—balding and with tats down both arms—slammed Aiden into the wall.

The taller one—black with a rough scar across his cheek—tried to stop her. Her shoulder throbbed as he wrenched her arms behind her. She fought to pull away, but she couldn't get the momentum she needed to throw him off of her.

The other convict pulled a knife on Aiden as he tried to fight back, then slammed him against the wall again. Aiden slid to the ground, leaving behind a trail of blood against the wall where he'd been stabbed.

12

Nikki stumbled backward as Aiden slid down the wall onto the floor. His phone tumbled out of his hands. How in the world had this happened?

She plunged toward the inmate blocking her way to Aiden and slammed her elbow into the man's throat. He stumbled backward, caught off guard for a fraction of a second before turning back toward her and smashing her against the wall. Her lungs gasped for air as he grabbed her. She'd underestimated his strength. He was solid muscle, with at least thirty pounds on her.

I need you to help me get out of this, Jesus. Please.

She couldn't stop fighting yet. She had to find a way to get her and Aiden to safety. Thick arms reached around her from behind. With a rush of adrenaline, she squatted, then pressed against him with her back, using momentum to throw him off of her.

The taller inmate pulled out a gun and aimed it at Aiden, stopping her in her tracks. "You run, I kill your friend."

She glanced back at Aiden. He was staring up at her, panic in his eyes. Face pale, hands shaking next to him, while blood pooled at his side on the floor. He'd never make it if he didn't get immediate medical attention.

"We need to get out of here now, Finn." The gunman's jaw tensed. His expression hardened and focused. "Tie her up with the belt. She's coming with us."

Finn shoved Nikki's arms behind her, then tied them securely with the belt.

"Wait." She tried to move back toward Aiden, but the inmate only tightened his grip on her arm. "He's going to die if he doesn't get help."

"Do I look like I care? You're our ticket out of here, and we're going. Now."

Their ticket out of here?

A wave of panic swept over her. How had a simple interview for a missing persons case landed her in the middle of a hostage situation? A guard and a prisoner were already down. They'd somehow managed to smuggle weapons into the prison in preparation of a hit. Which meant this wasn't necessarily a crime of opportunity. Neither were they worried about anyone getting in their way. They hadn't hesitated at stabbing Aiden. And they wouldn't hesitate getting rid of her either if they felt for an instant she was a liability instead of leverage.

She glanced at her captors. Sirens were blaring. They were starting to lock down the building. Whatever happened over the next few minutes, this wasn't going to end well without a miracle.

Aiden looked up at her as they started dragging her away from him. "I don't know what you want, but leave her out of this. Please."

"If you leave him to die—" she started.

"Shut up."

Footsteps pounded ahead of them.

"Cipher . . ." Finn looked at the other inmate. "We're out of time. They're coming down the east corridor."

"If you hadn't stabbed them . . . ," Cipher said.

Finn pressed his fingers against Nikki's bruised shoulder in a tight grip, shoving the knife he'd stabbed Aiden with against her back. "If I hadn't stabbed them, we'd be dead."

She fought to concentrate as they ran down the opposite corridor with her, searching for a way to stop what was happening. But if she tried to run, they'd kill her. And if she didn't run . . .

Tyler had been right. She never should have continued with this case. She should have told the FBI to handle this case on their own and gone home and slept for the rest of the week. Because she hadn't been ready to get back on the field. Not emotionally. Not physically. And there was no way she was ready to handle something like this.

Except she had to be.

She couldn't let them win.

She could hear her father's voice.

Dig deeper, Nikki. You're braver than you think.

She fought to focus as she started praying, digging up strength she was going to need in the following seconds.

You're stronger than you feel, Nikki.

Someone shouted behind them. Had the guards found Aiden? She glanced behind her. Even if she did manage to escape the two men, she was now turned around with no idea how to get back to the entrance.

Cipher yanked open a heavy metal door and shoved her into a room, then quickly barricaded the door behind them. She glanced around, weighing her limited options. He'd secured them in the library. Blue laminate floor. Eight or so round tables with chairs. Shelves of books along the wall. The overhead lights were dimmed, casting eerie shadows across the room.

"What are we doing here?" Finn asked.

"Thanks to you, the plan has changed."

"Changed?" Finn's frown deepened.

"You've got two choices." Cipher leveled the gun at Finn. "You can do exactly what I say from now on and get out of this place with me, or you're on your own."

"Wait a minute. Escape?"

Nikki glanced at Finn. If escaping wasn't their goal, then what in the world had been their plan in the first place?

"There's no way they'll let you leave," she said. "They're locking down the building."

"She's right." Finn glanced at the door. "How long do you think it's going to take for them to find us?"

"You really think things can get worse for me here? And even with three men down, there's not much more they can do to me. Besides, this is that chance I've been looking for. We've got the leverage we need. A hostage."

"And if they catch us . . . then what?" There was fear in Finn's eyes. "They'll add the death penalty. Is that what you want?"

"Maybe you should have thought about that before smuggling in weapons and stabbing those men." Cipher turned to Nikki, ignoring his question. "What's your name?"

Nikki hesitated, glancing from one man to the next. Cipher was clearly in charge, and she hadn't missed the panic in Finn's voice. But an escape? They might have a hostage and a weapon, but did he really think the officers were going to let him walk out of here? She knew that whoever was put in charge of negotiating was going to do everything they could to neutralize the situation short of an escape.

"Your name!" he repeated.

She looked at him, fighting to erase the fear she knew hovered in her own eyes. "Nikki Boyd."

He grabbed her arm, pushed her into one of the chairs, then

squatted down in front of her. "You were with the deputy, so I know you're not here visiting an inmate. Which means you got to be law enforcement."

She caught the darkness in his eyes and felt a chill slither down her spine. There was no doubt in her mind that he wouldn't hesitate to kill her if she got in her way. "I'm with TBI. Their missing persons task force."

Finn started pacing in front of them. "She was here to interview Peters."

Cipher's frown deepened at Finn's comment. "Aren't you the smart one."

"Is that who you attacked?" Nikki asked, trying to put things together.

Cipher stared at her like he was about to strike, but she wasn't finished. The more information she could get out of them the better.

If she made it out alive.

"If that's true, then who ordered it? Brian Russell?" Nikki studied Cipher's face, knowing she was pushing her luck. But Justin had told them that Russell had connections in prison. And that Russell wanted to ensure that the evidence Erika had would disappear.

"Shut up and quit asking questions," Cipher said.

But she didn't miss the flicker of recognition in his eyes. Justin had been right. Russell's connections were far-reaching.

Nikki's phone started ringing. She tugged on the belt still securing her wrists. Jack would be worried, wondering what had happened to her.

"I should answer it," she said, glancing at her captors. "They know I'm in here and are going to assume something's wrong when I don't walk out."

"Where's your phone?" Cipher asked.

"In my back pocket."

She winced at his touch as he pulled it out.

"It's my partner," she said, glancing at the screen as it stopped ringing. "He's here and he's going to keep calling until I answer."

"Then we're going to call him back," Cipher said.

"Call him back?" Finn stopped pacing in front of them. "And what . . . tell him where we are? You're an idiot. Every guard in the prison would be in here in a matter of seconds."

Cipher held up his gun and pointed it at Finn's head. "If you think I'm an idiot, then you should have stayed back in your cell."

"We've got a string of bodies and a hostage, and you think they're going to let us walk out of here?"

Cipher flipped off the safety. "Shut. Up!"

"Why? Because you know I'm right?"

"Maybe Cipher is right," Nikki said, feeling the need to play into the man's ego without making him feel backed into a corner. "We can call my partner, and if you let me go now, I'll put in a word for you. Tell them you didn't hurt me and that you're willing to put an end to this. That will go far with the DA, I promise."

"We're not giving ourselves up," Cipher said. "And you're still going to call."

"Then what do you want me to say?" Nikki asked.

"When your partner answers, you will ask to speak to whoever's in charge. They should have a hostage negotiator in place at this point. Tell them I want a car with a full tank of gas, a fresh set of clothes for both of us, twenty thousand dollars in unmarked bills, and a clear way out of here. You'll come with us, then we'll dump you off somewhere once I know we're in the clear."

She caught the antagonism in his steely eyes and knew he wouldn't keep his word. He'd dump her off somewhere, all right—after he killed her. Which meant she needed to find a way to stop this before it went any further.

But how?

"And if they don't agree to your demands?" she asked.

"Then I kill you. Because like I told you, I have nothing to lose at this point." He shoved her chin up with the barrel of his gun, forcing her to look at him. His veins pulsed beneath the dragon tattoo running down his neck. "And if you try to send them some coded message or say anything I don't tell you to say . . ."

Nikki nodded, her own heart pounding, and swallowed hard. *Give me the right words, Jesus . . .*

Cipher pressed the button for the last number received, then put the call on speaker, his weapon pointed at her chest.

Jack answered on the first ring. "Nikki?"

"Jack . . ." She could hear the sirens blaring in the background, making her head pound.

"Nikki, are you okay?"

"I'm okay, but I need to speak with whoever's in charge of the lockdown."

"Wait a minute. Where are you?"

"Please, Jack. Just do what I ask."

She could hear voices in the background as Jack talked with whoever was with him.

A moment later, she heard another man's voice. "This is Lieutenant Long. Is this Special Agent Nikki Boyd?"

Cipher nodded at her to answer, still hovering over her.

"Yes. I'm here with two of your prisoners as their hostage. You're on speakerphone, so anything you say they'll be able to hear."

"Are you injured?" he asked.

"No, but Aiden Lambert is. He was stabbed in one of the hallways, and he's going to need immediate medical attention."

Cipher squeezed her arm. She closed her eyes, wishing she couldn't see Aiden's face staring up at her. Wishing she could stop thinking about his family, their unborn baby. How were they going to deal with his death?

God, you've got to save him . . .

"We've found him, and he's receiving medical care. Where are you?"

Cipher leaned down and whispered into her ear. "Stick to the demands. Nothing more."

"They have a list of demands," she said, pulling away from his hot breath.

"I'll be working with you to make sure this ends as soon as possible and to ensure your safety."

Nikki bit her lip. They couldn't ensure her safety. No one could. There were things that happened in life that no one could control or stop.

"Nikki, are you still there?" The agent's voice pulled her back to the present.

"I'm here."

"What are the demands?"

She glanced back up at Cipher. "A car with a full tank of gas. Two sets of clothes. Twenty thousand dollars in unmarked bills."

There was a pause on the line. "It's going to take time to get that together. Especially the money."

Cipher stepped away from her with the phone. "You've got exactly thirty minutes to get us what we asked for, or I will kill her."

He hung up the call and tossed the phone into a chair beside her.

Nikki glanced at the other man, her mind automatically going to her training. She wasn't going to be able to completely rely on the men outside this room negotiating her release. Not in this situation. She was the one here, dealing with them face-to-face. She was the one who needed to try to prove to them she understood where they were coming from and get them to trust her.

Finn paced in front of them. "You do realize, don't you, that even if you get out of here, she'll never let you see Chloe."

Nikki glanced at Cipher. "Who's Chloe?"

"It doesn't matter."

"His one regret of being in here," Finn said.

"Your daughter?" Nikki asked, needing to find a way to connect.

The hard lines on Cipher's expression softened slightly. "She turned five last week."

"You must miss her."

Cipher shrugged. "I just hate that her life's no different from my childhood. No father, mother working seventy, eighty hours a week."

"You could still end this now," Nikki said, "before things get worse. At least you might be able to see her from here."

"Before things get worse?" Cipher shook his head. "You think we're stupid? There's only one way to end this."

He was wrong, but there was still one thing she needed to know.

"Why did Russell hire you?" she asked.

"We were just supposed to rough Peters up," Cipher said. "See what he knew."

"And if he did know something?" she asked.

Cipher's gaze dropped.

Nikki felt a shiver rip through her. They were supposed to make sure he didn't talk.

"That guard got in the way," Finn said.

"So you stabbed him as well?" she asked.

"We did what we had to do."

Cipher turned the gun back on Finn. "Shut up! You've said enough."

"Why?" Finn stepped forward in challenge. "You think I trust you to get us out of here alive? Because I think she's right. They're not going to let us walk out of here. Even with a hostage."

"Then you walk out of here and let me do this on my own, you coward."

The veins in Finn's arms bulged as he lunged at Cipher, grabbing for the gun.

"Stop, both of you." Nikki jumped up from her chair, still trying to free her arms. The safety on the weapon was off. If the gun fired, whether accidently or on purpose, Finn wasn't the only one liable to get hit.

The sound of the gun firing ripped through the air. It was too late. Finn staggered toward her, his face frozen in pain. Blood spread across his chest where he'd been shot. He grabbed her arm, trying to catch his balance. But instead, he crumbled to the floor, pulling her with him.

"You didn't have to shoot him!" she said, scooting away toward the wall. "Let me help him. He's going to bleed to death if we don't do something."

"He's an idiot and the reason I'm in this mess. I never should have agreed to let him help me."

Nikki leaned against the wall, shaking. She was tired, her nerves were on edge, and she wasn't in any mood to cooperate.

"You killed him," she said, staring at Finn's lifeless body.

"I had to. He lunged at me. And you'll be next if you don't shut up."

The phone rang again.

Cipher hesitated, then picked up the phone as he pointed his weapon at her. "Tell them the gun went off by accident and everyone's fine."

"And if they don't believe me?" she asked.

"Make them believe you," Cipher said, taking the call and putting it on speaker.

"Nikki . . . we heard a gunshot. Is everyone okay?"

Nikki glanced up at Cipher. "We're fine. The gun went off by accident."

"We're working on getting what you asked, but we don't want this situation to explode. Give us one more minute."

One more minute?

She looked at Finn's dead body, then to the door, trying to read between the lines. They knew the men had tried to kill at least three people. They knew shots had been fired in the room. And that both men had nothing to lose.

They didn't want the situation to explode.

They needed another minute.

What were they trying to tell her?

That they weren't going to wait any longer.

Anticipating their next move, she closed her eyes and turned toward the wall. A second later, a sharp burst of light filled the room as men in boots swarmed into the room.

13

All Nikki could hear were garbled shouts around her. Someone brushed against her, but she couldn't see anything beyond the bright lights of the flash grenade across her line of sight. They were shouting at Cipher to stand down and drop the gun. Shouting at him to put up his hands and not move.

"Agent Boyd." Someone's hands were on her shoulders, then undoing her hands from behind. "I'm Lieutenant Long. The SWAT team has things neutralized. You're safe now."

She nodded, shaking and disoriented. A wave of nausea swept through her. If only she could block out the flashes of light and the noise . . . She pressed her forehead against her knees. "All I can see is light and spots."

"Give it a few minutes and the spots will go away. Another fifteen or so and your ears will hopefully stop ringing."

Hopefully? He'd better be right.

"You sound like you've done this before." She touched her temples, wishing the ringing in her ears would stop. Her head was killing her. And the flashing wouldn't stop.

"A stupid dare at the academy," the lieutenant said, stepping away from her. "Your partner's here."

"Nikki, it's Jack. Are you okay?"

"I think so." She could hear the snap of handcuffs as they secured Cipher and then the shuffle of boots as they led him out of the room.

"There's blood on your hands and face," Jack said.

The room began to slowly come into focus as the bright lights faded. She looked down at her hands. Jack was right. They were covered with blood. Finn was lying beside her. Still. Lifeless. There was a bullet hole in his chest, with blood pooling onto the ground. It could have been her lying there on the hard floor. Things could have ended so differently.

A domino effect of wrong decisions had brought them both here to this moment. She started rubbing his blood off her hands, onto her shirt. She wanted it gone. Wanted all the reminders of what had happened today gone.

"The paramedics are here, Nikki." Jack's fingers tightened around her arm. "They need to make sure you're not injured. Is that okay?"

She held up her hands. "It's not my blood. He shot his partner."

God, all I wanted to do was help people. To make sure families didn't suffer like ours did when they lost someone, but this . . .

Dig deeper, Nikki.

You're stronger than you feel. Braver than you believe.

He gives strength to the weary and increases the power of the weak.

The words echoed in her mind. There had been so much loss. So much death. And they still hadn't found Erika.

"They started fighting about what to do. Finn tried to grab the gun," she said, trying to make sense of everything that had happened. "The weapon went off."

"We'll worry about what happened later. Do you think you

can stand up?" Jack asked. "There's a chair over here where you can sit while the paramedics check you over."

Her legs shook as he helped her up and led her to a chair, where a woman with short brown hair and a sympathetic smile cleaned up her hands and face. But the bloodstains on her shirt were still there. All she wanted to do was go home and change and forget today ever happened.

"You were right," Jack said, still hovering beside her as the paramedic finished up. "It's not your blood."

"Do you hurt anywhere?" the woman asked.

"Just my head. It's pounding."

"That's typical after a flash bang. We'll give you some pain medicine. Anything else?"

Besides feeling like she was in a brain fog? "I don't think so. I just . . . I just want to get out of here."

The room was closing in on her. She was fighting to breathe against the panic. The coroner zipped up Finn's body to her left. She didn't know where they'd taken Cipher, but he was gone. Did he regret what he'd done at all, or had it been worth trying to escape?

Maybe that didn't matter. All that really should matter at this moment was that it was over and she was safe. But not everyone involved was okay.

She glanced up at Jack as her mind started clicking through the events of the past hour. "What happened to Aiden? I was with him when he was stabbed." Her heart pounded. If he hadn't made it—

"He's at the hospital," Jack said.

"Is he going to be all right?" she asked.

"From what I understand he's been stabilized and will be okay."

Jack was still right next to her, holding her hand, trying to steady her, but she could feel her hands trembling and her heart racing as she struggled to convince herself it was over and she was safe now.

"What about Justin? Is he the one they stabbed?"

Jack nodded.

"And . . ." Nikki pressed.

"All we know at this point is that he's been taken in for emergency surgery."

"It's all connected," she said, as she took the pain medicine and water offered by the paramedic. "They stabbed Justin. It had to be a hit, hired by Russell."

"You're sure about that?" Jack asked.

Nikki nodded. "Yeah, I'm sure."

Which meant they needed to question Cipher. Find out what he knew about Russell. Maybe lead them to Lily's father.

"Agent Boyd." The lieutenant was back again, standing in front of her in his tactical gear. "I'd like to ask you a few questions while everything is fresh in your mind. Is that okay? We need to know what the inmates said while you were with them."

Her head pulsed as she tried to focus on his request. She wanted to help. Wanted to figure out as much as he did what had just happened. But all she really wanted to do was go home. To see her family. To see Tyler. Anything that was normal. How had this simple missing persons case turned into such a nightmare?

"Nikki?" the lieutenant asked again. "Is that okay?"

She nodded, then let Jack walk with her down the hall to an office. Fluorescent lights buzzed overhead. The air conditioner hummed in the corner. Her ears were still ringing. At least they'd turned off the sirens.

She sat down in one of the chairs next to Jack.

"Can I get you something to drink before we start? Maybe some coffee. I promise this won't take long."

She was nodding again. Following orders. Still feeling numb. She waited another couple minutes while someone went to get her some coffee. It was dark outside now. Street lamps lit up the parking lot. She glanced around the room. She should feel safe. But she didn't. She wanted to go home, not sit and talk about what had happened.

The lieutenant came back into the room. "Sugar and cream?"

"Thanks."

He set a large cup in front of her. "I promise not to take long. I just want to ask a few questions, then Jack will take you home."

She took a sip of the coffee. It was bitter and weak, but hopefully the combination of caffeine and painkillers would knock out her headache.

The FBI wasn't going to want her to discuss the details of the case, but at this point she didn't care. They'd withheld information that might have impacted her case. She was through playing games. Especially when lives were at stake and people were willing to kill for what they wanted.

"I'd like you to walk through what happened after the interview you had with inmate Peters," the lieutenant said.

She glanced at Jack, who nodded for her to go ahead. "Jack and I had just finished interviewing Justin Peters in connection with a case we're working on. As we were leaving, I saw Deputy Commissioner Aiden Lambert in the hallway."

"Why did you talk to him?"

"I've known him for a long time. He's been one of my resources in a cold case I've been working on." Nikki took another sip of the coffee. The lieutenant didn't need to know that the cold case was her sister. "While we were talking, he received a call on his phone. He told me there had been an attack on one of the prisoners and that one of the guards had been hit. He said he needed to get me out of there."

Memories surfaced like colors shifting through a kaleidoscope. Fuzzy, then coming into clarity for brief moments, then fading away. The blade of the knife Finn had used to stab Aiden as it caught the light. The feeling of the air being knocked out of her lungs when she'd hit the wall. The blood pooling beneath Aiden.

"Then two of the prisoners came up behind us. They seemed . . . almost panicked. Like whatever plan they'd had was falling apart and they didn't know what to do."

"What happened next?" the lieutenant asked.

"Aiden moved in front of me, but Finn reacted faster. He slammed Aiden into the wall . . . and then he stabbed him."

"So you don't think that the attack on Aiden or the ensuing hostage situation you were involved in was premeditated?"

"No—it started as a hit on Peters."

"Do you know what the attack on Peters was about?"

Nikki glanced at Jack, wondering how much she should say. "You'll have to talk to the FBI about that. It's their case. But what can *you* tell me about Cipher?" she asked, ready for some answers herself.

"He stays out of trouble for the most part. But he's a part of a gang, and we know now—thanks to the gun he had—that he still has connections to the outside."

Like Brian Russell.

Nikki set her coffee down, her brain finally clearing enough for her to begin putting the pieces together. They needed to talk with Cipher. If he could lead them to Russell . . .

Lieutenant Long leaned across the table and handed her his card before standing up. "If you can think of anything else that might help us with our investigation, please let me know. And if we have any more questions for you, we'll be in touch." He nodded toward the door. "The guard will escort you to the exit."

Nikki drew in a deep breath and nodded, but didn't get up. The pain medicine had finally managed to alleviate her headache, but she still felt unsteady. Today had come far too close to pushing her over the edge. Which was why there were times when it wasn't possible to simply look at a case from the outside and not feel personally involved. But no matter what today had thrown at her, she still wasn't ready to walk away. She was even more determined to find Erika and Lily before Russell did.

"What are you thinking?" Jack asked, tossing her empty coffee cup into the trash can.

"That I'm not ready to walk away from this case," she said, standing up. "I need you to help me convince Carter to let me keep working."

"You're kidding, right?" Jack stopped in front of her. "He'll never go for that. Not after all you've been through today."

"Which is why I want you to speak to him." She shook her head and stood up. "I need a good night's sleep and a few pain relievers, but I wasn't hurt. Just a couple of bruises. Erika's out there, and I want to see this through."

"Nikki—"

"I want to talk to Justin again," she said, not waiting for him to shoot down her idea. "I think he knows way more than he told us, and Cipher . . . he can lead us to Russell—"

"Can I give you some advice?" Jack asked, his hand resting on the doorknob. "Because you're not thinking clearly. Let me drive you home. Get a good night's sleep, and don't make any decisions until tomorrow."

"Fine, but just take me to the station, and I can pick up my car."

"Forget it," Jack said, heading out the door. "I'm driving you home. You can pick it up tomorrow."

It was dark outside by the time they stepped into the humid night air. The moon hung in the sky, just like it did every single night. It was the only thing that seemed familiar in a world that had spiraled out of control.

"Why don't I take you to your parents' house," Jack said, unlocking his car. "I'm not sure I should just drop you off at home alone—"

"I'm fine, Jack." She breathed in a lungful of air before getting into his vehicle, thankful to be out of the confinement of the prison. Thankful she was free and alive. "Trust me."

She stared out the window as Jack drove out of the parking lot and onto the main road. She appreciated his concern but knew that what would help her the most emotionally was making sure they found Erika and Lily safe. Cars flew by, their lights searing through her and reminding her of the flash grenade. She couldn't go see her parents. Not tonight. She knew they worried about her. And while they had supported her decision to change careers from teaching to law enforcement, she knew her mom in particular worried about that decision every day. They didn't need to know what had happened tonight.

Because children weren't supposed to die before their parents. But sometimes they did. Or sometimes, you didn't know what happened to those you loved, which was even worse.

Her phone rang. She glanced at the caller ID. It was her mom. She let it ring. If they found out what had happened, they were only going to worry more.

"I spoke with your parents tonight," Jack said. "They were trying to get ahold of you. They're still worried about you after the plane crash and want to see you."

A sliver of guilt shot through her. "What did you tell them?"

"I told them you were okay and that you might be working late tonight. And if you did, you'd call them tomorrow."

"Thanks," she said, leaning back against the headrest. "As long as they know I'm okay, I'll talk to them tomorrow."

"You should talk to them. Sooner rather than later."

She winced at his comment, knowing he was right. She hated leaving them hanging, but she needed time to process things, and they were going to bombard her with dozens of questions. She just wasn't ready for that.

"You sure you don't want to go to your parents'?" he asked, stopping at a red light. "Last chance."

"I'll be fine at home, Jack. I promise." It was time to pick a new topic. "Tell me about Holly. Things seem to be getting pretty serious between the two of you."

"You're changing the subject," he said.

"Aren't you the smart detective."

Jack laughed.

She listened to him talk about his allergist turned girlfriend, thankful for the distraction. She needed the reminder that sometimes life had happy endings. That somewhere in the midst of everything that had happened she could still find a slice of normal.

14

Fifteen minutes later, Jack pulled in against the curb outside her condo.

"Thanks for the ride," she said, grabbing her bag off the floorboard, then opening the passenger door.

"Nikki, wait." Jack laid his hand on her arm. "You successfully avoided talking about tonight. If you need to talk, or vent—"

"I'm too tired, Jack." Was it just this morning she'd been flying home, looking forward to a day with nothing more to do than reconnect with Tyler? Tomorrow she was going to have to deal with her own statement and paperwork, and at some point she'd have to talk with a shrink to make sure she was okay. But she was okay. Or at least she would be okay. She just needed time to sort everything out in her head.

"Look," Jack continued. "I just want you to know that I'm here. Gwen's here. We understand what you're going through.

130

What it's like to get caught up way too close on a case. Like when I got shot, for example."

She turned back toward him and saw the scar on his neck, barely visible in the streetlight. Four months ago, he took a gunshot to the neck and almost died. Sometimes she couldn't help but wonder if what they did was worth the risks. But in those deep moments of soul-searching she knew it was. It was worth it for Sarah and for anyone out there needing a second chance.

"You are right about one thing," she said. "Today did get to me. Physically . . . emotionally . . . I just need to regroup and find some perspective."

Jack shifted toward her in the driver's seat. "Which is why you need to take some time off. No one would think anything about you walking away from this one."

Nikki blinked back tears of fatigue. Maybe he was right. But she also knew how sitting around simply resting was going to make her crazy.

"Everything changed tonight. There's a little girl involved, and if we don't find her—"

"That's where you're wrong. Nothing's changed. And I don't say this because you're not a valuable member on our team, because you are, but you've got to take care of yourself first."

She got out of the car and hurried toward the front door of her one-bedroom loft nestled in a row of renovated houses in the heart of Nashville. Nikki slid the key into the lock, her hands still shaking as she struggled to open the door. Maybe Jack had been right. Maybe being alone wasn't the answer.

Jade, her Russian-blue cat, met her at the door. She pulled the key out and slipped the key ring into her pocket while trying to shove away the panic that refused to lessen.

Jade rubbed against her leg.

"Did you miss me, sweetie?" she asked, picking her up.

Had it really been four days since she'd been home?

Jade purred as she filled her food dish with tuna-flavored kibble. "I'm going to assume Luke took good care of you."

Jade had become the perfect companion for Nikki's job. Totally independent and yet affectionate when she wanted company late at night. And when she was gone for a few days, her brother Luke came by to make sure she was okay.

Nikki flipped on the black-and-crystal chandelier over the dining room table, then set her bag down on the island. The panic was beginning to slip away. There was something comforting in the familiar. Especially tonight, when every hour seemed to bring something unexpected—and usually horrifying. Twelve-foot ceilings, exposed brick walls, decorated mostly with deals she'd found on eBay and local flea markets with her best friend, Katie.

She could feel the physical ache of loss. She wished she could talk to Katie. Even though she had other close friends and family, none of them had completely been able to fill the void she'd left behind.

Except Tyler.

Of course, if Katie were still here, she never would have fallen for Tyler. Or discovered how Tyler "got" her. Because even Katie had never completely understood Nikki's job and why she was willing to take the risks that came with it.

She picked up a note from her brother off the counter and quickly scanned the familiar handwriting. Jade had behaved while she was gone. There was barbeque in the fridge for her—thanks to her mom, who was always worried about her eating habits. And he was going to be playing at the Bluebird Café for their open mic on Monday if she was off work.

She opened the fridge and found the takeaway box with her father's barbeque, a side of coleslaw, and two thick slices of her mama's homemade jalapeño corn bread. Leave it to her mom to make sure she ate a proper meal despite her own hectic schedule. But while she normally loved her father's prize-winning barbeque, her stomach turned at the thought of eating.

She closed the fridge without taking anything out. She hadn't been home since last week. Her carry-on was still somewhere at the airport, which meant at some point she was going to have to deal with all the paperwork required to get it back. The airline had promised to return all belongings once the National Transportation Safety Board was finished with the on-site investigation, but that could take days.

She paused before turning away. Her last doctor's appointment reminder hung crooked on the silver fridge, staring at her. She pulled the paper from the clip, read over the date and time, then crumpled the reminder between her fingers. Maybe it wasn't just her current case that had her nerves humming. Though a plane crash and prison riot were enough in themselves to shove her toward the edge. And now this . . .

She tossed the paper into the trash. It was that balancing act of work and her personal life that always seemed to leave her feeling pulled in too many directions. There was never enough time for family. She neglected friends. And in this case, she hadn't had time to even process the consequences of the doctor's phone call.

And there would be consequences. Having children was something she wanted, but it had always been somewhere on the distant horizon. She'd never found that right person she wanted to spend the rest of her life with. The one person she wanted to commit to raise a family with. Until Tyler. But she couldn't think of that. Not now.

The bottom stair creaked as she went upstairs with Jade following close behind her. Her phone went off again, but she didn't pull it out of her pocket to see who was calling. Already in the past hour, her mother had called twice. Tyler three times. She knew she should answer, but instead she'd let the calls go to voice mail like the others. She needed time alone to gather her thoughts. Of course, it wasn't as if she hadn't been thrown into vulnerable situations in the past.

Then why was she feeling so out of control?

Inside the upstairs bathroom, she let her gaze sweep over the black claw-foot tub, white tiles on the wall with dark grout, wood floor, candles, and a Moroccan rug for color, holding on to the sense of familiarity.

A heavy fatigue swept over her as she stared into the mirror, debating if she should take a bath or simply go to bed. Her face was pale and there was a distinct bruise on her left cheek from where she must have hit it during the crash. The soreness of her shoulder had only gotten more intense. She should take another couple Tylenol and maybe even a sleeping pill to help her rest.

She opened up the medicine cabinet and grabbed the bottle of nighttime pain medicine, then hesitated. She was afraid of the dreams she knew would come, but didn't want to feel drugged when she woke up in the morning.

But avoiding the dreams won out. She pressed open the cap, her hands still shaking, then dropped the bottle, spilling the pills across the bathroom floor. Fighting the tears, she braced her hands against the sink.

I don't know why this is hitting me so hard, God, but I need you here. I need some peace.

She'd had hard days before. Tough cases that had stretched her both emotionally and physically. It simply wasn't possible to do what she did without letting it affect her. She dealt with families whose lives would forever be changed by their situations. Situations that stretched her every time her team got the call.

But today . . . today had managed to suck everything out of her. And it had left her feeling a vulnerability she wasn't used to. She'd meant what she said to Jack about finishing the case. She knew herself well enough to know that sitting at home doing nothing would drive her crazy. But he was also right. She needed to sit this one out.

I'm not sure I can do it this time, God.

The crash . . . the prison . . . the shooting.

She reached down and started picking up the scattered pills and dumping them back into the bottle. The phone rang again. She pulled out her cell and frowned. Tyler's face stared back at her on the screen.

She didn't want to talk to him right now. She didn't want to talk to anyone. After a half-dozen rings, he'd leave a message, asking her how she was. She should answer. Let him know she was okay, because he'd be worried. Eventually—if it wasn't already—her name would end up being tied to the prison hostage situation in the news.

The ringing stopped.

She blew out a sharp breath, set the phone on the sink, and finished picking up the pills. She was being irrational and over-emotional.

The phone rang again.

On the third ring, she stood and picked it up. It was Tyler again.

"Nikki?"

"Hey." She sat down on the edge of the tub, and Jade rubbed against her legs, begging for her attention.

"If I woke you up, I'm sorry. I was worried—"

"I'm still up. I was just getting ready for bed." She stared at the red and gray patterns on the rug. "It's been a long day."

"I called down to the station when I couldn't get ahold of you, but Gwen said you'd gone home. I'm glad. You need some sleep after today."

"I know."

He was right. Everyone was right. She wasn't Superwoman, and made no claims to be. But she was determined, driven, and wanted to finish what she'd started. Because Erika deserved to be found.

"Are you sure you're okay? You sound . . . off."

"I'm just tired. That's all."

She could hear the TV in the background. Probably the news, knowing Tyler. "Gwen mentioned that something happened at the prison today, but she didn't give me any details."

She hesitated before answering. He was pressing for answers without being too straightforward. But if she told him what had happened, he'd only worry more. He'd tell her she needed to step down from the case and take care of herself. But she wasn't ready to do that. Not yet.

Am I wrong, God?

"There was an issue with a couple of the inmates. They locked down the prison and were able to neutralize the situation." She could hear the detachment in her own voice. It wasn't how she wanted to sound, and he didn't deserve her distance.

"Nikki. I saw the news a few minutes ago. One of the prisoners was stabbed along with one of the guards, and there was at least one hostage." There was a long pause on the phone. "You were involved, weren't you?"

The next few seconds brought with them a string of flashbacks and raw emotions. But as much as she wanted to hide the truth from him, Nikki knew she couldn't.

"Yeah. I was there."

She walked out of the bathroom and into her bedroom, wishing he were there and she could tell him in person.

"I . . . I ran into Aiden Lambert after we finished interviewing one of the persons of interest in the case. I was talking to him about Sarah's case. We were walking toward the exit and ran into a couple of prisoners who'd escaped."

"You . . . you were the hostage?" His voice broke, allowing

her to hear the emotion in his voice. He'd already lost so much, and now knew that losing her too was a legitimate fear.

"They held me for just under an hour." She wanted to tell him it wasn't really a big deal. That she'd never really been in danger, but she had. And forgetting was going to take a long time.

"Nikki . . . I'm so, so sorry. I try not to worry, but sometimes . . . When I hear about things like this . . ."

His voice trailed off. She understood his worry. And so had Jesus when he spoke about not worrying about tomorrow because tomorrow would bring its own worries. But sometimes today's troubles left her feeling as if she were drowning.

But at least she knew he understood. Three tours in the Middle East had brought him home with a bullet in his leg. And while he'd healed physically, she knew the emotional scars could quickly erupt when he least expected it.

"I'm okay," she said, unable to tell him she'd watched a man die in front of her.

"I know what it's like to find yourself in the middle of trauma you can't control, Nikki." He didn't sound convinced she was okay. "And these past twenty-four hours . . . It's okay to admit it's more than you can handle."

"You sound like Jack and my mother—"

"You know they're right. They should make you step away from this case, and you know that—"

"I have to talk to Carter in the morning and I'm sure he'll say the same thing. But I found out tonight that there's a little girl involved." She sat down on her bed, pulling a quilt up around her. "I'm sorry. This isn't your fault, I'm just . . . You're right. It's been a really tough day."

He wasn't the bad guy. But she was dealing with too much, including not knowing what his reaction might be when she told him the truth about the doctor. Not knowing if it would change their future together.

For weeks, she'd imagined him coming home and assuring her he wanted that future with her. A future that included a family.

"What time are you going back in tomorrow?" he asked.

"I'll probably be up early." She rested her elbows on her knees. "Even if I don't continue working the case, I'm going to have a pile of paperwork to fill out."

"I could stop by and bring you breakfast before you leave."

I miss you so much right now and wish you were here, but I'm just not ready for this.

There would be time for the two of them when all of this was over.

"You don't have to do that," she said instead. "You've just got home. Liam needs you and I—"

"It's not a problem. I've got a meeting at seven thirty, and we've both got to eat." There was a long pause on the line. "Unless you don't want me to come over."

"No . . . of course I want to see you." She lay back and stared at the ceiling. "We have so much to talk about and there's been so little time with this case and everything that's happened."

She didn't have a real excuse. She wanted to see him. Wanted him to reassure her that everything was going to be okay. With her case. Between them.

"I'm sorry, I'm just tired. I'm not thinking straight."

"I'll pick up something I know you'll love and come by before my meeting. No expectations. No need to talk about anything specific. Just a good breakfast to start your day and even better company."

She laughed. "Okay, because you're right about the company. I'll see you in the morning."

"Good night, Nikki."

"Good night."

She ended the call, then curled up against the row of pillows, too tired to change her clothes. She could see Tyler when she closed her eyes. The way she felt when he smiled. When he touched her. They were heading down a path she wanted to take, but what if she couldn't give him what he wanted?

What if she wasn't enough?

15

The nightmares came like she'd feared . . .

She was running down a narrow passageway, fighting to catch her breath. Her body was shaking from the dampness of the cement walls around her, but she couldn't stop. She could see Lily ahead of her. The little girl sat crying on a narrow ledge, wearing a white dress.

"Don't cry . . . I'm coming, Lily. Just don't move."

If Lily moved, she'd fall. Familiar waves of panic settled in around Nikki. If Lily fell, she'd lose her forever.

"Lily . . . It's going to be okay. I'm going to find a way across."

The ground shifted beneath Nikki's feet. A small avalanche of rocks scattered in front of her. She pressed her hands against the wall to catch her balance. A shaft of light from above showed the passageway dropping off abruptly in front of her. There was a dark chasm between them, which meant no way to get to Lily.

She searched the walls for a place for her fingers and toes to grip. If she could find a way to climb across the rock face, she might be able to get to her.

She turned back to the little girl. Lily was gone. This time Sarah sat on the ledge in her place.

"Sarah?"

Nikki blinked. No . . . It couldn't be Sarah. Sarah had been gone for so long. But she was sitting there with her angelic smile, her blonde hair pulled back in a pink ribbon. Sarah's favorite color had been pink. Her room had pink walls and a pink bedspread.

Nikki pressed her fingers into a fissure in the wall and began to make her way across the chasm, determined to get across. A rock fell, smashing into the wall beside her, and suddenly she was falling—

Nikki woke with a start. She opened her eyes, heart racing, sweating. She'd heard something. Or maybe it had just been a part of the nightmare. She rolled onto her side, confused as to where she was until her eyes focused on the familiar crack of light against the wall from the street lamp, reminding her she was home.

The past twenty-four hours came back to her in a rush. The plane crash. Seeing Tyler. The prison. Talking to Aiden about Sarah. Finding out about Lily . . .

She tucked the comforter tighter around her shoulders, closing her eyes again, willing her heart rate to slow down. She needed to sleep, but even with the pills she'd taken, nightmares had plagued her, waking her up every hour or so in a panic.

Nikki stilled as the bottom step creaked. The same way it did when she came up the stairs. Maybe she hadn't been dreaming.

She shoved back the comforter and slid her body around on the bed until her feet were hanging down against the thick rug on the floor. She heard another noise. She hadn't been dreaming. Someone was in the house.

Taking in a sharp breath, she fought to clear her head. She needed her phone and her gun. She reached into her nightstand for her service weapon, then grabbed her cell next to the lamp. A tree branch scraped against the bedroom window and cast eerie shadows against the wall.

Her fingers wrapped around the door handle. She paused again, listening for sounds, then opened her bedroom door.

The silhouette of a man stood at the top of the staircase, coming toward her with something in his hand. She reacted immediately, striking her elbow against his face. His nose cracked and he started toward her again. This time, she shoved his hand away from her, knocking a taser from his hand. Off balance, he stumbled down the steps in front of her, smashing against the wall at the bottom of the stairs.

He rolled onto his back and groaned.

"Don't move," she said, running down the stairs after him.

Nikki shoved one of the kitchen chairs against the wall with her foot, knocking over a floor lamp in the process. "Sit on your hands in that chair, and don't move."

He hesitated, then followed her directions as she started dialing for backup.

"This is Nikki Boyd from the Missing Persons Unit. I've got an intruder in my house, and I need immediate backup."

"We'll send a patrol car right away, ma'am. They should get there in the next two to three minutes. Are you injured?"

"No. Just get someone here as fast as you can."

She dropped the phone onto the table, wishing she had a pair of handcuffs within reach. Wishing she didn't feel so tired and vulnerable.

The man shifted in his seat.

"I said don't move, or I will shoot you."

"You can't shoot me," he said.

"Oh, really?" Nikki stepped forward until she was half a dozen feet from the man and held her gun out, pointed at his chest. Blood dripped down his face where she'd hit him and probably broken his nose. But she was tired and irritated and at the moment didn't care. "Here's the thing. Normally, I might not be tempted to shoot you, but you caught me on a really, really bad day. I was in that plane that crashed at the airport yesterday, then a couple guys at the prison decided to use me as bait. And now I wake up to an intruder breaking into my house and . . . well, I think you get the picture."

"I wasn't trying to kill you—"

"Then what were you doing?"

"I wasn't supposed to hurt anyone."

"Who were you after?"

He was flustered. He used his shoulder to wipe away the trail of blood from his mouth. "I just do what I'm told and get paid. I don't ask questions."

"You still haven't answered my question. Who were you looking for?"

"I was supposed to come here and take Erika Hamilton with me. I was told she might be in some kind of trouble."

"How noble," Nikki said. "So you were here to protect her with a taser."

"Yes . . . no . . ."

"Who's your boss?"

"I don't have to answer your questions."

Nikki's head pounded. "I'm asking you who's your boss?"

The man just stared at her, his lips pressed together tightly.

"Maybe I can help you," she said. "Does the name Brian Russell jog your memory?"

His eye twitched.

"So it is Mr. Russell."

"I didn't say that."

"You didn't have to," she said, hoping her instincts were right. "Why would you think his girlfriend was here?"

"You'd have to ask him. He gave me the address."

"And how do you get ahold of Mr. Russell?" When he didn't answer she took a step forward. "I asked you a question. How do you get ahold of Mr. Russell?"

The man's frown deepened. "He gave me a phone. That's how we communicate."

"Where is the phone?"

"Don't I get a lawyer or something?"

"Where's the phone?" she repeated.

"Front pocket."

She grabbed the phone and scrolled through the list of calls. There was only one number.

Nikki pushed call, then held the phone to her ear.

"He's going to kill me if he finds out I broke into a cop's house."

"I guess we'll have to take that chance."

She let the phone ring. No answer. No voice mail set up.

"Where is he?"

"Forget it. Shoot me if you want to, but I know my rights, and I'm done talking."

Someone banged on the front door.

Nikki moved to open it, her gun still trained on the intruder.

Two officers stepped into her house. "Are you all right, Detective?"

"I am now."

"Looks like you have everything under control."

Nothing felt under control.

One of the officers handcuffed the intruder, then turned back to her. "Do we need to call an ambulance?"

"I don't think so, though he got the worst of the fight. Someone might want to look at him. I'll come down later today and give my statement."

Brinkley walked through the open door as the officers left. He was wearing jeans and a short-sleeved T-shirt. She'd never seen him not wearing a suit.

"Brinkley?" she asked. "What are you doing here?"

"I couldn't sleep and heard the chatter on the radio. When I heard your name, I thought I should show up."

She frowned. "You didn't have to do that. I would have given you a report when I came in this morning."

"Who was he?" he asked, as the officers led him outside.

"I think he works for Brian Russell."

"Why come after you?"

"That's what I'd like to know. Apparently he was expecting to find Erika here." She shook her head. "You said there was a leak in your division. Why would someone think Erika was here?"

"I have no idea," Brinkley said.

"Then tell me what happened when they came after Erika that last time," she asked.

"There's not much to tell. She was staying at a safe house. Two agents were there with her. During the night—just after midnight—someone broke into the house. He had a taser."

"Sounds familiar." Nikki nodded at the taser lying on the floor across the room. "Send a photo of this guy to the agents who were guarding Erika last time and see if it's the same person who broke into the safe house."

"I will. Anything else you need from me?" Brinkley asked before heading toward the door.

"How about the truth?" she said, catching his gaze.

"The truth? What are you talking about?"

"I'm talking about the fact that you've lied to us since the moment I agreed to take this case."

"We didn't lie—"

"What would you call it? A bunch of half truths and omissions? No, you lied to me and used my team to try and get what you want."

"We gave you the information you needed to help us in this case. Your job was to find Erika. You were outside this case, enabling us to search for her without risking the possibility of coming in contact with our mole."

"So you just assumed we wouldn't find out about Erika's daughter?"

Brinkley tapped the edge of the island and caught her gaze. "I figured you'd find out, but it was part of the deal we made with Erika. She would only agree to testify if we ensured there would be no mention of her daughter."

"I understand her concern for her. But it makes me wonder what else you haven't told us." Nikki set her gun down on the counter. "Are you any closer to finding out who your mole is?"

"We're narrowing down our list of possibilities."

Nikki frowned. Vague as always.

"And how many more are going to die before you find your leak?" she asked.

Brinkley frowned. "We've done all along what we thought was best at the time."

"Well, guess what? Your air marshal is dead because of what you thought best. Kim is dead. And now Justin is in critical condition. Not to mention Aiden and our dead 'fake' marshal. When is this going to end?"

A flicker of anger sparked in his eyes. "Those deaths are tragic, but ultimately out of our hands."

"Maybe they wouldn't have died if you'd been more thorough in finding out the truth," Nikki continued. "Because you told me you were convinced Erika wasn't playing you. That she was scared of Russell and not you, and that there was no way she was simply pacifying you."

"Nothing that has happened in the last two days convinces me that Erika wasn't working for us. But I will do this," he said, throwing a measure of sympathy into his voice. "I'm going to have a patrol officer outside your house until we figure out what's going on."

She started to object, then nodded. She was through with taking chances.

"Good," he said. "I'm going to have to spend most of the day in court trying to see if I can postpone the indictment until we find Erika. Call me if you need me."

"I will." She followed him to the door. "But I should have said no to taking this case."

"I asked you because I knew you wouldn't say no."

"Apparently, you were right."

She shut the door behind Brinkley, locked it, then leaned back against it. She wasn't sure if it was worth it, trying to get another hour or two of sleep, or if she should just stay up. She wanted to make sure her team did their own interview of her intruder and have Gwen check over the phone. But she'd meant what she said. She shouldn't have taken the case. She should have spent the day with Tyler and Liam.

But Brinkley had been right as well.

She couldn't say no.

Nikki walked back upstairs, her legs still shaking, and stepped into the bathroom. There had to be a connection between the two break-ins. Erika at the safe house and now at her house. They had to have a way of tracing Erika.

The thought hit her like a freight train. Erika's watch.

She had Erika's watch.

She tried to remember what she'd done with it. It had to be in her bag. She looked at the time. It was almost six. Not too early to call Jack.

He answered on the fourth ring. "Nikki . . . what's going on?"

"Someone broke into my condo."

"What?" There was a long pause on the other end. "Are you okay?"

"I'm fine. He's in police custody now."

"Who was it?"

"I'm not sure yet. They've taken him down to the precinct for questioning, but I don't think he's going to say anything. At least not willingly. But I'm sure he works for Russell. It's the only thing that makes sense."

"But why would they come after you?"

"That's what I've been trying to figure out."

"And?"

"He thought Erika was here."

"I don't understand. Why would they think she was at your place?"

"You're the gadget expert. Could they have put a GPS on Erika?"

"It's possible, but we already know we can't trace her phone."

"What about her watch? The one she left on the plane."

"I guess it's possible. But I still don't understand how that connects to you."

"I have Erika's watch. I forgot about it until a little while ago, but it makes sense. The FBI said someone had managed to track her down at the safe house. What if it was her watch all this time?"

"It makes sense."

She shuddered. He hadn't tried to kill her. Just subdue her.

Which meant they potentially knew two things.

One, the bad guys still didn't know where Erika was, and two, they wanted her alive.

But why? Why go after her in the first place?

It had to be because she had information. Information that Russell would do anything to stop from getting out. He'd even tried to make sure Justin didn't have information he might be able to pass on to the authorities.

"Have you looked inside the watch?" Jack asked.

"Not yet. That's one of the reasons I'm calling."

"It's not easy to put a GPS tracker in a small piece of jewelry, but it would work with a watch. Especially with a bit of a budget, it would be possible."

"So what do I do to find out?"

"Get something sharp and try to pop off the back of the watch and let me know what you find."

Nikki found a small flathead screwdriver, then worked to pop off the back of the watch.

"Did you get it open?"

"Yeah."

"What's inside?"

"It looks like a small circuit board."

"Then I think you're right. Russell was tracking her."

"And they weren't after me. But how did the FBI miss something like that? They should have swept for bugs."

"I don't know. But Brian Russell has money. He didn't want to lose track of her. Especially if he found out she was testifying against him. He's going to do everything he can to stop her."

And then the plane crash threw him off.

"We saw her running scared at the airport," Nikki said. "If she saw someone she recognized, one of Russell's men, or feared she was being followed, it makes sense she'd run."

"Especially when they didn't protect her the last time," Jack said.

"I'm going to come in now," she said. "We need to speak with Justin again as soon as he wakes up. The man who just broke into my house—"

"You should go back to bed. Get some sleep before you even think about coming in. I'll come over and pick up the watch."

"I'll be fine. I'll get dressed and bring it in—"

The doorbell rang, interrupting her train of thought. She glanced at her watch. It was Tyler. How could she have forgotten he was bringing her breakfast?

"Someone's at the door, but I'll come in later this morning."

"Or you can take the day off," Jack countered. "Spend some time with your family."

But she'd already made up her mind. "I'll see you at the precinct."

16

6:10 a.m.

Nikki picked up Jade, then opened the door, wishing she could erase her conversation with the nurse at the doctor's office. With all that had happened over the past thirty-six hours, she'd barely had time to think about the consequences of the diagnosis. Or how infertility might affect her relationship with Tyler.

She shot him a smile. "Hey."

"Morning." Tyler stood in the doorway with a bag of take-out, two coffees, and the lopsided smile on his face that made her heart melt. Their relationship had evolved from best friends, and now she couldn't imagine going back to the way things were. He'd told her their relationship didn't have to be complicated. They were just two people figuring out love and life. But she couldn't see things going forward between them once he knew the truth.

And life seemed anything but uncomplicated at the moment.

"You know you didn't have to do this?" she said, shutting the door behind him. "The sun's barely even up."

"I figured you needed to eat, and it isn't like you've had time to shop for groceries since you've been back. Besides that, it gave me an excuse to see you again. I missed you."

"I missed you too." She breathed in the smell of onions and sausage and forced herself to shove aside her doubts for the time being. "And you know you don't ever need an excuse to see me."

"I hope not."

"And to be honest, you are a lifesaver," she said, setting Jade down. "I realized unless I want the barbeque my mom sent over yesterday, I'm pretty much out of everything, including coffee."

He set the food and coffees on the island, then pulled her into his arms. "Do you know how hard it's been knowing you're right across town, and I can't see you?"

He kissed her forehead, then her lips. Her fears started to melt. It seemed that the only place she felt safe lately was in his arms.

"How are you feeling?" He pushed back a strand of her hair that had fallen across her cheek. "You look tired."

She grabbed his hands and smiled. "I'm definitely better than yesterday."

"Any signs of a concussion?"

"None. I took a sleeping pill and slept hard until—"

"Wait a minute. Something happened here?" He was staring at the lamp that had crashed against the tile floor. "What's going on, Nikki?"

She looked up at him, wanting nothing more than to stay lost in his eyes and forget the reality of everything she was having to deal with. Just savor the fact that he was here with her. Because that was enough. Wasn't it?

"Nikki?"

She took a step back from him. "I had a break-in this morning—"

"A break-in? What are you talking about?"

"Brinkley's sending over a patrol car. Everything's okay now. I promise. It's connected to this case I'm working on. You remember the watch I had that belonged to Erika?"

"Yes . . ."

"There was a tracking device in it." Saying it out loud again sent a shiver down her spine. How had she managed to get so entangled in this case?

"Wait a minute . . . so you're saying they traced her watch here."

She nodded.

"Nikki, this has all gone too far. The plane crash, the prison, and now a break-in . . . Surely they aren't expecting you to keep working."

"No—"

"Good, because you need to go somewhere safe and let your team handle this."

"But *I* need to keep working." She looked up at him. "There's a woman out there who agreed to testify for the FBI against the father of her child. This man . . . he's got a lot of money and powerful friends, and he'll do anything to stop her testimony. I need to find them—both her and her little girl—before he does."

"I know what motivates you," he said, running his thumb down her cheek. "Which means I'm not going to change your mind, am I?"

"No."

"And I suppose you know I'd probably do the same thing in your situation."

"Isn't that part of the reason why we get along so well?" She managed a weak smile. "And on top of that, I'm hungry."

"You better be, because I wasn't sure what you were in the mood for, so I picked up a little of everything. Figured Liam would like the surprise of whatever was left over when he woke up."

"What is it?"

"A variety of breakfast burritos and some fruit salad," he said, sitting down on one of the barstools.

"Perfect." She opened up the bag. "Where is Liam?"

"My mom's staying with me for a couple days. I think she loved having him for these past few months and misses him when he's gone."

"I don't blame her," she said, pulling out a wrapped burrito marked spinach, mushroom, and feta.

"How's your mom and dad? This has to have been tough on them." Tyler took one with sausage and cheese and started unwrapping it.

"I haven't seen them, but I've talked to them on the phone a couple times. The whole family's a bit shaken. I watched the video of the crash again. It feels like a miracle anyone survived."

"Your mother called me."

Nikki grabbed the napkins, handed him one, then took a bite of her food. "You got a call from my mother?"

"She was worried. Wanted to make sure you really were okay."

Another pang of guilt struck. She promised herself she'd see them as soon as this was over. She hoped her mother really did understand why she couldn't just walk away.

Tyler was staring at his breakfast without eating anything. An uneasy feeling settled in her stomach.

"You okay?" she asked.

"Yeah, it's just that I . . ." He pushed his breakfast aside and looked up at her. "I meant it when I said I'd probably do the exact same thing you're doing, but that doesn't mean you can't think that this situation won't affect you. When the shock of everything that's happened the past twenty-four hours starts to wear off, it's going to hit you hard."

"Psychology 101?" She smiled, wanting to lighten the mood, but she knew he was right.

"I didn't have to take psychology to know that."

"I'm okay. Really. If I wasn't, I'd step away from the case, but I can handle this. And once we're done, I promise to take a few days off."

He reached for her hand. "And spend them with me?"

"You might have to fight for time with my mom, but yes. I promise." She looked up and caught his gaze. "But let's forget about that right now. You brought me breakfast and coffee, which means I've got about twenty minutes to begin putting a dent into the past three months I missed, and I, for one, don't want to talk about my work."

"Okay . . . it's a deal."

She sat down on one of the barstools next to him, knees touching. Wishing she had more than twenty minutes to catch up.

"And you? How are you? You haven't even gotten over jet lag yet."

"Liam keeps catching me up in the middle of the night reading. I think he just doesn't want me out of his sight. I missed him so much while I was gone."

"He struggled while you were gone, but in his own wise six-year-old mind, I think part of him understood."

Tyler picked up his coffee and took a sip. "Have I thanked you for checking on him so much?"

"Yes, and you're welcome. He's a great kid and you know I love him."

"Yesterday he gave me a long list of everything the two of you did together. I knew you'd be there for him, but you really went above and beyond the call of duty."

"Don't worry, I enjoy hanging out with him."

She added a couple spoonfuls of salsa to her burrito, then closed it up again. She really had enjoyed every moment of her time with Liam. Because being with him made her feel like Tyler wasn't quite so far away.

"Tell me about this job opportunity," she said.

"I got an offer from a private company, working as a director of their cyber security. It's a great opportunity, with high clearance levels."

"Meaning if you tell me, you'll have to kill me?" she asked.

"Something like that." Tyler laughed. "I have a meeting set up for Friday with their CEO. I'll learn more then. What I do know is that the job is here in Nashville, heading their cyber team to analyze critical threats."

"Wow . . . that sounds perfect."

"I think it could be. At least on the surface. I haven't given them an answer yet. It will keep me busy, but it only requires minimal travel, which means I'll be home with Liam most of the time. So the job would be challenging to me and yet give Liam the stability he needs."

"Sounds like a perfect match," Nikki said. "What about your house? Any interested buyers?"

"My Realtor's showing the house again now that I'm back. And I'm planning to start looking for something else. My mother brought up the idea of my buying a house with a mother-in-law apartment when we move."

"And what do you think about that?"

"It would be wonderful to have her right there. She loves helping me look after Liam, and it's a tremendous help to me. If she were closer, it would be even easier. I think I'd worry a lot less. Knowing she was always there if I needed her."

Nikki caught the hesitation in his eyes. "But you sound uncertain."

"I told her there were a lot of things to consider. Like us."

"What about us?" she asked. Nikki couldn't look at him while she asked. She picked at her burrito, eyes down, barely breathing. Finally she looked up and faced him, and faced her fear. "You've gone through a lot the past year and a half. Losing

Katie and the baby. Becoming a single dad. I don't want to be . . . the convenient answer to your life."

Tyler laughed. "I'm not looking for a nanny or a housekeeper, if that's what you're worried about." His smile faded. "You should know that by now. But if I'm pushing you—"

"No, it's not that." She took another sip of her coffee. How in the world was she supposed to tell him that they might not ever be able to have the life they'd talked about? That she might not ever be able to give him the family he wanted?

"Trust me, you're anything but convenient," he said, breaking into her thoughts. "Nikki, for the first time I'm able to think about life after Katie. I can actually see a future that makes me happy."

"What do you see?" she asked, looking up at him.

"You and me together. These past three months made me realize I want that. And not because it's convenient, but because of the simple reason that I'm in love with you. I want us to look at moving forward and someday . . . have a family together. I want Liam to have brothers and sisters."

She felt panic rush through her.

"Am I scaring you?" He took her hand and pulled her toward him. "If I am, I'm sorry, but—"

"No, you have nothing to be sorry about." She shook her head.

"You know, this is my fault. Everything's out of order." Tyler let out a low laugh. "I haven't even asked you out on an official date, and I'm talking like we're ready to walk down the aisle. I shouldn't be pushing you. I just . . . I missed you while I was gone, Nikki. Every single day had me wondering why I decided to go, even though it was probably the best thing I could have done. Just tell me we're heading in the same direction."

"We . . . we are. I'm sorry if I sound like I'm hesitant, because I'm not." Nikki paused, knowing that eventually she'd have to tell him the truth. But the last twenty-four hours had been a blur that had left her head spinning, both physically and emotionally. "This is just the first time we've spoken about us face-to-face."

"You're having doubts?"

She looked up and caught his gaze. "No, I'm just . . ."

She didn't know how to tell him.

He leaned forward. "If you want to take things slower, I understand. Anything you want is fine. I'm not trying to rush things between us—"

"I know. And what I'm going through right now has nothing to do with you. I'm just distracted and this case has drained me." She glanced at her cell phone. "In fact, I probably need to get going."

She wanted him to pull her into his arms. Wanted to forget everything that had happened. But she didn't know how to let it go. Didn't know how to tell him what she was thinking.

"Okay," he said. "But I need you to know that I'm here for you. If there's anything I can do . . ."

But it wasn't about the case.

She looked down at her half-eaten plate of food. This wasn't how she'd imagined his homecoming, but she wasn't sure she could deal with the added emotions right now. Maybe when she was away from this she'd be able to think clearer.

"I need to go." She finished off the rest of her coffee, avoiding his gaze. "But thank you for breakfast."

"Nikki—"

"I'm sorry. I really am."

More guilt washed through her. She was trying to avoid talking about what really mattered. But putting off the conversation wasn't going to change the facts.

"I'll let you know when we wrap up the case," she said, "and then I'll make up for all of this. I promise."

"Liam wanted me to ask you to come over so we can have pizza and watch movies."

"I'd like that."

"And we'll talk some more. Go out on that first date. Alone."

She couldn't help but smile. "I'd like that."

He stood up and drew her into his arms. "Just promise me you'll be careful." He locked his hands together around the back of her neck.

She nodded. Needing him to go. Wanting him to stay. "I promise."

He brushed his lips across hers, hesitating for a few seconds before pulling away. Being with him made her want more of him, but she didn't know if what she wanted was ever going to happen.

17

Nikki grabbed the lampshade that had fallen over during the struggle. The bulb had shattered and now lay scattered across the floor. She already regretted her decision to let Tyler walk out the door. The timing might be all wrong, but she should have told him to stay. Should have told him the truth about what the doctor had said instead of letting it continue to simmer inside her. How were they supposed to have a relationship if she couldn't be completely honest with him?

She grabbed the dustpan and brush from the small utility closet and started cleaning up the mess. She'd tell him when this was over. When she could talk to him without any distractions. He deserved the truth from her. Not her excuses.

A knock at the door interrupted her thoughts. She dumped the shards of glass into the trash can. If Tyler had come back . . .

She glanced through the peephole, then swung open the door. Gwen stood next to Jack holding three coffees in a cardboard takeout container. A patrol car sat against the curb outside the apartment building.

"I know you told Jack you were coming in later this morning, but when I found out what happened, I decided we needed to come by and see you now," Gwen said, taking a step into the room. She looked Nikki over from head to toe, as if she really did want to make sure she was still in one piece. "So how are you?"

"It's been a rough twenty-four hours." Nikki rubbed her temples, still feeling the tension pulsing through her veins. "But I'm okay. At least I will be."

"Rough?" Gwen shook her head. "Seriously, Nikki, that plane crash would have been enough to do me in. And then the prison incident . . ." She set the coffees on the island next to the one Tyler had just brought her. "Looks like someone beat us to your daily morning java jolt."

"Tyler came by with breakfast and coffee, but I could use another round of caffeine." She took a sip, hoping the energy boost would also settle her nerves, then pointed at the ones Tyler had left. "There's a lot of burrito left if you're hungry."

She didn't want to throw it out, but her own stomach churned at the thought of any more food.

"I already ate, but thanks," Jack said. "Holly's got me on this elimination diet to discover food allergies, and anything I do eat has to be organic."

"You, on an organic diet? Seriously, Holly really is rubbing off on you." Gwen laughed. "Though now that you mention it, I can't remember the last time I saw you with a burger and fries or cheese-crust pizza."

"True. And you also might have noticed," Jack said, patting his flat stomach, "that I've lost five pounds and feel—and look—at least that many years younger."

"Don't push it," Nikki teased, thankful to have the spotlight off herself for the moment. She pointed toward the back of his neck. "You still haven't managed to get rid of that rash."

"Rash? What rash?" he asked, reaching up to feel his neck.

Gwen laughed. "She's kidding, Jack."

Nikki smiled, then took a sip of her coffee. While she appreciated the distraction, she couldn't stop thinking about Erika and Lily. And how if she was just given the chance to talk to Cipher one more time they might get some of the answers they needed.

Jack leaned against the counter and caught Nikki's gaze. "What are you thinking?"

"That I need to go in and give an official statement this morning, but after that"—she set down her drink—"there's no way I'll go back to sleep, and I'm going to go crazy sitting at home."

"Which is why if I were you, I'd be putting in for time off and heading off for a few days in the Smokies, or maybe rock climbing," Gwen said. "Anywhere you can avoid thinking about what you've just gone through."

A few days away would do her good, but she couldn't forget her dream about Lily and Sarah. Nikki could feel her heart racing and her palms sweating. She took in some deep, calming breaths to tamp down the adrenaline surge.

She glanced at Gwen. "Did he tell you what else we found out while talking to Erika's brother last night?"

"That Russell and Erika had a baby? Yeah. But I don't get it. Is this situation her testifying against him, or are we looking at a custody case?"

Nikki shook her head. "My guess is both."

"Then why didn't the FBI tell us about her? The fact that there's a child out there who's also missing seems pretty relevant to the case, if you ask me."

"Apparently Erika insisted that Lily was kept out of things for her own safety." Nikki shivered despite the fact that the air conditioner was set too high. Someone was leaving a trail of bodies behind. And keeping secrets worth killing for.

"I knew you would want some information on him, so I stopped by the station on the way over," Jack said. "While I was there I found out something interesting. They just ID'd our fake marshal. He was definitely connected to Russell."

"So Russell was behind the swap."

"Looks like it." He dropped the file he'd been holding onto the island. "As for Cipher, unfortunately, he's not talking yet, even though there's a good chance he's looking at the death penalty now."

"His file?" Nikki asked.

Jack nodded. "His real name is Freddie Jenkins. He's a local thug for hire. The last time he was arrested, the judge gave him twenty-five years with no chance of parole."

Nikki drummed her fingers against her coffee cup. That might explain the motivation for him risking a prison escape. At his age, twenty-five years might as well be life. But the bottom line was that right now, Cipher was her only connection to Brian Russell. She'd spent the most time with him. If anyone could get him to talk, she believed she could.

"Cipher has answers. We need to talk with him."

"We?" Jack's brow rose. "Forget it. You know Carter will never go for that. Besides the fact that he was involved in the deaths of two people and injured two others, the DA has just taken over the case and doesn't think we need to be involved."

"You've got to be kidding." Nikki's frown deepened. "They don't want us involved?"

"No, but there's also another small detail, in case you forgot. Less than twelve hours ago he was holding you hostage at gunpoint. None of us want you around that man."

Nikki swallowed her frustration. She might understand their position, but she wasn't ready to simply walk away. "What if I can get him to talk—"

"Nikki—"

"Hear me out." They were both eying her like she was crazy, but at the moment she didn't care. "During the hostage situation,

I connected with him . . . even if it was only for a brief moment. If I can get him to talk, I might get information out of him that could lead us to Russell. Information we need right now in order to find Erika and her daughter."

Jack frowned. "We all agree that we need to talk to him if we can get the DA on our side, but let Gwen and me handle this."

"I know you can handle things, but—"

Jack's cell phone rang. He pulled it out of his back pocket and took the call.

"He's right, you know," Gwen said, taking a long sip of her coffee. "You've gotten us this far. Let us do the rest."

Am I just being stubborn, God, or would what I could do really make a difference?

"Who was that?" Gwen said as soon as Jack hung up.

"It was the hospital where Justin Peters is recovering."

"And . . ." Nikki prodded.

Jack glanced at Gwen, then back to Nikki. "Peters is awake and he wants to talk with you."

───────◆───────

Thirty minutes later, Nikki stepped into the large hospital elevator with Jack and breathed in the smell of disinfectant. For the most part, hospitals had never bothered her. It wasn't like walking through the claustrophobic halls of the prison, where hundreds of inmates had completely lost their freedom. But today, everything had her on edge. Maybe it was the lingering scent of death, bringing with it the reminder that she'd come far too close in facing her own immortality.

Life was so fleeting.

We never know which breath might be our last, do we, God?

Had those same thoughts run through Sarah's mind the day she'd been abducted? Had the day she'd been abducted been her last one alive?

Nikki pulled her mind back to the issue at hand. Gwen had stayed back at the precinct in order to try to set up an interview with Cipher. Which meant for now, Nikki needed to stay focused on what she wanted to ask Peters so they could put an end to this.

"You sure you're up to this?" Jack asked, punching the elevator button.

She gritted her teeth and nodded. She had to be.

The doors slid open on the third floor in front of the nurses' station. Except for a few beeps from monitors, the floor was quiet, with only a few nurses doing their normal rounds.

Jack held up his badge as he strode across the tile floor to address the thirtysomething nurse wearing purple scrubs and an eyebrow ring. "We're with the Tennessee Bureau of Investigation, here to see Justin Peters."

"Of course. I was told they were sending up two of their agents." She glanced down at a clipboard. "He's in room 303, to your left. Officer Poole is outside."

"Thank you."

Nikki started down the wide hallway, asking herself the same question for the past thirty minutes. Why did Justin Peters want to see her and what information did he have for her? Did he know where Erika was? Had he been trying to protect his sister and then realized he couldn't?

A guard sat slouched in his chair outside Justin's room. Chin against his chest. Arms in his lap. Sleeping.

Nikki frowned. So much for the security measures they'd put in place to keep Peters safe.

She hurried toward the guard, holding up her badge. "Officer Poole?"

No response.

She bridged the gap between them, irritation lacing her words. "Officer Poole . . ."

She touched the man's shoulder, but he didn't move. Her heart quickened. She felt for his pulse, then glanced up at Jack. "I can't find a pulse."

"We need medical attention over here now," Jack yelled.

Nikki felt the blood rush to her temples as she ran inside Peters's room behind Jack. What if they'd found a way to get to the guard?

Inside, Justin was handcuffed to the bed. His head was turned to the side, as if he were asleep, and his arm was hooked up to an IV. He was paler than the last time she'd seen him.

No, God . . . please. Let him be alive. We need him to be alive.

"Justin!"

As she had with the guard, she felt for his pulse, then hesitated. Nothing. She took a step back. The room started to spin. This couldn't be happening.

She stumbled backward. "He's dead, Jack. They killed him."

"Have Gwen send backup and alert hospital security. We're also going to need access to their video surveillance." Jack ran out of the room to where medical personnel were trying to revive the guard. A second team rushed into Peters's room.

Nikki could hear Jack's voice echoing in the hallway as she hung up her call to Gwen seconds later and moved out of the way of the doctor trying to resuscitate Peters.

"When's the last time someone checked on Peters?" Jack stood in front of a nurse whose face was whiter than Peters's.

"I . . . I checked on him myself," she said. "About seven twenty."

Nikki glanced at her watch. "That gives us a window of fifteen minutes."

Enough time for someone to slip out of the building without anyone noticing.

"Did you see anyone who shouldn't be here?" Jack asked.

"I don't think so . . . no . . . wait a minute. There was a man in a lab coat who walked through about ten minutes ago. I didn't think about it at the time."

"Can you give us a description?" Jack asked.

"He was about six feet tall. Short dark hair. He was wearing a typical lab coat and carrying some sort of small bag."

One of the doctors stepped up to where they were huddled. "I think the guard will make it, but the patient . . . I'm sorry, but he's dead."

Nikki's cell phone rang before she had time to process the information. It was Gwen. "The guard should make it, but Peters is dead."

There was a short pause on the line. "Do you have any idea what happened?"

"Only that he was murdered."

"Murdered?"

Nikki caught the surprise in Gwen's voice. And felt the desperation in Russell's latest move.

"Sounds as if you need some good news," Gwen said.

"What have you got?" Nikki asked.

"I just heard from the DA. She's agreed to let you interview Cipher."

Nikki hung up the phone and turned to Jack. "We just got a second chance."

Nikki walked into the prison interview room with Jack for the second time in less than twenty-four hours, her last interview fresh on her mind. It was as if they were playing a game of chess, and they were always one move behind. But this wasn't over yet.

Cipher avoided her gaze as she sat down across from him. A guard stood by the door. They weren't taking any chances this time.

"I need to ask you a few questions," she said.

"Like I told you earlier. I don't have to tell you anything. And even if I did, I don't have to answer you. Remember, I don't have nothin' to lose."

"I think you do. Things have changed since the last time I saw you. The DA's going for the death penalty. If you have any desire of taking it off the table, you'll cooperate—"

His jaw tensed. "Think about it. Life versus the death penalty. Doesn't really matter, does it?"

She needed to find a way to get through to him. "Then just listen. I'm trying to find a woman and her daughter who are missing. I believe their lives are in danger. The woman's name is Erika Hamilton. She has a daughter named Lily. Brian Russell might have mentioned them to you. You might have even met her."

Cipher looked up at her and caught her gaze. At least she had his attention for the moment. "I know who they are, but I never met them."

Maybe she was trying to accomplish the impossible. Trying to speak to a conscience that was no longer there.

But if she could find a way to connect to him . . .

"You mentioned you had a daughter. I'm sure you would do anything you can to protect her. Erika was only trying to do the same thing. Provide for her daughter. But if I can't find her, I can't help her."

Cipher ran his hand across the back of his head. "Do you think any of that matters to me? I lost everything the day I stepped into this prison. And nothing I can do can ever change that. I won't see my daughter grow up, and every day I'm reminded of what I'm missing."

"Do you think Brian Russell has regrets?" she asked.

"I know his girlfriend turned against him. What did you expect him to do?"

"Tell me how you know Russell."

"I used to work for him. Before I landed here. I owed him a couple favors, so when he came to me needing help, I agreed."

"And that *help* was taking out Justin Peters?" Jack asked.

"I wasn't supposed to kill him. Just scare him. Brian needed some information out of him."

"What information?" Nikki asked.

"Information Erika may have shared, or told Justin where she'd hidden it. Then that guard showed up, Finn stabbed him, and everything fell apart. Using you as a hostage seemed like my only way out."

"Did you know Peters is dead?" Nikki asked.

Cipher stared at her. "They can't pin that on me. When I left him, he was alive."

"Someone killed him in the hospital. We're assuming Brian Russell was behind the attack."

"I didn't have anything to do with that."

"Then help us find Russell. We know he's in town. And we need to talk with him. Think about your daughter, Cipher. Think about the lengths Erika's gone not just to save herself, but her daughter. You can understand that, can't you? You want your own daughter to be safe. To have a normal life."

Maybe she was imagining it, but she thought Cipher's eyes softened slightly.

"I don't care what Russell's involved in," she continued. "Right now, my job is to find Erika and Lily, and to do that I need to find Russell. And right now, you're my best lead. If you help me find him, I promise I'll make sure the DA knows you cooperated in this case."

"I owe him."

"You don't owe him anything." She leaned forward, keeping her voice even. "He controls you, even in prison, and doesn't care what happens to you. You're nothing more than a puppet.

He's free, and you'll still be here when this is over. Forget a ticket out of here."

Cipher studied a dark spot on the table between them. "If he finds out I told you, he'll kill me too."

"He won't find out where we got this information," Nikki said, praying she'd said enough to convince him.

He gave her a small smile and crossed his arms. "Why don't you try looking for the holdings of Arana Corporation. You never know where that might lead."

She glanced at Jack, praying that what Cipher had just given them was going to be enough.

18

At a quarter past ten, Nikki sat at her desk staring at a photo of Brian Russell, while Gwen searched for more on the corporation name Cipher had offered up. She'd spent the past hour going through the list of names Erika's brother had finally given her before he died, hoping to find the person Erika had entrusted Lily with. But so far her search had come up empty.

And there was another thing that bothered her. In spite of Justin's strong feelings against Russell, something wasn't adding up. How could a man who was known for helping people, and who had his own personal fortune, end up so high on the FBI's radar? He'd been interviewed by everyone from *Time* to *People* magazine. He'd been listed in *Forbes* as one of American's fifty top philanthropists, making him the poster boy of a number of charities he not only donated to but helped raise money for.

Nikki looked up as Jack dropped Erika's watch onto her desk, pulling her away from her thoughts.

"What'd you find out?" Nikki sat up and rubbed the back of her neck, trying to work out the kinks that had settled.

"I traced the GPS tracker you found in Erika's watch to a company that primarily works government contracts."

"That ought to narrow things down," she said.

"I'm waiting for a list of civilian purchases." Jack leaned against the edge of her desk. "What about you? Any luck?"

"I've contacted most of the people on Justin's list, but no one I've talked to claims to know where Erika and Lily are. But here's the strange thing. If it wasn't for Justin and Cipher and Russell's ex-wife's damaging testimonies, I'd actually think that the FBI was on a witch hunt."

"What do you mean?" Jack asked.

"Every person I've spoken to about Brian Russell has said pretty much the same thing. None of them believe he would do anything to hurt either Erika or Lily."

"And these are friends of Erika?" Jack asked. "Friends who have to know that despite Russell's charitable lifestyle he's also a womanizer?"

Nikki shrugged. "I'm just as surprised as you are. Though Erika might have kept their relationship problems to herself. Because trust me, no woman wants her friends to know she's fallen in love with the wrong man for the second time."

Gwen looked up from her computer where she was working and tapped her pen against the table. "I confess, I kind of keep hoping the man's innocent. I read about him last year in *Time*, and quite honestly I'm surprised they don't put the guy up for sainthood. And besides his long list of good deeds, just look at him. He's this perfect specimen—you gotta love that five-o'clock shadow. With a face like Bradley Cooper, what's not to like?"

"Apparently you're not the only one who thinks that way," Nikki said, frowning. "The list of women he's dated over the past few years—Erika included—is pretty extensive and, according to a couple articles online, every one of them talks like he hung the moon. And on top of that, despite the FBI's long list of accusations, the guy doesn't even have a parking ticket."

"It does sound more like a witch hunt," Gwen said, turning back to her computer screen.

Nikki's gaze fell back on Brian Russell's photo. The man had degrees from Harvard, then Vanderbilt. He'd served on a number of boards for various nonprofits, one of which had grown into one of the largest private nonprofits in the south.

"So the man sounds perfect," Jack said. "But we all know, being wealthy doesn't solve all your problems. Or keep you on the right side of the law."

"True, and I did find a few hiccups along the way." Nikki glanced down at her notes. "Two years ago, he checked into a rehab center for a problem with prescription drugs after shoulder surgery. Though no one seems to hold that against him. And according to a recent interview I read, he claims he's been clean ever since. There's one other stain I could find on his reputation. When he was seventeen, he got a girl pregnant."

"What happened to the child?" Jack asked.

"His mother got involved. Made the problem go away."

"What about his father?" Gwen asked.

"He's been out of the picture since he was a baby." Nikki's mind started running the threads together. "Maybe that plays into this situation."

"What do you mean?" Jack asked.

"He feels guilty over his girlfriend's abortion. There was no father figure in his life. We know that Russell and his ex-wife weren't able to have children. It would make sense for him to want to hold on to Lily."

"And give him motivation to get rid of the woman standing in his way."

"Guys, hold on," Gwen said, pushing her chair back from

her desk. "You both might be on to something, but I think I just tracked down Russell's address here in Nashville. Cipher was right. The owner of the property is listed as a corporation, but with a bit of digging. I tied it back to Russell."

Nikki grabbed her keys out of the top drawer of her desk and glanced at Jack. "Then it sounds like it's time we make a personal visit and ask Mr. Russell our questions ourselves."

Twenty-five minutes later, Nikki parked her Mini Cooper on the street in front of one of Nashville's upscale neighborhoods. She hadn't included Brinkley in the loop this time. Until they found Russell, they were going to move ahead on their own.

The sprawling two-story house matching the description Gwen had given them stood at the end of a circular drive. Manicured lawns and pristine landscape were surrounded by a fence and steel gate to keep out unwelcome guests. A silver Mercedes-Benz sat in the driveway.

"What do you think this place costs?" Nikki asked, pushing the buzzer on the wrought-iron gate that stood at least eight feet tall. "Two and a half, three million?"

"At a minimum," Jack said.

She pushed the buzzer again.

Finally a woman's voice came over the intercom. "Can I help you?"

"This is Special Agent Nikki Boyd and Special Agent Jack Spencer with the Tennessee Bureau of Investigation. We need to speak to Mr. Russell."

"I'm sorry, but Mr. Russell isn't here right now."

Nikki glanced at Jack. "Then we'd like to speak to you for a moment."

There was a long pause before the woman answered. "All right."

A second later, the smaller side gate opened automatically. Nikki made her way with Jack down the long drive to the house, where there were half a dozen brick steps with a wrought-iron railing leading to a wide front porch. A swing hung on either side.

An older Hispanic woman, wearing a double-breasted black dress with white lapels, met them at the porch, the frown on her face intense. "You said you were with the police?"

Nikki held up her badge. "I'm Special Agent Nikki Boyd and this is my partner, Jack Spencer. You said Brian Russell isn't here? It's very important that we speak to him. Do you have a way for us to get ahold of him?"

The maid's face paled as she pressed her hands against her chest. "This is about the car, no?"

Nikki caught the fear in the woman's expression. "I'm sorry . . . what car?"

The maid glanced at the circular drive. "Mr. Russell's BMW."

"What about the car?" Jack asked.

"It's nothing serious. There was just some . . . *confusión*. I thought maybe there had been an accident."

Nikki glanced at Jack, then back to the woman. "If you would help us get in touch with Mr. Russell, I'm sure we'll be able to clear up any . . . mix-up."

"I'm sorry, but he's not here."

"And do you know when he'll be returning?"

"Mr. Russell had an appointment with his accountant today, so I've been expecting him, but I haven't heard from him." The maid fiddled with the lapel on her dress. "You must understand, *por favor*, I am just the housekeeper. Mr. Russell doesn't keep me informed of changes in his schedule. I do my job and make sure the house is ready when he shows up."

"Do you have a number to contact him?" Jack asked.

She pressed her lips together. "I have his cell number. I suppose he wouldn't mind if I give it to you."

"Wait a minute." Nikki read off a number on her phone. "Is that the number?"

"*Sí* . . . Yes. That is his number."

It was the same number they'd already been using.

"What is your name?" Nikki asked.

"Maria Lopez."

"Maria, how long have you worked for Mr. Russell?"

"Eleven, almost twelve years."

Eleven years was a long time. Enough time for her to become protective of her boss. And to know some of Mr. Russell's intimate habits and secrets.

"At this house?"

"Oh no. In Houston. But when he bought this house, he asked me to come here to help get the house ready until he hires staff."

"Let me ask you something else." Nikki held up a photo on her cell phone. "Do you know a woman by the name of Erika Hamilton?"

"Erika . . . *Sí*. He brought her here a couple times. She's . . . she's always been sweet to me. Asks me how I'm doing. Not everyone does that."

"When is the last time you saw her?" Nikki asked.

"It was . . . last Wednesday. I remember because it was her birthday. I made her favorite cake—chocolate fudge."

"Was that here?"

"No. She's been staying at Mr. Russell's house in Houston."

"And what about her daughter, Lily?" Nikki asked, sliding the phone to the next photo. "Do you know her?"

Maria's smile broadened. "*Sí. . . sí*. She's a sweet *chamaquita*—little girl. Looks so much like her mother. At least in her eyes. I watched her a few times when Mr. Russell took Erika out. Never can get her to go to sleep unless I hold her, but I don't mind. Just like my own Matías when he was little."

"Was Lily with Erika the last time you saw her?"

"Lily was at the party as well, but I think Erika was worried about something. I just tried to make her favorite foods and keep her happy." Maria's smile faded. "Something is wrong, isn't it? *Por favor* . . . if she's in trouble—"

"We just need to locate Mr. Russell and Miss Hamilton," Nikki said as she handed the older woman her card. "If you'd have Mr. Russell call us when he returns. It's very important that we speak to him."

The fear was back in her eyes. What was the woman afraid of? Mr. Russell? Or something else?

Maria slipped back into the house, shutting the door behind her as they started back toward the gate.

"Do you think she knows something?" Nikki asked.

Dogs barked in the distance.

"I don't know, but something feels off," Jack said.

Nikki felt the hairs on her arms rise, and she picked up her step.

She glanced around. Two Doberman pinschers were tearing around the corner of the house across the manicured lawn and were headed right toward them.

"Jack . . ."

He looked back. "You've got to be kidding."

They were halfway toward the front gate that was still shut.

"Maria!" Jack shouted.

But the dogs were closing in on them. Nikki could hear their loud barks as they got closer. There was no time to call for backup. No time to even have Maria call them off.

"Run!"

Nikki sucked in a deep breath of air to fill her lungs, forcing every last ounce of energy into her legs. The gate was still closed and the dogs were closing in on them, barking ferociously. Lungs about to burst, she could hear them rustling through a narrow row of bushes as they raced across the side lawn and onto the driveway behind them.

God, I've got nothing left here.

Today had managed to zap every ounce of energy from her—both physically and emotionally.

"Do you think they're friendly?" Jack shouted, lengthening his stride beside her.

"I'm not planning to find out."

The security gate loomed ahead of them. Nikki tried to yank back on the side door, but it was still locked. Why hadn't Maria opened the gate for them? Glancing back one more time, she made her decision. The dogs would be at the end of the driveway in a matter of seconds. To the sides of the gate, the stone wall surrounding the property was too high. The only chance they had was to scale the front gate.

Scrambling up the fencing, Nikki used her legs to push herself straight up, then over the top. Momentum carried her over the rest of the way. Seconds later, she dropped down on the other side of the fence and onto the sidewalk next to Jack.

Heart racing, Nikki braced her hands against her thighs to catch her breath while the dogs barked frantically against the fence less than a yard away. She glanced back at the dogs, glad she hadn't waited to find out if they were friendly.

Today had already held too many close calls.

"You okay?" Jack asked.

"Yeah," she said, trying to slow her breathing. "What about you?"

Jack tugged on the side of his gray dress shirt. "Besides the hole in my brand-new shirt? I'll live."

"You think we should bring in the maid for more questioning?"

"I think she's too scared to tell us whatever she knows."

Nikki slid into the driver's seat of her car, heart still racing from the surge of adrenaline. She couldn't shake the frustration. Justin Peters was dead, and they were no closer to finding

Erika and Lily. They needed Brian Russell, and she was tired of playing games.

"What are you thinking?" she asked, dangling the keys in her hands.

"I'm wondering if the FBI knows about this house."

"Think we need to let Brinkley in on our discovery?"

"Only if it helps us get a search warrant to let us in."

"What if it's already too late? What if he's already found Erika?"

"We'll get him, Nikki."

She banged the palm of her hand against the steering wheel. "If this isn't just a witch hunt . . . if Brian Russell *is* guilty, then I'm not sure we will. You know these kinds of guys as well as I do. They surround themselves with lawyers and corrupt accountants who spend their time making sure the boss doesn't get caught. They're immune to the system."

"He might think he's immune, but no one truly is."

She started the engine. A driver heading their direction turned on his blinker toward Russell's driveway.

"Wait a minute," Nikki said as she pulled away from the curb. "That's a BMW."

Jack leaned forward as the car made a U-turn in front of them, then headed back down the street. "I can't tell who's inside with the tinted windows."

Nikki pressed on the accelerator. "You'd think that at least one thing could happen today that didn't involve a chase or a crash."

"Sorry," Jack said, "but it's not going to be this time."

Nikki sped down the street after the car, past winding acres of green trees and million-dollar estates. She took a sharp right turn behind the BMW, then slammed on her brakes to avoid another vehicle speeding around a corner toward them.

A second later the black BMW they were following exploded in a ball of yellow and orange flames.

19

Nikki's Mini Cooper skidded to a stop fifty yards from the burning car. Her mind scrambled to compute what she'd just seen. For one, this was no accident. Someone had just triggered a bomb and blown up what she was going to presume at the moment to be Brian Russell's car. And if Russell was dead, another link to finding Erika and Lily had just disappeared.

"What in the world just happened?" Jack jumped out of the car.

"I don't know."

Nikki followed him onto the sidewalk and quickly called for backup. Black plumes of smoke filled the air, along with yellow-and-orange flames and the acrid smell of burning oil. She took a hesitant step backward, wishing she could see inside the driver's window. But no one could have survived the explosion. The front of the car was already a twisted metal shell, and even standing at a safe distance, she could feel the heat of the flames as the vehicle continued to burn.

She punched in Gwen's number.

"I need you to do a title search on a black BMW as quickly as possible," Nikki said as soon as Gwen picked up.

"Okay. Go ahead."

Nikki gave her the Tennessee plate number, barely legible now at the back of the burning car.

"Give me a second for the results. What's going on?"

"We're near Brian Russell's residence. A car just exploded."

"Exploded?"

"We think it might have been Russell's vehicle."

"Wait a second. I've got it," Gwen said. "And you're right. He purchased it just over a month ago here in Nashville. Was he in the car?"

"No way to tell who was in the car at this point."

"Anything else I can do?" Gwen asked, her voice barely audible over the sirens now blaring in the background.

"Yeah. Get a judge to sign a warrant for us to search the premises of Brian Russell's Nashville home."

A minute later, first responders arrived at the scene—an ambulance and a fire truck. Twenty minutes later, the quiet upscale street had been marked off with yellow tape and turned into an official crime scene that partitioned off the tree-lined road. And official personnel weren't the only ones on the scene. Neighbors gathered in the background, and the explosion had brought the media and their cameras into the swanky neighborhood.

Nikki ignored the shouts of an over-eager journalist while she waited to speak to the assistant medical examiner, who was busy with his on-scene evaluation of the body.

"Do you know him?" she asked Jack.

"I worked with him a few times while running homicide. His name's Dr. Torres. He's good at what he does."

Dr. Torres and his assistant carefully removed the body from the burned-out car and placed it onto a stretcher. If they were going to talk first with the man, now was the time.

"Is there any way to identify the body at this point?" Nikki asked, walking up to the ME and introducing herself. "There's the possibility that this ties in with a critical missing persons case."

"Heard you were working missing persons now, Spencer," he said, nodding at Jack. "I'm also going to assume you both realize that what's left of the body is badly burned. The intensity from the explosion would have killed them immediately."

"What are you thinking?" Nikki asked. "Homemade bomb?"

"Looks like shrapnel here," he said, pointing to a sliver of metal. "But I'll leave that side of the investigation up to you."

"Understood, but we really need to know who was in this car."

"You're going to have to give me some time. Like I said, there isn't much to go on, but judging from what's left of the clothing and hair, my guess would be that it's a woman."

"Wait a minute." Nikki glanced at Jack. "A woman?"

"I should be able to confirm the actual identity once I can do an official autopsy, but for now, I'd say yes. There's a distinctive woman's ring on the victim's right hand."

"So if it isn't Russell," Jack said, "then who is it?"

"Wait a minute," Nikki said. "Can we see the ring?"

She breathed in the strong scent of burning flesh and pressed the back of her hand against her mouth and nose.

"Our victim's right hand must have been somewhat protected against her body during the explosion." Dr. Torres wiped off the smudged stone. "It's a ring. Unique. I'd say a purple amethyst with diamonds in the center."

Nikki took a photo of the ring with her cell phone.

"I'm sorry, but that's all I'm going to be able to give you at this point. Touch base with my office in twenty-four hours, and I'll try to have something for you."

Nikki frowned. Twenty-four hours was going to be too late.

"It's definitely not Brian," Jack said, walking away.

"Do you remember seeing that ring on his ex-wife when she came in?" Nikki asked.

"No, but that doesn't mean she wasn't wearing it. I might be a detective, but when it comes to women's jewelry—"

"Wait a minute." Nikki pulled Jack away from the line of reporters while the ME loaded the victim into his van. "The housekeeper said there was some kind of mix-up with this car. She's got to know something, and she might even be able to recognize the ring."

"We'll need to let Brinkley know what's going on," Jack said as they headed for Nikki's car.

"Why?" Nikki held up her hand, avoiding the press's request for a comment. "He has this annoying habit of showing up where the action is. I have a feeling it won't take him long to find out about this."

"Maybe, but tell me this," Jack said. "Who do you think might have wanted Russell dead? Assuming he's the target."

"If the FBI's right about what he's involved in, it seems like a pretty long list to me," she said, pulling out her keys. "For starters, Dimitry Petran."

"Silence is a powerful motivator."

"Exactly. If Russell is getting sloppy, why not just take him out?" Nikki looked back at the burnt-out BMW. "And whoever was in this car got caught up in the middle."

Maria met them at the gate this time.

"We need to talk to you again."

"If this is about the dogs, I'm sorry. You have to believe me

183

when I say it was an accident. I had no idea they'd gotten out. They are usually locked up except for at night, but today . . . I don't know what happened."

"Someone let them out," Nikki said, gauging her demeanor. The woman looked terrified. "Perhaps the owner of the car parked in your drive, or perhaps Mr. Russell himself."

"No . . . no, he would never do anything like that."

"Who else is here, Maria?" Jack asked.

"Just Mr. Russell's accountant, Mr. Olson. He dropped by to pick up some papers."

"And Mr. Russell. Have you heard from him yet?"

"No. I'm sorry."

"When we were here earlier, you said there was a mix-up with Mr. Russell's BMW. We need to know what you meant."

Maria's gaze flickered to the driveway. "I already told you, it was nothing important."

"I think it is. In case you don't know what just happened, a car exploded down the road from you. A black BMW with a license that matches your boss's."

"No . . ." Maria's shoulders heaved. "That's not possible."

"Who was driving that car? Because we know it wasn't Mr. Russell. Maybe a girlfriend—"

"No." Maria's gaze dropped. "No, you must have made a mistake."

"A woman is dead," Nikki said. "We need to know who was driving that car."

Maria kneaded her hands in front of her. "She wasn't supposed to take the car. I shouldn't have let her, but she can be so persuasive. She promised me he wouldn't find out, so I gave her the keys."

"Who wasn't supposed to drive the car, Maria?"

"Mrs. Russell."

"Brian Russell's ex-wife?"

Maria nodded. "She came by to see me this morning. Told

me she needed to take her car into the shop and needed to borrow Mr. Russell's car. I told her she would have to talk to him, but I couldn't get ahold of him and he was already gone for the day. She told me it would be our little secret. That she'd have it back before he returned. So I let her take it."

"When was she supposed to return it?"

"Today. But she never came back."

"Do you recognize this?" Nikki held up the photo of the ring she'd taken at the crime scene. Purple amethyst with rose-cut diamonds in the center.

"*Sí*. That was hers. Mrs. Russell's. It was a family ring. Belonged to her great-grandmother, I think." Maria looked up. "So you are telling me that Mrs. Russell is dead."

"I'm sorry, but yes."

"Why would someone try to kill her?" Tears welled in the woman's eyes. "She wasn't even supposed to be driving that car."

"Maybe they weren't trying to kill her," Jack said. "Maybe they were trying to kill Brian Russell."

"I don't understand. Why would anyone want to kill him?"

Nikki's phone rang. She grabbed it on the second ring.

"I've got your warrant," Gwen said. "And a team is headed your direction right now to help you search."

Nikki hung up, then nodded at Jack. "Maria, do you know what a search warrant is?"

"A search warrant . . . they talk about it on those cop shows."

"It gives us permission to search a residence. And we have one for Mr. Russell's home."

"Mr. Russell isn't going to like this."

"I'm sorry, but it's the law."

Movement out of the corner of her eye caught Nikki's attention. A middle-aged man, balding, heavyset, and with wire-rimmed glasses, headed for the silver Mercedes-Benz in the driveway. He was carrying a briefcase.

"Who's that?" she asked.

"That's Mr. Olson. Mr. Russell's accountant."

Jack stayed with Maria while Nikki hurried down the driveway.

"Where are you going in such a hurry, Mr. Olson?" Nikki held up her badge. "I'm Special Agent Nikki Boyd with the Tennessee Bureau of Investigation. Would you mind stepping away from your car?"

Mr. Olson set down his briefcase. "Is there a problem, Officer?"

"We're looking for Brian Russell. Do you know where he is?"

"No." Mr. Olson's face reddened. "It's been a few days since I've seen him."

"Were you supposed to meet him here?"

"No. I just came to pick up some papers he left for me."

"That's odd. Maria told us Russell had arranged to meet you today. And your car was here when we stopped by the first time. I'm wondering if you had anything to do with letting out the dogs." Nikki nodded toward the side of the house. Jack and Maria had walked up to stand next to her.

The man wiped his brow with the back of his hand. "No, of course not. Maria told me about the incident—I was in Brian's office, collecting the paperwork."

"We have a warrant giving us permission to search Mr. Russell's house. Since you clearly have some of his papers, I'd like you to come inside with me for a chat while the house is searched so you can tell me exactly what Mr. Russell told you to pick up."

"I really don't think that's necessary. He just asked me to go through some paperwork in connection to one of the charities he works with—"

"It wasn't a suggestion, Mr. Olson. And Maria, if you'll open the gate, please, for the other officers who have just arrived."

The inside of the house was as opulent as the outside. Hardwood floors, a stone fireplace, and modern kitchen open to the living room and dining room.

Mr. Olson hesitated in the entryway.

"Why don't you have a seat?" Nikki pointed to one of the high-backed chairs in the dining room while officers in uniform began to search the residence under Jack's direction. "You seem nervous. Is there something you want to tell me?"

Mr. Olson looked around the room, his right hand gripping the handle of the briefcase, then finally took a seat.

"You're Mr. Russell's financial advisor," Nikki began, sitting down across from him.

"Yes."

"Can I assume the two of you are pretty close?"

"I've known him for a long time." He pulled out his cell phone. "Which is why I need to contact his attorney. He'll want to know what's going on—"

Nikki leaned forward. "Mr. Olson, an attorney isn't going to change what happens next. And I'm going to need to give the briefcase you're holding to my partner."

"You can't do that."

"I can," Nikki said. "Because the papers you have in your briefcase—papers you told us are Mr. Russell's—fall under the search warrant we have."

The man's grip on the case only tightened.

"There isn't a problem, is there, Mr. Olson? I mean, if your client has something to hide—"

"No . . . of course not. Take the papers." He dropped the case onto the table between them. "But you won't find anything in them that incriminates Brian."

"We'll let the FBI decide that, but in the meantime, I want to tell you what I think happened. Mr. Russell asked you to come by the house to pick up some of his files from his office. Files that had the possibility of being incriminating. Files that he didn't want the police to find in a search. Is that what happened?"

"Of course not, he told me—"

"So you have heard from Mr. Russell then."

"Yes . . . no—"

"Where is he, Mr. Olson?"

"I swear, I don't know."

Nikki frowned. "Here's the thing. Russell is in a lot of trouble. So we can wait until we go through the evidence we find during the search warrant, or you can help me out and I can put in a good word for you with the DA. Because either way, you're connected with what's going on here, and there is a good chance that you'll be spending time in prison. It's up to you to determine how long you're there."

"No . . ." He grabbed a handkerchief from his back pocket and wiped off his brow. "No, you don't understand. I can't go to prison."

"Unfortunately, you should have thought of that before you got involved with Mr. Russell. Because the FBI has evidence of a money trail that suggests the nonprofits he supports don't just pay for water wells and hospital equipment in third-world countries."

"I've heard the accusations. None of that is true."

"Then perhaps if you'll tell me where Mr. Russell is, we'll be able to clear this up."

The man shook his head. "You don't understand. Mr. Russell doesn't know I'm here."

"I thought he told you to pick up some papers."

"I . . . I lied. If he knew I was here—" Mr. Olson twisted the silver band on his right hand. "I borrowed a few thousand dollars from the account over the past year. My mother was sick. Insurance wasn't covering everything she needed. I didn't know what to do. If Brian finds out what I've done, I'll lose my job . . . my reputation—"

"How much money did you take, Mr. Olson?"

The man's Adam's apple bobbed. "A few thousand."

"How much?" she repeated.

"Seventy-five grand."

Seventy-five thousand dollars?

The man was clearly in over his head, but was he denying the FBI's accusations?

"Am I under arrest?"

Nikki's phone rang and she quickly pulled it out of her pocket and let out a swoosh of air. "We'll have to deal with your confession next," she said to him while lifting the phone to her ear.

"Any luck on your end?" Gwen asked.

"They've gone ahead with the search," she said. "We'll have to hand the evidence over to Brinkley, since our priority is finding Erika."

"I'm calling about Erika," Gwen said. "I've been going through the numbers on her phone records. One of the numbers she called twice belongs to a woman by the name of Helen Pope. She lives about an hour and a half from Nashville and works in a local diner in a small town. I've been trying to get ahold of her, but it looks like her phone's turned off.

"I was able, though, to track down Helen's boss. He told me she hadn't been in to work for the past three days, which, according to him, is completely out of character for her."

Nikki frowned. "What else did he say?"

"That he had some information but insisted on talking to someone in person."

"Maybe this is the break we've been needing," Nikki said. "Assuming Erika's still alive, she's going to go somewhere familiar. Somewhere she can trust."

Nikki hung up the call, then signaled to Jack. "Gwen just got us another lead on Erika. You up for a road trip?"

"You bet. And you were right. Brinkley just showed up. We can let him wrap things up here."

Nikki nodded. So much for her attempts at finding a bit of normal.

20

Just before two, Nikki stepped into Harper's Diner, located on Main Street. The quaint small town reminded her of visiting her aunt's house for the weekend while she was still in high school. Friday nights meant watching the local football team, then going to her aunt's restaurant for fried pies or milk shakes. It was probably some of those very memories that had inspired her father to start his own restaurant back in Nashville. And every time they went back to visit, Aunt Bell was ready to give her father tips on running his restaurant.

"I feel like I'm in Mayberry," Jack said.

Harper's Diner was like stepping back in time. The walls were covered with photos from Elvis to John Wayne, Coca-Cola memorabilia to country singers who tried to put themselves on the map. Red-and-white-checkered tablecloths, cozy booths, the twang of a guitar playing in the background; it had all the charm of an old small-town restaurant.

"I always forget how much I love these small towns. They're a bit of nostalgia wrapped up in a bunch of southern charm." Nikki eyed the long line of locals waiting for service at the counter.

"I don't know about that. I'm more of a city boy, in case you hadn't noticed."

"Why doesn't that surprise me?" Nikki laughed. "If we had time, I'd buy you a basket of fried catfish, onion rings, and a slice of pecan pie, and make you sit down and enjoy it."

"And put me in an early grave. I can feel the grease starting to flow—or not flow, more likely—through my veins, just standing here."

Nikki breathed in the smell of fresh coffee and fried foods and felt her stomach rumble despite the lunch she'd grabbed on the way here. "Suit yourself, but man, are you missing out."

One of the waitresses grabbed two plates of burgers and fries and headed toward a couple sitting in the corner of the room. She hummed while zigzagging between tables.

"I bet that's the proprietor," Jack said, nodding at the man with red hair and an even redder beard behind the counter.

Nikki made her way toward the long counter that ran almost the length of the entire restaurant.

"Raleigh Harper?" she asked, holding up her badge.

"You can call me Ray," he said, finishing up wiping down the front counter while a young girl that didn't look like she was a day over seventeen took orders. "You're the cops from Nashville."

"We're here to get some information on Helen Pope."

"Order up." A chubby waitress squeezed past him, balancing four plates of catfish in her hands.

"Give me a couple minutes, Brooke."

"Sure thing, boss."

"Can I get you anything to eat?"

"We're fine, but thanks," Jack said.

"Okay then. I think there's a table in the back that's free." He led them through the expanding line of customers ready to place their orders. "Sorry for all the noise. You came at the busiest time of the day."

"No problem." Nikki watched a little girl digging into an ice cream sundae, then slid into an orange booth next to Jack. "Thanks for agreeing to speak with us. We're trying to contact Mrs. Pope, and haven't been able to get ahold of her."

"You're not the only one. Like I told the detective on the phone, I've been trying to find Helen for the past couple days. To be honest, I'm starting to get worried."

"My partner told me you had information you didn't want to share over the phone," Nikki said.

"I hope I didn't cause too much trouble, having you drive all the way here." Ray leaned forward, resting his forearms on the table. "The local sheriff went out to her house to check on things." He pulled a note out of his front pocket and flattened it out on the table between them. "I found this note from Helen three days ago. She must have come into the store to see if I was here, then scribbled this note on the back of one of the order pads we use."

"She didn't try to call you?"

"There were a couple missed calls, but I'd been working the late shift and was exhausted. Decided to turn off my phone."

Nikki picked up the paper and read the message.

Sorry to leave you hanging, Ray, but I won't be able to work for the next few days. Call Cassandra. She could use the extra work. Will be in touch.

—Helen

Ray tapped on the edge of the paper with his finger. "That's Helen's handwriting. I'm sure of it."

192

"So this was unusual for Helen to take off, simply leaving a note?"

Ray leaned forward, shaking his head. "That's the thing. Helen's never late, and she rarely takes a day off. And if she does need a day off, she gives me a heads-up at least a week or two in advance. She knows how hard it is to fill her position."

"What about her husband? Have you heard from him?"

"I've tried calling him a couple times as well. That's the other thing that's odd. Just like Helen would never just not show up, Frank's usually one of my first customers. He gets here about seven every morning, orders coffee, black, and a blueberry muffin. Been doing that for as long as I can remember. Besides that, about the only time her husband leaves town is to go hunt, and we've still got a couple more weeks until the season starts. Something's not adding up. They would have told someone. As it is, they've just . . . vanished."

"When exactly did you find this message?" Nikki asked.

"Sunday morning when I came in to open up. It was early . . . I'd say five fifteen. Five thirty at the latest."

"And had she worked the late shift the night before?"

"No. The last time I saw her was when she got off before the evening rush Saturday night."

"Did she seem different in any way that day?" Jack asked.

"No. Not that I can think of. And trust me, I've gone through every conversation we had that day, thinking I had to have missed something, but honestly, everything seemed normal. She worked hard, and told me she'd see me the next afternoon for her next shift."

"What about her husband?" Nikki shifted in her seat. "Any issues between the two of them?"

"They fight off and on like any married couple, but they love each other."

"And how long has Helen worked here?" Jack glanced at

four kids digging into two baskets of onion rings in the booth across from them.

"As long as I can remember. In fact, when my mother started running the restaurant thirty-odd years ago, Helen had been running this front counter for at least a decade. Customers love her."

"You said you'd spoken to the sheriff?"

"The sheriff went out to their place yesterday. Came back and told me their car was gone and the place was locked up tight. Told me not to worry, that they probably went to visit family or something out of town. But it's been three days now with no word from Helen." Ray leaned forward. "Do you know if something happened? I only ask because when that woman called from your department, I was already worried something had happened to them. You have to understand that Helen's like family. If anything were to happen to her . . ." He shook his head, the worry lines around his eyes deepening.

"To be honest, Mr. Harper, we don't have information on the Popes. We were actually trying to get into contact with Helen regarding another woman who's missing." Nikki pulled out her cell phone and showed him the photo of Erika. "Do you know this woman?"

"Of course." Ray slicked his hair off his forehead. "Her name's Erika. She comes around here every now and then with her little girl. Such a cute little thing. Everyone here loves that girl. She always orders a pineapple milk shake. But I don't understand. What's happened to Erika?"

"She is missing, and we believe her life could be in danger," Jack said. "How often did Erika come up here?"

"Seemed like less often the past year or so, but always during the holidays. And whenever she could snatch a free weekend away from work. She had a good job, I understand. Worked for some ritzy art gallery."

"You said the sheriff went by their house?" Nikki asked, glancing at a man in uniform across the room.

"He did. If you want to talk to the sheriff, he's here right now. On Wednesdays we've got catfish on the menu, and he's almost always here."

"Why don't you ask the sheriff if he minds if we ask him a few questions while we're here," Jack said.

Ray nodded, and a minute later Nikki and Jack slid into seats across from Sheriff Vic Porter after a quick introduction.

"Hope you don't mind if I finish eating," the sheriff said, wiping off his mouth with his napkin. "Ray's wife makes the best fried catfish in the county. You seriously ought to try a plate before you head back to Nashville. But I know you're not here for chitchat. I understand you're looking for Helen Pope." The sheriff glanced at the counter where Ray was back at work. "I'm not sure what Ray told you, but I have no evidence at this point of any foul play regarding the Popes."

"I understand, but a friend of hers, Erika Hamilton, has gone missing," Nikki said, showing him her photo. "We're trying to determine who she might have contacted for help, and wondering now if there might be some kind of connection to the fact that Helen seems to have vanished as well."

"It is strange." The sheriff shoved his empty plate to the middle of the table and leaned his long form back against the booth. "I've known Helen and her husband, Frank, for as long as I can remember."

"Ray said you stopped by their place yesterday," Nikki said.

"Things looked normal. No sign of forced entry. No sign that anything was wrong. But it's not like the two of them to just up and disappear."

"Ray said Helen hasn't shown up for work for three days."

Sheriff Porter rubbed his goatee. "And you think their disappearance could be related to Erika and Lily."

"I don't believe it's a coincidence," Nikki said.

"Can't say that we've had a lot of people go missing in these parts. Don't have a lot of serious crime at all, to be honest. Haven't had a murder in ten years. I mainly deal with burglaries and thefts and, every now and then, the occasional domestic violence."

"Ray said they didn't have any children, but what about other family . . . or friends they might have gone to see?"

The sheriff held up his hands. "Hard to say. From what I know, most of their friends live around here. Don't recall them talking about visiting family. In fact, I'm sure Ray already told you that Frank didn't like to travel unless it was to go hunting."

"Did he have a cabin he went to regularly?"

"There's one he goes to quite a bit up the road that a friend of his owns, but I already gave Mac a call. He says he's not there."

Nikki frowned. It had been less than forty-eight hours, and Erika's trail was already running cold. Which implied two things. One, Erika didn't want to be found, or two, Brian Russell had already found her.

The sheriff sat back in his seat. "I can take you out to their house, if you'd like. Maybe you city police will find something I didn't, but it's highly unlikely."

Nikki and Jack followed the sheriff out to the Pope property in her vehicle. The ten-minute drive took them past the occasional old barn and pasture, reminding Nikki of how much she loved being out of the city. She and Tyler needed to plan another day rock climbing.

"You doing okay?" Jack's question pulled her out of her musings.

"A bit tired, but yeah. I'm fine," she said, listening to her tires grind against the gravel road. "Should have ordered some coffee to go from the diner."

"Or one of those milk shakes I saw you eyeing."

"I should have, considering I'm not the one on the restricted organic diet."

"Can you imagine yourself living in a place like this?"

"Definitely." Nikki smiled, enjoying a few moments to forget why they were really there. "My brothers and I used to visit my aunt in a small town like this one every summer. We'd work in the mornings on the farm, then ride our bikes into town for ice cream. I loved it."

"I have to say, I never imagined you a country girl."

She caught Jack's sideways glance. "I love the conveniences of the city, but you have to admit it wouldn't be a bad place to raise a family. Everyone knows everyone and looks after each other."

"Even places like this aren't perfect."

"Maybe not, but no murders in the past ten years."

"Which means that the most excitement you find here is handing out parking tickets."

"Something I could handle right about now."

She pulled into the long drive of the Pope property behind the sheriff's car, parking in front of a weathered two-story house that sat back from the road. There were a couple of sheds and at least a dozen old cars in various states of repair lying around the property.

"Frank was a mechanic," the sheriff said as he climbed out of his car. "He was always working on one of these old cars. Always collecting parts he might need one day. Think the man simply didn't have enough time in the day to fix them all. On top of that, he's got a couple sheds full of vintage car parts."

"That's what's in these old sheds?" Nikki asked, as they headed toward the house on the damp grass.

"Yep. He sells some stuff on eBay, but I think he ends up keeping most of it."

"Ought to send the American Pickers out here," Jack said. "Just might find a pot of gold buried in those sheds of his."

"I've told him that a time or two before." The sheriff cut across the front yard toward the porch. "Helen could probably quit working and they could retire to Florida—or anywhere they wanted, for that matter—if he got rid of most this stuff."

Nikki started up the front steps. "What did he say about that?"

"He planned to live and die in this house and won't budge. And to be honest, I can't imagine Helen leaving her job at the diner. After decades of working that front counter, I think it's more than a paycheck."

"I'll check things out around back," Nikki said.

She peeked through a side window into the kitchen, giving her a partial view of the living room. Everything looked to be in place. There were no dishes in the sink, and the kitchen had been cleaned up. She continued around the side of the house, then slowed down as she approached the back door.

Large slivers of glass lay on the back step. Nikki looked up at the door. The window above the handle had been smashed.

"Jack . . . Sheriff . . . ," she hollered. "I've got something."

21

Avoiding the pile of glass on the back step, Nikki quickly put on a latex glove, then reached for the door handle, careful to avoid smearing any fingerprints.

The sheriff and Jack appeared around the side of the house as she swung open the door. "Someone's been here. They broke the glass and unlocked the door."

"I swear this wasn't like this when I came by here yesterday." The sheriff rested his hands against his hips and frowned. "The house was locked up, with no sign of forced entry. No sign of tampering with any of the locks. But this . . . ."

"I noticed the grass is damp." Nikki bent down and picked up one of the shards of glass. "When did it rain last around here?"

"A little over an hour ago," the sheriff said.

"These are all dry, which narrows down our time frame."

Gun raised, Nikki stepped inside the house in front of the

men, then the three began clearing the premises. They met back in the living room a couple minutes later.

"A child's been staying here," Nikki said, holstering her weapon. "There are toys on the living room floor. A booster chair in the kitchen."

She reached down and picked up a worn teddy bear lying on the floor next to the couch. She ran her fingers across the pudgy stomach of the soft bear before turning it over. There was a name tag hand sewn on the back of the animal.

Lily.

Nikki glanced at the back door with the shattered window. When the sheriff had come by, there had been no sign of an intruder. Which put the time of the break-in within the last hour. Memories of her dream washed over her afresh. Lily sitting on a narrow ledge wearing a white dress . . .

Where are you, Lily—

"Nikki?"

She looked up at Jack, still holding the stuffed bear. "Lily was staying here. Her name's sewn into the label. And look at this"—she pointed to a picture of a small girl on an end table—"I bet that's Lily. She looks just like Erika."

"Looks like you were right about all of this," the sheriff said, "but what do you think happened? There's no sign of foul play. No blood. No signs of a struggle. No obvious signs that a crime took place, except that someone broke in and searched the house. Seemingly after Frank, Helen—and Lily—left."

Nikki held the bear against her chest, taking in the scene before responding to his question. "Erika decides to help the FBI in order to take down Russell and make sure she gets complete custody, but she needs Lily out of the way and safe until things with the FBI are over."

"So she brings her here," Jack said.

"If she was trying to protect her daughter, it makes sense

why she didn't tell anyone Lily was staying with them." Nikki looked up at the men. "But if we could make the connection between Erika and the Popes, so could Russell."

"We could have a team sent out here to search for prints, but I'm not sure we'll find anything."

Something crashed outside, turning Nikki's gaze toward the nearest window.

"Someone's out there," she said, running for the back door.

Halfway down the steps, she saw a man wearing a black hoodie and carrying something small in his hand slip into the shadows of a red barn toward the corner of the property.

"I'll head around to the back in case he tries to flee that direction," Jack said, running beside her. "You two go through the front."

Nikki made it to the barn before the sheriff, then paused for a few seconds at the barn door, waiting for him to catch up. The door squeaked open as Nikki pushed against it with her foot and stepped into the dimly lit space. Gripping her flashlight like an ice pick, she steadied her gun in her right hand. She paused long enough to let her eyes adjust to the darkness. Like the outside of the property, the space was filled with old cars and a tractor, a pile of metal signs, and more old parts. The only light, besides her flashlight and that of the sheriff's beside her, was random holes in the wall letting in narrow rays of sunlight across the dusty floor.

A floorboard squeaked to the left. Nikki re-angled her flashlight, throwing a beam of white light across the barn floor. The hairs on the back of her neck stood up as a rat ran across her shoe. She stumbled backward, barely avoiding a huge cobweb in the corner. The rodent skittered off under one of the cars.

Seriously?

Nikki refocused in the dim light. This might have been a workspace for Mr. Pope in the past, but it seemed pretty clear that he didn't spend a lot of time out here anymore. The space looked like it had been neglected for years.

Something creaked again on the other side of the barn. And this time, it was too loud to be a rodent.

Nikki signaled at the sheriff on her right, then, staying in the shadows, made her way along the edge of the building, looking for signs of their trespasser. She glanced up at the loft above her. Whoever was in here had to be connected somehow to Lily. Sunlight burst through the back of the barn as their suspect slammed out the back door and headed across the property toward the street.

Where was Jack?

"Jack!" Nikki shouted, lungs heaving as she took off after their trespasser. "We found our runner."

But there was still no sign of Jack.

Nikki ran beside the sheriff, shouting at their trespasser. "This is the police! Stop where you are and put your hands in the air where I can see them."

The man turned, paused for an instant, then continued tearing across the field. Nikki caught sight of Jack, who was chasing a second man a couple hundred yards ahead of her.

With a forced burst of energy, Nikki bridged the gap between her prey and herself. Seconds later, she was able to wrestle him to the ground before pressing her boot into the man's back so he couldn't move. Taking a step back, she pointed her weapon at the man's torso while the sheriff handcuffed him, then pulled off his hood to reveal dark, curly hair and stud earrings.

Sheriff Porter shoved him over with the toe of his boot. "I've got two questions for you, son, and I want the truth on both counts. Who are you, and what are you doing on the Popes' property?"

"I wasn't doing anything. Just looking for the main road back to Nashville."

"With your friend?" Nikki asked.

"We're traveling together."

"Right . . . ," Nikki said. "And you ended up here, poking around a stranger's barn? You must not have seen the NO TRESPASSING signs. Besides that, you're a little out of the way from the main road back to Nashville."

His eyes kept shifting toward the driveway. "I was doing a bit a sightseeing and got lost. Thought whoever lived here wouldn't mind if I came and might be able to give me some help. I thought I heard someone in the barn."

"You didn't answer the first question," the sheriff said. "What's your name?"

"That's okay. I can answer the question for you." Nikki flipped open the wallet that had fallen out of the man's pocket in the scuffle. "Driver's license says Brad Collins. Thirty-five years old. Tennessee license."

"Whoever he is, I can tell you he's not from around here. And here's the thing, in case you didn't know." The sheriff knelt down next to the man. "We do two things to trespassers around here. Arrest 'em or shoot 'em. I'm guessing you have a preference?"

"I wasn't trespassing. Or at least I didn't mean to. I told you I was lost and looking for directions."

"We'll see about that."

Jack jogged back to where they were standing, out of breath. "Your partner in crime's gone. Drove off in your getaway car."

"There was no crime and no getaway car."

"Save your excuses for the judge," the sheriff said.

"Did you get a license plate?" Nikki asked.

"A partial. I'll call it in to Gwen right now and see what she can get."

"Sheriff . . . why don't you take Mr. Collins back to your office. I want to make a final sweep of the house, and we'll be right behind you."

The sheriff nodded, then helped his prisoner up. "You got it."

Nikki headed back for the barn, her flashlight in hand.

"Looking for something specific?" Jack asked.

"The guy had something in his hand when I first saw him. Which means he probably dropped it in the barn." She shined her flashlight across the wall near the door. "Maybe a light switch would help."

A second later, she flipped a switch and the barn was flooded with light.

"Do you have any idea why he was in here?" Jack asked.

"All I can figure is that he thought going through the barn would block our line of sight from the house to the road."

They started looking around a pile of discarded car parts where Collins had been when Nikki first saw him.

"Wait a minute . . . I think I might have something." Nikki reached for a piece of paper that was wedged beneath an old car part. It was a photograph. "Take a look at this," she said, holding up the ripped photo.

"What is it?"

Nikki flipped it around. "It's a photograph of Erika Hamilton."

"Erika . . . You're sure he dropped it?"

"I can't be 100 percent sure what was in his hand, but it fits. And if he did have this photograph, it definitely points to the fact that our Mr. Collins was here looking for Erika."

"And if they're still looking for her, it means they haven't found her."

"Maybe not," Nikki said, "but neither have we."

Twenty minutes later, the sheriff handed Nikki a cold milk shake. "Compliments of Ray's Diner."

"Thank you," Nikki said, taking a long sip of the fudgy chocolate shake that was definitely made with real ice cream.

She might end up comatose from a sugar overdose, but it was going to be worth it.

"You're sure you don't want anything, son?" the sheriff asked Jack.

"I'm good, but thanks."

"Did you find anything else then?" the sheriff asked.

"A photograph of Erika Hamilton, the woman we're looking for," Nikki said, dropping the photo onto the sheriff's desk between sips.

Sheriff Porter took off his hat, then sat down behind his desk. "I've just sent two of my deputies out to board up the broken window at the Pope home."

"That's a good idea," Nikki said. "So what's our suspect saying?"

"Nothing so far."

"What information do you have on him?" Jack asked.

"We ran his name through our database. He's former military, now working as a security consultant for B. B. Williams."

"Who exactly is that?" Jack asked.

"According to their website, you can hire them out for individual private security needs."

"What about searching for a missing person?" Nikki asked.

"I'd say that's definitely possible."

Nikki glanced at Jack. "I think it's time we tried talking to the man."

"Be my guest," the sheriff said. "Hopefully you'll get more out of him than I did."

If possible, the sheriff's department interview room was even drabber than their precinct's back in Nashville. Brad Collins sat in front of a dingy gray wall, his hands in front of him and tapping on a worn metal desk.

"Mr. Collins," Nikki said, sitting down across from the man. "I don't think we were properly introduced back at the Pope residence. My name is Special Agent Nikki Boyd. I'm sure we can clear this whole incident up quickly and have you on your way back to Nashville if you can just answer a couple questions."

"I hope so, because I've yet to be given the chance to call my lawyer."

"You said you were looking for directions," Jack said.

"We were in the area to see about doing some hunting in a couple weeks."

"Why did you and your friend run from the police?"

"People were yelling at us. Wouldn't you run?"

"Not when I was told to stop by the police," Nikki said. "And not unless I had something to hide."

Collins blew out a sharp breath of air. "I don't have anything to hide. Or anything more to say, for that matter."

"Okay." Nikki bit back her frustration. Seconds were ticking by, and they were getting nowhere. She slid Erika's photo across the table. "What about this woman. Have you seen her before?"

Collins looked away. "Never seen her before."

"Really?" Jack said. "Because we have reason to believe you were at the Pope residence, looking for her."

"I said I've never seen her before."

"Here's the problem, Mr. Collins," Nikki said, leaning forward. She needed the guy to tell her the truth. "We know you were looking for her, because not only were you trespassing, there are fingerprints on this photo, fingerprints on the back door that was broken into, and fingerprints in the house. And because of your military background I can match them all to you. Which means when something happens to her—for instance, if we found her murdered on the Popes' property—I can connect it to you—"

"Murder? Now hold on." Collin's face reddened. "You found her murdered? Nothing was supposed to happen to her. I was only hired to find her."

"Really." Nikki smiled. "Now we're finally getting some answers."

"Who hired you?" Jack asked.

"That information is private—"

Nikki tapped on Erika's photo. "I think we're past that."

His jaw tensed before answering. "Brian Russell."

"And what did he ask you to do this time?" Nikki asked.

"He told me he was worried about his girlfriend, Erika. Said she'd taken a trip a couple days ago to visit her family here, and he hadn't heard from her. He was worried she might have gotten in an accident. I guess a couple other guys working for him weren't successful, so he hired Jason and me to bring her home."

"Why not just go to the police if she was missing?"

"Far as I know, he did go to the police, but I don't know. I didn't ask."

"So you weren't hired to kill Erika."

"Are you crazy? No way."

"Have you ever worked for Russell before?" Jack asked.

"I've done a few specific jobs for Brian over the years. Mainly security jobs."

"What kind of security are you talking about?"

"Mr. Russell was well off, which meant it wasn't uncommon for him to hire private security."

"And the Popes. How do they fit into all of this?"

"Apparently they're close friends of hers. He said she might have gone to them if she was in trouble."

"In trouble . . . how?" Jack asked.

"You'd have to ask Mr. Russell that."

"And do you know how we might be able to get ahold of him?"

"I . . . I've got a number I can call if I need to get ahold of him."

Nikki's cell phone rang. She glanced at the caller ID. "It's Gwen. We need to take this." She and Jack stood up. "Thank you for your cooperation, Mr. Collins."

"Wait a minute. The woman . . . Erika Hamilton . . . is she really dead?"

Nikki paused in the doorway. "I don't know."

She stepped into the hallway and put the phone on speaker. "What do you have, Gwen?"

"911 just took a call from a frantic woman about a car that matches the description of Kim Parks's car. It was spotted driving east toward Knoxville."

"That's not far from here." Nikki felt her breath catch. "What happened to the car?"

There was a pause on the line. "It was reported going off the road and into the gully below."

22

Nikki glanced at her speedometer, then let her foot off the gas as she took another windy curve along the narrow mountain highway. "How much farther?"

"According to the GPS, it looks like just under half a mile," Jack said. "You'll see a narrow turnoff to your right where you can pull off."

Nikki bit the side of her lip, trying not to think about what might have happened if Erika's car had gone off the road on one of these sharp curves. The metal guardrails wouldn't have been enough to stop her if she were going too fast.

A minute later she pulled off the road onto the turnoff, parked, then turned off the engine. A blue sedan sat behind a police car along the narrow ridge. Nikki jumped out of her car ahead of Jack and ran down the gravel shoulder. She glanced down at the deep gully. There were skid marks along the side of the road leading to where the guardrail had been hit. More than likely, this wasn't the first time this had happened.

And if this really was Erika, and she'd gone over the edge . . .

Nikki showed the officer her badge and quickly introduced herself and Jack to him and the young woman wearing gym clothes who had to be their witness. She was breathing hard and her face was streaked with tears.

"I'm Officer Blyth," the officer said with a thick southern drawl. "Didn't expect TBI to show up. This is the third time a car's gone off the edge in the past year. Sure wish we could do more to stop this from happening, but people refuse to slow down."

"You were the first responder?" Jack asked.

"I just got here a couple minutes ago," he said. "This is Susanne Lane. She was driving down the highway and saw two cars speeding through these curves. I've been taking her statement, but she's understandably pretty shaken up. In the meantime I've called for backup, both an ambulance and our rescue unit. I thought about going down there, but it's going to take some special equipment."

"You did the right thing," Nikki said.

She knew what the officer was thinking. *If* there was a survivor. The chances of someone living through an accident like this were slim.

"I want to see the car that went off the road," Nikki said, "then we'll need to ask you a few questions, Ms. Lane. I also want an updated ETA on the arrival of the ambulance and rescue team."

"I'll put in another call to dispatch right now," Officer Blyth said, pulling out his radio.

Nikki moved to the edge of the cliff with the pair of binoculars the officer had handed her. From the angle where she stood, she couldn't see inside the car. Something orange lay in the bushes.

"It definitely could be the car we believe Erika was driving," Jack said. "I can't see the license plate, but it's the same make, color, and model as Kim's car."

"There's no movement," she said.

"She's got to be either inside the car or maybe in the bushes."

Nikki turned to Ms. Lane. "Did you see the car go through the guardrail?"

"No." The woman's face was splotchy from crying. "I'm sorry. I know I'm a mess." She blew her nose on a tissue. "I haven't been able to stop shaking or crying, because I . . . I didn't know what to do. They were both driving recklessly, but then that one car . . ."

She leaned against the side of her vehicle and started sobbing again.

"Ma'am," Jack said. "I know this is hard for you, but we need you to tell us what you saw."

"Okay." She nodded, then drew in a deep breath. "I . . . I was on my way home. There were two cars driving in front of me pretty fast. One was chasing the other one and even hit it a couple times. I slowed down, not wanting to get involved. I figured it was just a couple of teens, but then as I came around the bend, I noticed that the first car was gone and the second car was driving away from this turnoff."

"Did you ever assume that the first car had simply driven off?"

"Yes, except when I saw that the guardrail had been hit, I had to look. Just to make sure there wasn't a car down there. But when I got out and looked—" Ms. Lane blew her nose again. "I'm sorry. When I got out and looked, I realized that the first car had gone over the edge."

"But you didn't see the second car push the first car over the edge."

"No, but I did see the skid marks and pieces of broken taillight near the guardrail." She drew in a ragged breath. "By then the other car was long gone, so I called 911 and waited for someone to show up."

"Can you remember what the other car looked like?"

"I'm sorry, I don't know cars. It was . . . dark blue. Yes, I'm sure."

"Were you able to see the license plate?" Nikki asked, knowing it was a long shot if the woman wasn't even sure about the car's color.

"No. It all happened so quickly. I called my husband. He's on his way here now. I didn't know what else to do."

"You did the right thing," Nikki said. "Could you tell who was in the car? A man . . . woman . . . a child?"

She shook her head. "They were driving so fast . . . everything happened so fast. I don't know."

Nikki glanced up the road toward Nashville. Backup should be here by now. "Officer Blyth. Did you get an ETA on the rescue team?"

"Apparently there was a three-car collision about five miles east of here. It's going to be at least another fifteen minutes."

"That could be too long." Nikki shrugged off her sweater. Erika—or whoever had gone off that ledge—had already been down there at least ten to fifteen minutes, judging by the 911 call Ms. Lane had made. Another fifteen minutes could be too late.

"I'm going down there," she said, making her decision.

"Wait a minute." Jack caught her gaze. "It's too risky. We need to wait for the rescue team to get here. They've got the equipment needed to get down there safely."

She knew what he was thinking. Chances were slim anyone could have survived this crash. But that didn't matter right now. If there was any chance at all Erika was alive, she needed to get down there now.

"We don't have time to wait." She started back for her car,

not waiting for his response. "Because if there's any chance whoever's down there is alive—"

"Nikki . . ."

"I'm going down there, Jack," she said, hollering over her shoulder.

"So the rescue team will have a second victim to rescue."

She stopped, turned around, and faced him. "It's not exactly the first time I've done this."

"But this is different."

"Why? I've got gear in the back of my car, still stashed there from the last time I went climbing. I'll need your help to get me set up. Then, as soon as backup arrives, it will be quicker to get her up with someone already on the ground. It makes sense, and you know it."

She continued on to her car. The last time she'd gone rock climbing, she'd ended up wishing the whole time Tyler was with her instead of halfway around the world. She'd gone back home after barely half a day, and had never taken the time to take her gear out of her trunk. She'd decided to wait until they could go again together. But she didn't need to be thinking about him and their future. Not right now.

She popped open the trunk and hurried to pull out her gear. She owed it to Erika to do everything possible to find her. Alive.

"You're sure about this?" Jack asked, moving to help her get everything set up and ensure it was all secure, despite his reservations.

She pulled on her gloves. "There's a chance she's still alive, but if we have to wait for the rescue team, it might be too late."

"Okay, but promise me you'll be careful. You've been through a lot these past couple days, and I know how tired you are."

"All I want right now is to find Erika and Lily."

The officer ran over to where they stood, with a first-aid kit in his hands. "You might need this. Can you take this down there with you?"

Nikki secured it with a Velcro strap, then finished making sure the harness sat snugly around her waist. "Got it."

"The EMTs should be here soon," Jack said. "All you need to do is get her stabilized if she's alive, and wait for help to bring her up."

"I will," she said. "And Jack, I'll be okay. I promise."

Seconds later, Nikki leaned back, rope tight, and peered over the edge of the embankment. She'd always loved rappelling, primarily because she loved the adrenaline rush. And the chance to get away from the busyness of her life. To spend a few hours of quiet in God's creation.

Today, though, wasn't the best scenario when it came to climbing. The rocky cliff, full of foliage and debris, was going to make it hard to ensure her rope didn't get caught on one of the branches. She braced her feet against the side and tightened her fingers on the rope, reminding herself again that if Erika was alive, this was their chance at getting her stabilized before the rescue crew came.

A minute later, Nikki breathed out a sigh of relief as she reached the bottom of the embankment. She dropped onto the ground, undid the emergency kit, then slid out of the harness she was wearing. A branch scratched her arm as she moved away from the rock face, drawing a thin line of blood as she made her way through the brush toward the wreck, but she barely felt it.

Someone hollered at her from the top of the embankment. She looked up at Jack and gave him the thumbs-up, then headed toward the banged-up car. Pushing aside a large bush from the driver's side, she managed to pull the door partway open and glance inside.

The car was empty.

The window of the driver's seat had shattered. If Erika hadn't been wearing her seat belt . . .

She glanced in the back. There was no car seat. No sign at all that Lily had been in the vehicle.

Nikki turned around. The most logical explanation was that Erika's body had been thrown out of the driver's window. She headed west, toward the sun that was already beginning to dip toward the horizon. There was a streak of color ahead of her. The orange she'd seen from the road.

She'd been right. Erika lay twenty feet from the crash, where she'd been thrown from the car. Her body lay twisted at a strange angle. Her eyes wide open and laced with fear.

"Erika . . . it's Nikki Boyd." She crouched down beside her and smiled. "We met on the plane yesterday morning. The flight from Houston to Nashville. I was sitting next to you, do you remember?"

"You had the photo of that cute guy." Erika smiled back, but there was pain in her expression. "I thought about you today. Did he meet you at the airport?"

"Yes, but there are a lot of people worried about you. You left the airport in a taxi before anyone had a chance to make sure you were okay." Nikki checked her pulse. It was weak, but steady. "I want you to stay still. Help is on its way."

"If you'll just help me up. I can't . . . I can't feel my legs."

"Erika . . . Don't try to move. There's a rescue team on its way right now. They'll be able to get you out of here."

"Okay."

"Does anything hurt?" She looked for signs of trauma. Erika's neck lay at an odd angle and there was a trickle of blood across her forehead where she'd hit her head on something. Beyond that, there were scratches across her face and arms, but no obvious open wounds.

"No, but I'm not going to make it, am I?" Erika asked.

"Of course you are. You're going to be fine." Nikki fought back the stream of tears threatening to erupt. Because she knew Erika wasn't going to be fine. "But I do need to ask you a question. Was Lily in the car with you?"

"How do you know about Lily?"

"I work for the Tennessee Bureau of Investigation. I've been looking for you since the plane crash."

Erika's chest was heaving with every breath. Her eyes blinked, then shut.

"Erika . . . Erika . . . stay with me."

She opened them again, but it was obvious it was taking more and more effort. "It's getting harder to breathe. I never should have told the FBI I'd testify against Brian for them. They promised me I'd be safe. And I thought I could keep Lily safe, but now . . . I can't keep running from him."

"Who pushed you off the road, Erika?"

"I don't know. Someone Brian sent, or maybe—" She stopped to catch her breath. "Maybe Petran sent someone. It was pretty clear the FBI couldn't really keep me safe . . . me or Lily."

"Can you tell me where Lily is?"

"I had to keep her safe."

"I know, Erika. And I need you to hang in there. Because we're going to get you to the hospital, and then we're going to go find Lily. But I need you to tell me where she is."

"Helen has her."

"Helen Pope?"

Erika nodded. "Maybe I never trusted him completely. I don't know, but I kept secrets from Brian, and he doesn't know about the Popes. But when I called . . . I couldn't get ahold of them." Erika was whispering now. "I told them to run, but you have to find her before he does. Please. You have to keep her safe. That's all I ever wanted."

Nikki crouched closer beside Erika in order to hear her better. How was it that she'd survived the airplane crash only to die barely twenty-four hours later in a car crash?

"Erika . . . Erika? Please stay with me . . . Please."

Nikki pressed her ear next to Erika's mouth to feel for a breath. Nothing.

Nausea swept through her.

Erika had died. Her friend Kim had died.

None of this should have ever happened.

"I was supposed to save her, God."

Nikki stared up at the overcast sky. This was her job. The thing that got her up every morning, because she knew she was making a difference. Stopping someone's mother from having to go through what her mother had gone through. Find them and bring them home and ensure that those responsible never had the opportunity of doing this again. She'd promised to protect and uphold the law. That's all she'd ever wanted.

And what about the chance encounter on the plane. Hadn't that been an act of God? If she'd tried looking for Erika in those early moments after the crash, if she'd found her sooner . . .

But now she was dead.

Nikki's phone rang in her back pocket. She stood up, stepped back from Erika's body, and answered the call.

"What did you find?" Jack asked.

"She was thrown from the car. I was able to talk with her. I just needed a few more minutes, but she's gone, Jack."

There was a long pause before Jack responded. "Was Lily in the car?"

"No. We were right. She's with the Popes, though Erika hasn't been able to contact them." She stared straight ahead at the twisted metal. "But they killed her. We were supposed to stop this from happening."

"We can't stop them all, Nikki. Even as much as we want to. You know that."

217

She knew she was starting to sound hysterical. Knew she had to get control over her emotions. Because if she didn't, she'd never be able to work a case again.

Nikki drew in a deep breath. "If Lily's still alive, she's never going to know her mother. It just . . . it wasn't supposed to end this way."

"Russell wants Lily alive, which means there's a good chance she's still out there. Safe."

"I hope so."

But they needed to find her before Russell did.

23

Nikki stood in front of the timetable they'd posted for Erika, trying to pinpoint where Lily might be . . . and to make sense of what had happened over the last few days. The room smelled like Chinese takeout, but all she could think about was how had Erika Hamilton gone from informant with promised FBI protection to dead in the bottom of a gully?

She'd spent the past hour combing through the information they had discovered, along with the file the FBI had given them. They needed to know where the Popes would take Lily, but so far, not only were there still holes in their timeline, every lead she'd followed up on had ended up being a dead end.

"You know this wasn't your fault," Jack said, stepping up beside her. "Erika's death . . . there's nothing else you could have done."

"Maybe. I just didn't expect things to end this way. I feel like I had the chance to stop this, and I couldn't."

She knew as well as anyone that sometimes you can't stop bad things from happening. Sometimes all you can do is trust God and hold on when life sucks you into the darkest places.

But she'd been on the plane with Erika. She was the one who'd first discovered she was missing. She was the one who'd been pulled into the case by the FBI to find her. And now Erika was dead. "I just wanted to save her."

"We still can find Lily," Gwen said, looking up from her desk.

"And if we don't?" Nikki let out a deep sigh. "Russell's been one step ahead of us this whole time, and it's as if the Popes have vanished."

"Maybe that's what Erika wanted," Jack said.

"I know that's what I would have wanted." She rested her hands on her hips. "But no one simply vanishes. They have to be somewhere. Someone has to have seen something that will help us find the Popes."

"Let's walk through the timeline again. Maybe we've missed something."

"Okay." She took a step closer to the board, praying for the answers they needed. "Here's what we know so far. According to Justin, Erika's biggest fear was losing Lily. If Russell went to prison, then she could keep full custody of Lily and not worry about him taking her away. So for her, working with the FBI was her only way out."

"Her motivation," Jack said.

"Yes, but before she agreed to work with the FBI, she had to make sure Lily was at a place where she'd be safe. Which was—according to Erika—with the Popes. Maria told us there was a birthday party for Erika last Wednesday night in Houston. Lily was there as well."

"So how did Erika get Lily to the Popes?" Jack asked.

Nikki nodded. "We know that on Friday morning, Erika told the FBI she would agree to testify against Russell. This was after several attempts on their part to get her to talk. They took her to a safe house, where they spent the next two days listening to her evidence.

"After two days of interviewing with the FBI, someone broke into the safe house and attempted to grab Erika. Fortunately, the agents managed to stop him, but he got away."

"And we now know," Jack said, "that the description of the attacker is the same as the man who broke into your apartment."

"Exactly. Then at some point after the attack, early Sunday morning, she warns the Popes to run. We know this because Helen Pope left a note for her boss at Ray's diner saying she'd be out of town for a few days."

"I think there was someone else involved. Someone else who helped Erika. It's the only thing that makes sense. Someone had to take Lily to Tennessee—"

"I think you're right. She ensures Lily is safe in Tennessee while she goes back to the FBI to get ready for the grand jury." Gwen shoved her chair back from her desk. "But I can give you another reason I think someone else is involved."

Nikki stepped away from the timeline to give Gwen her full attention.

"What do you mean?" she asked.

"I've been going through that cell phone you found in Erika's car at the crash site. There were files hidden inside it. Most people, when they want to hide something, use encryption, which will obscure the data, but it's still obvious there is something there. That's not what Erika did. She encrypted the data and then managed to hide its existence."

"What did she do?" Jack asked.

"She—or someone—used a stego technique that makes it almost impossible to even tell that there is any private data with the file," Gwen said. "According to her FBI file, she told them that she had more information. Hard evidence that included information that could put Brian Russell away for life, but she wasn't ready to give it to them yet. The file on her phone must be what she was talking about."

"Can you tell what she hid?" Jack asked.

"Only partially, but from what I've been able to see so far, there are spreadsheets, accounting ledgers, lists of names—you name it, it's here. It's going to take time to go through it, as some of it still needs to be decoded, but if this is legit, it's going to be enough to put Russell away for life."

"What about Dimitry Petran? Can you connect anything to him?"

"Like I said, there is still a lot that will have to be decoded, but so far I haven't seen anything that hints at his involvement."

"That's not going to make the FBI happy. But either way, why didn't she just give this information to the FBI when she met with them last weekend?" Jack asked.

Nikki shrugged. "Maybe she didn't have all the information yet. Maybe she wasn't ready to give up the only leverage she had."

"She didn't know who to trust," Gwen said.

"Here's another question," Jack said. "How easy is it to hide data this way?"

"You'd have to have some pretty advanced skills. That's why I said you might be right that someone else was involved."

Nikki glanced at Jack. "So who else could she have trusted?"

"I might be able to help you with that one as well." Gwen said. "Erika ditched her first phone, but we know she made calls to three different numbers. The first one was to Kim Parks. The second number was the unregistered 931 area code she called after the crash."

"The Popes?" Nikki asked.

"Yes, but they never picked up either."

"Erika told me she'd tried to get ahold of them, but she couldn't get through."

"And the third number?" Jack asked.

"It was registered to someone right here in Nashville. She also called the same number using the disposable phone she picked up."

Nikki felt her heart rate speed up. If this turned out to be the lead they needed . . . "Do you have a name?"

"Brandon Folly. He works for the Russells in their IT department, keeping up their websites for all of their businesses." Gwen pulled off her reading glasses. "And here's something interesting. When I couldn't reach him, I tried calling the office here in town. He's already gone home for the day, but he called in sick last Thursday and Friday."

Nikki quickly did the math. "Enough time for him to drive to Houston, pick up Lily, and take her to the Popes."

"This is starting to make sense," Jack said. "Not only were he and Erika co-workers, he had the skills she needed."

"She made three calls to him," Gwen said, glancing back at her notes. "One was yesterday about three. Then again late last night. Both of those calls lasted just under ten minutes. The third call she just left a voice message."

"What did she say?" Nikki asked.

Gwen hesitated. "I can let you listen to it."

Nikki nodded.

Brandon, I need you to call me back as soon as you get this. Please. I think he's following me and I don't know what to do.

Nikki felt the knots in her stomach tighten as she listened to Erika's voice. But she was going to have to process what she just heard later. For now, their one focus had to be finding Lily before Russell did.

"I'm tracking down where Brandon lives," Gwen said.

"Thank you." Nikki turned back to Jack, then frowned as

Brinkley walked through the doorway. "And in the meantime, it looks as if it's time for another chat with the FBI."

Agent Brinkley had changed from the jeans and short-sleeved T-shirt Nikki had seen him in that morning at her house to a dark-gray suit and green tie. Along with his expensive suit was the familiar smug look on his face.

"I got your message that you need to see me, Special Agent Boyd." His voice boomed through the room as he acknowledged Jack and Gwen before stopping at her desk. From the look on his face, he'd already heard the news. "I also just got word that both Peters and Erika are dead."

Nikki pressed her lips together. "One of Russell's men was sent to finish the job before we could talk with Peters, and Erika . . . her car went through a guardrail about an hour and a half from here."

"Which I'm sure was no accident either," Brinkley said.

Nikki studied his expression, unable to tell if there was a flicker of compassion in his expression or simply frustration. "There's evidence her death wasn't an accident."

"What about the evidence she promised to give us?"

"The evidence?" This time Nikki didn't try to mask the anger in her voice. "The woman is dead, her daughter's still missing, and you're worried about the evidence."

Brinkley combed his hands through his thinning hair. "I didn't mean it that way. I'm sorry Erika's dead. I really, really am, but there's a lot at stake here."

"Yes, there is." Nikki stepped in front of him. "Like a child who just lost her mother. She turns four this month, and she doesn't even know she's just lost her mother. In fact, it won't be long until she won't even remember her."

She'd talked to Tyler's son about losing his mother, Katie.

Liam was six and already struggling to remember his mother's face.

Daddy tells me I'll see her again one day in heaven. But sometimes I think I'm forgetting what she looks like.

Brinkley's frown deepened. "I really am sorry."

"Save your apologies," Nikki said. Anger over the events of the past two days welled up in her gut. "If this had been handled differently—if you had told us everything at the beginning—Erika might still be alive today."

"And you really think any of that would have made a difference?"

"She was scared and running for her life because she felt you couldn't protect her. But I guess all of that doesn't matter anymore, does it, because she's dead. Even though you threatened her with jail time if she didn't cooperate, and—"

"I convinced her of the importance of her testimony and advised her in her best interest."

"In her best interest or yours?" Nikki asked, not even trying to mask her anger this time. "Because Erika's willingness to work with you cost her her life."

"The bottom line," Agent Brinkley said, "is that she wanted Brian Russell in prison. So did we."

"Then you'll be happy to know that Gwen found the information you wanted. Spread sheets, accounting ledgers . . ." She nodded at Gwen. "Gwen is still going through all the information, but it looks like Erika held up her end of the bargain."

"Where did you find it?" Brinkley asked.

Gwen handed him the phone. "She swapped phones at some point and had this one with her during the crash."

"Maybe we'll be able to take down Russell after all. But what about Lily?" Brinkley asked. "Any leads on where she might be?"

"Gwen's tracking down someone right now who we hope

will have some answers," Nikki said. "There is one other thing you need to know. I believe we found your leak."

"You found the leak? Who?"

"A few months ago, Russell bought Erika an expensive watch. She was wearing it on the plane, but it fell off at some point and I found it as I was getting off. I never had the chance to give it back to her. But after one of Russell's men showed up at my house—"

"You realized he was using it to track her," Brinkley said.

"We found a GPS tracker inside the watch," Jack said. "He would have been able to track her to the safe house."

"So Erika was the leak and she didn't even know it." Brinkley glanced down at the phone. "You keep looking for Erika's daughter, and I'll give the files you have to my team and see what we can come up with. One way or another, we're going to take this guy down."

"You okay?" Gwen asked Nikki as Brinkley stalked back out of the room.

"Erika's dead and he's worried about the evidence." She shook her head. "It doesn't really matter. We've got a little girl to find."

"I'm searching for Brandon Folly right now," Gwen said, scooting back to her desk.

Nikki's phone beeped. She glanced down at her phone to read the text message she'd missed.

Tyler

i know this has been a rough day for you. you don't have to respond now. just know I'm thinking about you and I love you.

Nikki bit her lip to hold back the tears. "I need to make a quick call."

She hurried out of the room, past the break room to the front office, then outside, where she punched in Tyler's number and let it ring. Traffic rushed by along the busy street outside the precinct.

No answer.

He was probably busy. Like herself, he had a lot on his plate between looking for a new job, selling his house, and raising Liam.

She started to hang up as he answered.

"Nikki?"

"Tyler . . . hey. I didn't think you were going to pick up."

"Sorry I almost missed your call. My Realtor called to discuss a house she'd shown me."

"You don't sound too enthusiastic. What did you think?"

"It was . . . a house. The master bedroom was purple and the living room was this, I don't know, a pukey green color."

Nikki laughed. "You know you can easily fix paint color."

"That's exactly what my Realtor said. I guess I'm not much on house hunting."

Maybe if we were looking together for our own family . . .

She pushed away the thought for now.

"It's definitely a big decision," she said.

"Forget about the house. I've been thinking about you all day but didn't want to interrupt. How are you?"

She looked up at the cloudless sky and drew in a deep breath. "Honestly, I've had better days. Erika Hamilton . . . the woman who was on the plane with me—"

"You found her?"

"Yes. But she's dead."

"Oh Nikki, I'm sorry. I really am."

"I know, and I shouldn't let myself get so caught up, but this case . . . it's really gotten under my skin."

"After all that's happened, I'd think there was something wrong with you if it hadn't affected you." There was a short pause on the line. "So what happens now? Are you wrapping things up?"

She wanted to. Because she wanted to see him. Wanted to stop the world for a few hours to let him hold her and tell her there were still some things that were good and right and normal in the world. "Not yet. Erika's daughter's out there somewhere, and we still haven't found her."

"I'm worried about you. You didn't get much sleep last night—"

"I'll be okay. We've got a good lead. We believe we know who has her, and if we're right, she's safe. I'm hoping we can track her down in the next few hours."

"Is there anything I can do?"

"Invite me over for dinner as soon as this is over. I'll bring Chinese takeout."

"You don't have to worry about any of that." She caught the emotion in his words. "All I want to see is you."

Nikki smiled. There was something about hearing his voice that was helping to smooth over the rough spots of the day. She wasn't going to think about the doctor's report or what the future might hold for them. Not now. Only that he was there for her and he loved her. "I'm going to need to go. But I'll call you as soon as we're done here."

A minute later she walked back into the precinct, determined to see this through. She wasn't going to let Brian Russell win this round.

"Any luck on finding Brandon Folly?" she said, walking up to Gwen's desk.

Gwen handed Nikki a piece of paper. "His work said he was sick and left early. He's still not answering his phone, but I was able to track down an address."

24

Brandon Folly's apartment was located in a large complex about twenty minutes from the Moreau Gallery, where he headed up Brian Russell's IT department. The buzz of a lawn mower whirred in the background as Nikki and Jack walked down the sidewalk toward building C.

"What's the apartment number?" Jack asked.

Nikki glanced at the address Gwen had given her. "Two seventeen. Should be a couple breezeways ahead on the second floor."

A couple stood outside on their partially enclosed patio barbecuing their dinner. The smoke from the grill filled Nikki's lungs, triggering an unwanted memory. She froze. The plane had smelled like smoke and burning plastic when it crashed. She bit her lip and glanced at the small plume of smoke, fighting the urge to run.

"Nikki? You okay?"

"Yeah." She nodded. "It's nothing."

She starting walking again, knowing all too well the emotional responses that often followed a traumatic event. Hearing Tyler's voice had helped soothe her tattered nerves, but her emotions were still on edge. Which was normal. Or at least that's what she was trying to tell herself. She knew it was going to take time for the stress reactions from the past couple days to completely fade, but for now, she needed to ignore everything that was vying for her attention and simply focus on finding Lily.

I just need you to help me through the next few hours, Jesus. Help me find Lily, and bring closure to this situation.

Because like a lot of the cases she worked that became personal, this wasn't something she could do in her own strength. Not today anyway. Fatigue from both the emotional toll and lack of sleep was starting to catch up with her. And she couldn't afford to lose her focus.

Nikki paused in front of one of the two-story buildings. "This should be it."

She hurried up the flight of stairs to the small landing outside apartment 217, then knocked on the door.

Nothing.

Fifteen seconds later she knocked again, this time louder.

"If he really is sick," Jack said, "maybe he ended up going to the doctor."

Nikki took a step backward and glanced down the breezeway. "Somehow I don't think he's sick. If he heard that message from Erika—and is involved the way we believe he is—he's going to want to find her."

"Which is going to make *him* extremely hard to find," Jack said.

"Why don't you try his cell again?"

Jack punched in the number Gwen had given them, then shook his head. "He's still not answering his phone."

"So what now? He's not at home, he won't answer his phone . . ." She glanced at the door across the breezeway from Brandon's apartment. The door had been decorated with an orange, yellow, and red fall wreath and a welcome sign. "Maybe the neighbor knows something."

A minute later, an older woman opened the door across from Brandon's a crack, the chain still in place. "Can I help you?"

"I'm sorry to bother you, ma'am." Nikki held up her badge. "We're looking for your neighbor, Brandon Folly. Have you seen him today?"

"Just a minute." She quickly shut the door, slid off the chain, then opened it again. "You asked about Brandon? He's such a nice young man. Always offers to carry my groceries up the stairs for me."

"What about today?" Jack asked. "Have you seen him?"

"I did, actually." She pressed her hands against the pair of pink pants she wore. "I didn't speak to him, but I saw him leave in a hurry. Not that I'm nosy or anything, I just try to keep an eye on him. Make sure he's okay. He doesn't have family around here, so I try to bake him cookies every once in a while."

"How long ago did he leave?"

"Just a couple minutes ago. I'm sure if you hurry, you might even be able to catch him."

Nikki glanced at Jack. How had they missed him?

"Do you know what kind of car he drives?" Nikki asked before turning away.

"I know it's a newer model, and it's red."

"Thank you."

Nikki ran down the stairs toward the double row of parking in front of the apartments. She scanned the lines of cars, pausing at a red Honda Civic. A man wearing a gray beanie was putting a bag in the trunk.

"That's got to be him," Jack said.

"Brandon Folly?" Nikki called out, approaching the car from behind.

The man looked up and caught her gaze. Late twenties, beard, dark-brown hair . . . He was definitely a match to the photo Gwen had given them.

He slammed the trunk shut. "I knew you'd find me."

"We're with TBI. We'd like to speak with you for a few minutes," Nikki said.

"TBI. Right. And I'm an Israeli with Mossad." He reached behind him, pulled out a gun, and pointed it at them. "Don't come any closer."

"Whoa . . ." Jack stopped beside Nikki a dozen feet from where Folly stood. "Why don't you put that weapon down so no one gets hurt. We're just here to talk."

"Forget it." Folly kept his arms steady, pointing the weapon at them at chest level. "Because I don't have what you want."

"I thought this guy was an IT geek," Jack said quietly enough so only Nikki could hear him.

"An IT geek who thinks he's the Terminator." Nikki weighed their options. The last thing they needed at this point was a gun battle in the middle of an apartment complex, but something told her that Brandon wasn't just angry. He was scared. And probably not convinced they were really with TBI.

"In case you were wondering," Brandon continued, "I've taken defensive handgun classes and can hit a bull's-eye at fifty feet. I do even better close up."

"Okay. Then what happens next, Brandon?" she asked. "Because all we came to do was talk."

"Just talk? Right." His jaw tensed. "I know what you want, but like I said, I don't have it. So turn around right now, get out of here, and tell your boss to leave me alone."

"We're telling the truth, Brandon. I can show you my badge." Jack started to pull back his suit jacket.

232

"Stop."

Nikki heard the click of the safety being released and felt her own heart hammer. His hands were steady, but all it would take was a slight pressure against the trigger to discharge the weapon.

"Please put the gun down," Nikki said. "He's telling the truth."

"That he's got a *real* police badge? That doesn't mean anything. You can buy those on eBay. Besides, I've heard a lot of cops wear fake badges so they won't lose the real ones."

"We're with the Tennessee Bureau of Investigation, Missing Persons Task Force, and we're here to talk to you about Erika Hamilton." Nikki studied his reaction. "We know she's in trouble, and that you've been trying to help her."

His face paled at the mention of Erika's name. "How do you know that?"

"If you put down your weapon, we'll tell you. But we're here because we need your help."

"I don't understand." His eyes narrowed. He was clearly thrown off by what she'd just told him. He'd obviously been expecting Russell's men to come after him. Not the good guys coming to him for help. "Why would you need me?"

"Because we know Erika's been on the run since the plane crash. We also know that she was coming to Nashville to testify against Brian Russell, and that you helped her hide the evidence she has against him."

She wasn't ready to tell him Erika was dead.

"I don't know." The conflict was clear in his eyes. "Just because you're the authorities doesn't mean I can trust you. She was in an FBI safe house and they got to her. If they can find her at a presumed safe house, no place is really secure."

Nikki drew in a slow breath. "I understand you're scared, but please understand something. We're on your side."

"I . . . I don't know who to believe anymore." His hands

were shaking, and with the safety off . . . "Besides. You don't know what it's like to watch someone you love go through this. How guilty I feel—"

"I understand." Nikki bit her lip. "I lost my sister ten years ago, but it still feels like yesterday. Someone kidnapped her, and we never found her. I've always felt it was my fault because I was late picking her up that day."

He dropped his hand to his side, so the barrel of the gun was pointing toward the ground. "We can talk, but not here. We're too exposed."

"Give me the gun first," Jack said, stepping toward him.

Brandon hesitated, then flicked the safety back on before handing the gun to Jack. "Are you going to arrest me?"

"We're not here to arrest you," Jack said. "We really do need your help."

They followed him back to his apartment, then waited for him to open the front door, certain that his neighbor across the breezeway was watching until he shut the door behind them. Inside, the small apartment looked like a typical bachelor pad, with a pizza box on the table and a few scattered Coke cans. From the TV setup, it was obvious that he was heavily into gaming.

"I don't have a lot of time," he said, offering them a seat on the leather sofa. "If you're telling the truth, then you know she's running because they're after her and the evidence she has."

"The evidence she has for the grand jury," Nikki said.

He hesitated, then sat down on a cushioned leather chair across from them. "She never should have agreed to help the FBI, but she thought . . . she thought if Brian was in jail, she'd be free of him."

"How do you know Erika?"

He drummed his fingers against the arms of the chair. "We met first at work when she was here in Nashville. I helped her out a few times, computer stuff, and we got to know each other.

We were just friends. And then after a while I started noticing that something wasn't right."

"What wasn't right?" Jack asked.

"She would come to me and ask questions about digitally tracking people, tagging people with GPS trackers, spyware, and monitored phone tracking."

"Did she ever tell you why she wanted to know those things?"

"At first she just told me she was curious and found the subject interesting, but I eventually figured out that she was afraid of someone."

"Brian Russell?" Nikki asked.

Brandon nodded. "No matter what most people think about him and all his money, she deserves so much more."

"So you're in love with her?" Nikki asked.

"Yes, and she feels the same way about me."

"And did you know about Lily?"

Brandon nodded again. "Brian has money and power, and Erika . . . she thought if she left Brian, she would lose Lily."

"And so you decided to help her."

"There wasn't much I could do. Not until she came to me with evidence that Mr. Russell was involved with some very illegal things."

Nikki leaned forward. "What did you do with that information?"

"I encrypted the information she had and hid it in her cell phone. Because that evidence is the only leverage she has. As soon as Brian goes to jail , she'll have full custody of Lily; and we're going to get married. We just . . . we couldn't tell anyone. Not even her brother knows."

"According to her phone records, you spoke with her a couple hours after the airline crash," Jack said.

"She told me about the crash, and that when she got off the plane, she saw one of the men who tried to grab her at the safe house. She realized she was being tracked. She'd gone to her friend Kim's house to pick up some clothes and money and to use her car."

"Did you know Kim is dead?"

Brandon nodded. "Erika found out. It totally freaked her out. That's why she wouldn't let me pick her up. She was convinced they'd find me and kill me too."

"When's the last time you spoke with Erika?"

"We spoke briefly again last night on the burner phone she'd bought. Then today, she left me a message. When I called her back, she didn't pick up."

"A message that said she was scared and being followed?"

His legs were shaking, rattling the glass on the table next to him. "How did you know?"

"Because we have her phone," Jack said.

"Wait a minute . . . I don't understand."

"That's how we found you. You were one of three people she called on her burner phone."

"If you have her phone, you should know where she is."

Nikki glanced at Jack. It was the part of her job she hated the most. Telling people that the person they cared about wasn't coming back. Because she knew how it robbed them of any hope that one day everything would be the same again.

"Brandon." Nikki leaned forward. "I'm so sorry to have to tell you this, but Erika was involved in an accident a few hours ago. Her car ran off an embankment. She died shortly after."

"Wait. No . . . Erika can't be dead." Brandon rubbed his hand behind his neck, then stood up. "It's not possible. We were going to meet later today. I was trying to figure out a way for us to leave the country."

Nikki found herself choking up as she watched his frantic denial. "Brandon . . . I really am sorry. I was with her when she died."

"No. I don't believe you." He started pacing in front of them. "She's okay. She has to be."

"Listen to me, Brandon. I know this is hard for you, but Agent Spencer and I work with missing persons and we need your help. We need to find Lily. Do you know where she is?"

"Yes. She's been staying with Erika's friends. The Popes. I drove her to Tennessee. It was the only place Erika believed Lily would be safe. "

"The problem is, we can't find the Popes," Jack said.

Brandon rubbed the back of his neck. "Erika called them and told them that they weren't safe. Told them they needed to disappear. But I don't know where they went."

Nikki let out a sharp breath of air. Surely this wasn't going to turn out to be another dead end.

He sat back down and caught Nikki's gaze. "I tried to do everything I could to stop this from happening, but now . . . I just can't believe she's really gone."

Nikki nodded. "I'm sorry."

"He's going to pay for this," Brandon said, not trying to mask the anger in his voice.

"Brian?" Jack asked.

"Yes, and I know where to find him."

"Where? How?" Jack asked.

"I'm in IT. I work with computers."

"How does that help us find him?"

"A few weeks ago, I started tracking his phone. It's been off until a few minutes ago. I was actually on my way to see him now."

"With a gun?" Nikki asked.

"I wasn't going to shoot him. Just talk to him."

Right. Somehow she didn't believe him.

"Where is he?" she asked.

"He's checked into a suite at the Fairmont Hotel."

25

Nikki stared out the car window while Jack sped down I-40 toward the Fairmont. "So Erika finally finds a decent guy who appears to love her—and who as far as we know isn't a serial killer or a cold-blooded criminal—and now it's too late for them."

"Not exactly a fairy-tale ending," Jack said.

Nikki's cell phone rang and she answered it, then switched her phone to speaker so they both could hear Gwen.

"Your new friend Brandon was right," Gwen said. "I was able to trace Russell to a suite at the Fairmont. Room 795. He checked in under the name Patrick Gray, which interestingly enough is one of the aliases he uses, according to the information from Erika."

"We're on our way there now," Nikki said.

"But you need to know something else. Since you spoke with Maggie about arranging his flight here, I've been trying to track down the plane he arrived in. And guess what? Russell owns the plane under the name of Patrick Gray."

"The house . . . the plane. Why's he hiding assets under a bogus name?" Jack asked.

"Haven't figured that out yet, but he's definitely hiding things."

"Do you know where the plane is right now?" Nikki asked. If they could locate it, they could have a team waiting at the airstrip to pick up Russell just in case he'd already left. "Because that's his ticket out of here."

"Not yet, but I'll keep trying to track it down. How far away are you from the hotel?"

Nikki glanced out the window of the passenger seat, thankful it wasn't rush hour. "I'd say five minutes, tops."

"Go find out if Russell's at the hotel. I've called in backup to meet you there."

Nikki checked her watch. "I had a uniform escort Brandon to the precinct. He should be there in the next fifteen minutes. Work with him to finish translating the files on Erika's phone. The FBI will appreciate the help, and we might be able to use the information as well."

"And we'll need a warrant to search Russell's room," Jack said.

"Already on it," Gwen said. "I'll have it faxed to you at the hotel as soon as it's ready."

Nikki's fingers gripped the armrest as Jack pressed through traffic.

They were one step closer to grabbing Russell, but if they missed him again . . .

We need to get him this time, God.

Because they needed to find Lily and end this.

"What are you thinking?" Jack asked.

"That I want this to be over. And yes, I wish Erika could have gotten her fairy-tale ending."

"While I hate what's happening, I never pegged you as the sappy romantic type. You're more of a realist."

"I don't believe there's a magic formula or a fairy godmother waiting to give you a perfect Oscar de la Renta dress and pair of Prada shoes for the ball, if that's what you mean. And even with a happily-ever-after ending, you still have to do the dishes, take out the trash, and work hard on your relationship." She glanced at Jack's profile and caught the determination in his face. She wasn't the only one ready for this to be over. "We need to get this guy. And make sure we find Lily before he does."

Two minutes later, Jack parked the car near the entrance of the hotel, and they were making their way toward the swanky lobby she'd only heard about on the news. The Fairmont was a newly reconstructed hotel, located conveniently near downtown, giving it access to some of the city's main highways, Music Row, and Vanderbilt. Inside the large glass entrance, huge chandeliers hung from lofty ceilings above a cozy lounge area where guests sat chatting on cushioned chairs.

Nikki stepped up to the black-and-gold front counter and showed her badge to the woman, who was dressed in a neat black suit and too-white smile. She read the name on her jacket lapel.

"Emma, I'm Special Agent Nikki Boyd, and this is Special Agent Jack Spencer. We're with TBI."

"TBI . . . Wait a minute." She glanced toward the lobby, then leaned forward. "Please . . . If this is about the recent complaints of . . . solicitation, we can't have our clients knowing there's been any issues with the police."

Nikki glanced at Jack. "I don't know anything about solicitation complaints, but I do have a warrant. If you look at your fax machine, it should have just come through. We need access to room 795."

"Seven-ninety-five. That's the room of . . ." She punched something into her computer, then frowned. "That would be Patrick Gray. He checked into one of our executive suites yesterday."

"Is there a problem?" Nikki asked.

"No, it's just that he's so . . . charming. It's hard to believe he could be in trouble with the law. I could point out a dozen men I wouldn't mind you arresting. But not Mr. Gray."

"How long did he check in for?" Nikki asked.

"Originally for three nights, but I know he's not in his room right now. He left the hotel about thirty minutes ago."

"Did he say where he was going?" Jack asked.

"I'm sorry, but no. Only that he was planning to check out later this evening."

Nikki looked at Jack. If Russell was getting ready to leave Nashville, it was more than likely because he'd found out where Lily was.

She held up a photo of Brian Russell. "Is this him?"

"Yes." Nikki caught the slight blush that ran up the woman's cheeks. "He's quite the charmer, I have to say. Is he in trouble?"

"The warrant, please, Emma?" Nikki asked.

"About that." The woman bit her lip. "I've never had to deal with a warrant before, so I'm going to need to call my manager."

"Here's the thing." Jack took a step forward. "There isn't time to call your manager. Mr. Gray is a very dangerous man, and the life of every guest in this hotel could be in imminent danger if we don't find him quickly."

"But he seemed so . . . nice." Her eyes widened. "What do you want me to do?"

"Just check your fax machine for the warrant now, and we'll take care of the rest," Nikki said. "That, and we'll need someone to let us into the room."

"Of course. I'll take you up there myself. " She signaled to a tall blonde who'd just hung up the phone on the other end of the counter. "Cover for me, will you, Camy?"

The three of them took the elevator up to the seventh floor in silence. Nikki tried to ignore the worry lingering in her gut as they stepped off the elevator and headed down the hallway, but everything they were doing hinged on finding either the Popes or Russell. And if Russell managed to get to Lily first, she had no doubt he was going to disappear with the little girl for good.

They stopped in front of room 795 and Nikki knocked on the door. "Housekeeping."

No answer.

Nikki nodded at Emma to use her key, then stepped inside the suite. There was no doubt they were in Nashville from the music theme of the space. A closed suitcase sat on a wooden luggage rack and a man's shaving kit sat on the bathroom counter. It took less than thirty seconds to clear the suite, but there was no sign of Russell.

Nikki pulled back the blackout curtain to reveal a view of the Cumberland River and downtown Nashville. If he hadn't left, where was he?

"You were right. He's not here," Jack said to Emma. "Did he meet with anyone that you know of while he was here?"

The blush was back on her cheeks. The girl would probably swoon if he walked into the room right now. "He came down to the lobby right after I started my shift and had lunch at the Grill with an older man. A bit overweight. When I walked by the restaurant to check on something, though, they seemed to be talking about something serious."

"His things are still here, so we can assume he'll be back, but I think we need to call for backup before he returns," Jack said. "The last thing we need is for this to go south."

"I'll get an ETA from Gwen, and we can meet them in the lobby to make a plan," Nikki said.

"What do you mean, *go south*?" Emma's face paled. "You

weren't serious when you said he was dangerous, were you? I mean . . . he seemed so nice. I didn't think you were serious."

Jack frowned. "We're going to arrest Mr. Gray for smuggling, money laundering, and murder, if that gives you an indication of how dangerous he is."

Emma's jaw dropped. "What should I do?"

"Come with us back downstairs and do your job."

Two men stepped off the elevator as they moved back into the hallway. Nikki recognized both of them immediately. The man on the right was Phil Olson, the accountant they'd talked to at Russell's house. The man on the left was Brian Russell.

Nikki motioned for Emma to get back inside the room as she pulled out her weapon. They needed this to go down quickly and quietly, with no one getting hurt. And they needed Russell alive.

"TBI," Nikki shouted, starting down the hallway. "Put your hands up where I can see them, now."

The elevator doors had already closed, but Russell tried punching the button again. When the doors didn't open, he pulled out a handgun and fired. A bullet whizzed past her head, slamming into the wall behind her.

Adrenaline rushed through Nikki as Jack shoved her into one of the recessed doorways.

She pulled out her radio. "When's that backup getting here, Gwen? We have shots fired."

"Two minutes out."

They couldn't wait two minutes.

The room door behind them opened and an elderly gentleman stepped out.

Nikki motioned for him to be quiet. "Get back inside your room, sir. Quickly."

"We need to move now," Jack said. "They've gone into the stairwell."

Scenarios played through Nikki's mind as she sprinted down the hallway beside Jack, and none of them ended well. Not with an active shooter and the potential for a hostage situation in a hotel filled with innocent bystanders.

Seconds later, Nikki threw open the heavy metal door to the stairwell, letting it slam against the wall, then glanced up the flight of stairs. She could hear footsteps echoing in the stairwell. Russell and Olson were heading for the roof.

"Why are they going up there?" Jack asked.

Nikki sucked in a breath of air as they raced up the stairs two at a time. "I don't know, but they've got to have an exit plan in place."

"The only way off this building I can think of up there is by helicopter."

"Then that's their plan." Nikki was back on the radio again with Gwen. "Check for air traffic around the Fairmont. We think they might have a helo coming for them on the roof."

Nikki pushed harder up the stairs until her lungs were about to burst. They were gaining on the two men, but it wasn't enough. Not if there was a helicopter waiting for them on the roof.

She glanced up. The two men were almost to the top floor, but Olson was starting to slow down. She could see his bulky form through the rails of the stairs as Russell left him behind.

"We need to stop them," she said.

"I've got a clean shot." Jack held up his weapon and fired.

Olson cried out and grabbed his leg.

"You got him."

But not Russell.

The door to the roof opened above them, letting in a gust of noise that filled the stairwell. A second shot echoed through the space.

Nikki pushed through the burn in her calves and lungs. "I think Russell shot him."

She rounded the last staircase a step ahead of Jack, then paused midway up.

Olson sat slumped on the top step. Blood had saturated his pants where a bullet had sliced through his calf. The second bullet—the bullet Russell had to have shot— had gone through his chest.

Nikki hurried to the top of the stairs. "Russell needed to silence him."

Jack crouched down to check Olson's pulse. "He's still breathing."

"Stay with him and find out what he knows before it's too late," she said, heading for the door to the roof. "We still need Russell."

"Be careful, Nikki."

A gust of wind hit Nikki's face as she shoved open the door. The spotlights of the helo in the darkness momentarily blocked her vision. All she could hear was the engine roaring like a jet plane about to take off.

She squinted until her eyes adjusted. Russell was climbing into the cockpit. She had seconds to stop him, if even that. She fired off a round and motioned for the pilot to shut off the engine and get out of the helicopter, but it was too late. The pilot lifted off the roof and seconds later they disappeared into the darkness, with only the fading lights of the helo visible.

Ignoring the sick feeling of frustration spreading through her, Nikki headed back to the stairwell and Olson.

God, don't let him die on us. Please.

They needed to know what information Russell believed to be worth the life of his accountant.

Inside, Jack sat down next to Olson, pressing his jacket against the man's chest to stop the bleeding.

"Is he still alive?" she asked.

245

"Yes. I've called 911, but I doubt he'll make it long enough for an ambulance to arrive."

Nikki crouched down next to him. "Looks like your friend left you to hang on your own."

Olson groaned. His face had paled and his breathing was shallow. "I need to get to a hospital."

"Help is coming, but I need you to answer some questions first. Does Russell know where Lily is?"

"It doesn't matter." He was gasping for air. "It's . . . it's too late."

"Listen to me. Your friend just left you high and dry. He's not coming back." She leaned over, close enough she could smell his soured breath. "Before you die on us, I need you to answer our questions. A little girl's life is at stake."

"I can't die."

"If you do manage to live," Jack said, "you're going to spend the rest of your life in prison."

"No . . . none of this was my idea."

"That doesn't matter at this point. You're a smart man, Mr. Olson. Have you ever heard the term 'aiding and abetting'?" Jack didn't wait for him to answer before continuing. "It means you don't have to be present when a crime is committed to be charged as an accessory when you have knowledge of the crime. Which means we could tie you to a string of murders, including Erika Hamilton and Kim Parks, even if you didn't pull the trigger."

"No." Olson groaned. "I had nothing to do with them."

"Don't bet on it. Your days of hiding behind Mr. Russell are over."

"He knows where Lily is, but you're . . . you're too late."

"Where is she?"

"He's . . . he's already organized his security team to extract her. They'll both be out of the country in the next few hours."

"Where are they going?"

"Brian dealt with all the details. He didn't tell me everything."

"Then tell us what you do know. Which airport?"

"I don't know, but Russell tracked her and the couple she's with to a fishing and hunting club about two hours from here." His breathing was getting more labored. "They're staying at a cabin there . . . don't think he knew which one. Just that they were there on the property."

"And the plan?"

"His team . . . his team was going to find her, extract her, then meet him at a nearby airstrip . . . he has a private plane waiting to take them both to . . . to Venezuela. He has new passports with fake identities . . . all set up for the two of them."

"If we show you a map, can you show me where they're headed right now?" Nikki asked.

"Yeah . . . I think so."

Nikki heard the faint sound of sirens in the distance. "We need to find a way to stop Mr. Russell from carrying out his plan."

26

Nikki stood at the bottom of the stairwell, watching the paramedics work to revive Mr. Olson, then call his time of death.

She let out a sharp sigh. Whatever doubts any of them had about Russell's guilt had just been eliminated. He'd shot a guy to keep him from talking, then left him to die.

Her phone went off in her back pocket. She signaled for Jack to follow her, then she stepped into the hotel hallway to take the call, hoping Gwen had the information they needed.

"First of all, as we assumed," Gwen said, after Nikki had switched to speakerphone, "there was no flight plan on that helo."

"Okay." Nikki started pacing the mosaic carpet. "Then please tell me you've got something. Olson's dead, and the information he gave us is the only lead we have right now. We're not getting any more where that came from."

"On the positive side, it looks like the information he gave us was correct. I was able to trace the Popes to the hunting and

248

fishing club Olson mentioned. It's located about two hours from here. The Popes have a friend who's a member and signed them in as guests. Problem is, we're looking at a couple dozen cabins scattered across hundreds of acres, and no one seems to know where they're staying."

Erika must have planned it that way. Have the Popes and Lily stay with a friend of a friend of a friend. But it was going to be like looking for a needle in a haystack.

Nikki leaned against the wall and shook her head. She wasn't settling on another dead end. Not when they'd gotten this close. "Someone there has got to know something."

"I'm going to keep looking, but at least we've got things narrowed down enough to make a search."

Nikki frowned. If you could call having to search hundreds of acres narrowing things down.

"There's also an airstrip on the property," Gwen continued.

Nikki glanced at Jack, feeling the flow of adrenaline pushing away any fatigue. "We're going to need transportation there."

"Already done. Highway patrol can get you there on their jet ranger."

"How long before we can leave?"

"They're fueling up now. Fifteen . . . twenty minutes, tops. Brinkley and his partner want in on this as well, and he's already working on sending in ground support from local law enforcement to both watch the airstrip and start the search to make sure Russell gets picked up."

Nikki checked her watch. They'd still be at least thirty minutes behind Russell, but if he didn't have the actual location of where the Popes were either, maybe they could still end up with the advantage.

"You okay about this?" Jack said as she hung up the phone.

"Taking down Russell and finding Lily?" she asked, heading back to the stairwell.

"Going up in the air again."

She paused at the door and pushed down the niggle of fear that kept threatening to creep in. "I've flown dozens of times, and they say flying's safer than driving."

"True, but that doesn't dismiss the fact that yesterday's crash had to have taken an emotional toll on you."

"Yesterday's crash was just a freak accident," she said, pulling open the door, knowing she was trying to convince Jack as much as herself. And from the look on his face, he knew exactly what she was doing. "What would the odds be for something like that to happen to me again in less than forty-eight hours?"

Fifteen minutes later, Nikki strapped herself into the twin-engine helicopter, her body straining against the seat belt as they lifted into the air. What *were* the odds of this helo going down? One in a hundred thousand? One in a hundred million?

It didn't matter. Unexpected waves of memories washed over her like a giant tsunami. The explosion rocking the back of the plane. Her stomach heaving as the plane dropped in altitude. She closed her eyes and grabbed onto the armrest, fighting to breathe. She could hear people screaming around her and feel the panic in the air.

"Nikki?" Jack nudged her.

She waved him off, then closed her eyes again. Breath shallow, her heart pounded with the vibrations of the helo. A wave of nausea struck as they climbed in altitude. She thought she'd be okay. But maybe taking another flight less than forty-eight hours after the plane crash had been a bad decision. Because all she wanted to do right now was vomit.

While the helo headed east, the crash continued to replay through her mind again and again. The final rapid drop in altitude. The plane skidding to a halt after the first impact.

The vacant eyes of the air marshal who'd sat two seats over. The panic.

God, sometimes I feel so . . . weak. I can't do this on my own. I'm too tired, too scared, and yet for some reason you put me here to fight this battle.

It was a fight for those who couldn't fight for themselves. A fight for justice and all that should be right in the world when it wasn't. It was all she really wanted to do. Make a difference. Whether she was a schoolteacher or working beside the FBI to save a young girl.

Which meant doing everything she knew right now, at this moment, to save Lily.

She pictured Lily's smile and brown hair from the pic she'd seen at the Popes' house. She'd been awarded the job by the governor of the state to bring home those who were missing. Lily might have lost her mother, but they weren't going to lose her too.

She forced her breathing to slow down and faded into a dreamless sleep.

───────────── ■ ─────────────

Fifty-three minutes later, local law enforcement met them on the ground. They'd already set up a base in the clubhouse. Every second they spent searching was another second Russell had to find Lily first.

"We've been watching the airstrip and so far there's been no sign of them." Sheriff Adamson laid out a map of the surrounding land on the table. "We've also started a grid search of the property, but so far, no luck. There are thirty cabins spread out over the acreage."

"We want in on the search," Nikki said.

"Wouldn't expect otherwise. We've got six more deputies who just showed up to help as well." The sheriff turned to the uniformed men standing behind him waiting for their instructions. "I've got GPS coordinates of the cabins. Split up and go find our girl."

Jack took the printout from their team, then addressed the men. "Brian Russell is to be considered armed and dangerous. He's on the run for murder, among a bunch of other things, and won't hesitate to shoot whoever gets in his way."

"One of my deputies has offered to drive you," the sheriff said, pointing to a uniformed officer who barely looked old enough to be on the force. "Keep your radios on channel four and check in every thirty minutes. If you locate either Russell or the Popes, let us know your location and we'll send in backup, especially in the case of Russell."

"I'm Deputy Banks," their driver said, escorting them to his car. "We don't usually have this much excitement out here. Normally it's just poachers, speeding tickets, and a break-in to deal with every now and then."

"How long have you been on the job, Deputy?" Brinkley asked.

"Nine months. My father was the last sheriff, and his father before that. Law enforcement runs in the family."

He unlocked the car and Nikki slid into the backseat next to Jack while Brinkley took the front passenger seat.

"Hope the three of you are up to this," the deputy said, starting the engine. "There's a good chance this is going to be a long night."

Nikki chuckled under her breath. He had no idea. She knew she was running on pure adrenaline and at some point she'd crash, but for now she just wanted to find Lily, make sure she was safe, and make sure Brian Russell spent the rest of his life in prison.

The first cabin on their list was located on the northeast corner of the property. The one-story log cabin was rustic looking, with no cars in the drive. No lights. And no signs that anyone had been there for weeks.

Nikki banged on the front door with Jack while Brinkley and Deputy Banks circled the property.

Three minutes later, they climbed back into the car.

Three cabins later, they still hadn't seen anyone.

"With it not being hunting season yet, the properties tend to stay pretty vacant," Deputy Banks said, heading for the next cabin. "So I'm not surprised at all at how quiet it is out here."

Nikki fingered the door handle. They'd just checked out their fourth cabin and found no one. Plus, none of the other teams had called in with anything. Had they somehow missed Russell?

"There's a light on in the next cabin," Brinkley said, leaning forward.

The deputy pulled into a narrow drive, surrounded by a grove of trees. There were fresh tire tracks in the driveway, and a car with a flat tire.

The four of them made their way toward the house, weapons raised. The front door was closed, but splinters in the frame showed that someone had busted it open.

And someone was inside.

"FBI," Brinkley yelled, bursting through the door in front of them.

A middle-aged woman hovered next to a man on the couch. A large bruise on the woman's forehead was quickly forming into a nasty lump. The man sat next to her, holding his arm covered with blood.

The woman held up her hands. "Please, he took Lily . . . you need to go after them. They took our car."

"Mr. Pope? Mrs. Pope? I'm Special Agent Nikki Boyd with the TBI. Are you both okay?"

"I'll call it in," Jack said, as she hurried to where they sat.

Mrs. Pope's hands were shaking in her lap. "We're fine for now, but Lily—"

"Did Brian Russell take her?" Nikki asked.

Tears slid down Helen Pope's cheeks, and she wiped them away with the back of her hand, then nodded.

"It was him along with a couple of his men," the older woman said. "They broke down the door, shot Frank, and grabbed Lily. I tried to stop them." Her hand went to her forehead. "They knocked me onto the floor and left with her."

"Mrs. Pope, this wasn't your fault," Nikki said. "And we're going to do everything we can to get Lily back. That's why we're here. To make sure she's safe."

"Do you have any idea where they were going?" Brinkley asked.

"No. They just said something about a plane waiting."

"How long ago did this happen?" Nikki asked.

"Not long." Mrs. Pope reached up to wipe her cheek with shaky fingers. "Maybe five minutes. I've been trying to call for help, but service is sketchy out here, and they took our car."

Five minutes. That meant they still had a chance.

"We need to figure out where they went," Nikki said.

"Ma'am," Deputy Banks said, "why don't you sit down while you talk to the officers, and I'll get some ice out of the freezer."

"And I need to look at your arm." Nikki knelt beside Mr. Pope, who was sitting on the couch. Blood was slowly seeping through his plaid shirt.

"They shot him," Mrs. Pope said again.

"Forget about me." Frank Pope pulled away from her and started to stand up. "It's nothing but a flesh wound. I'll be fine. You need to be out there looking for our little girl."

"We are, Mr. Pope," Nikki assured him, "and we've got most of the sheriff's department and even the FBI involved looking for Lily, so don't worry. We're going to find her. It might just be a flesh wound, but we still need to get it checked out. For now, I want you to sit here and try to relax."

"Relax—"

"Frank. Let her help you."

"I took worse than this back in the Gulf War. There's no way I'm going to start blubbering over something like this. Not when Lily's out there. Though I did wing him."

Nikki looked up at him. "You shot Russell?"

Mr. Pope nodded. "Got him in the shoulder. It wasn't enough to stop him, but maybe it will slow him down. Those roads can be rough out there, and if he's bleeding, he's going to be hurting pretty bad about now."

"And that's what got you shot," his wife countered.

"What did you want me to do, woman? They busted in here before we could even react. If I was twenty years younger, I'm telling you, those men wouldn't see the light of another day."

"Stop talking, Frank. You need medical help before you bleed to death."

"Mrs. Pope, your husband's going to be okay," Jack said. "We've got paramedics on the way right now, as well as extra backup. We're going to find Lily."

"Looks as if we've got the bleeding stopped for now," Nikki said. "Okay, ma'am, we're going to get both of you the help you need right away. Do you think you can tell me exactly what happened? Anything that might help us figure out where they were going."

Mrs. Pope's hands were still shaking as she leaned back on the couch holding the bag of ice against her forehead.

"How many men?" Brinkley asked.

"There were two besides Russell."

"Do you know where they were going?"

Mrs. Pope shook her head at the FBI agent's question. "He

didn't tell us anything. Came in here with his men and swooped up Lily before we could do anything. She calls us Pappy and Nana. We consider her our granddaughter."

"He took the car keys," Mr. Pope said. "From on top of the mantel. I think theirs had a flat tire."

"But there's one thing you haven't mentioned yet," Mrs. Pope said, leaning forward. "If you're here looking for Lily, you must know where Erika is. Have you found her?"

Nikki hesitated.

"She's dead, isn't she?" Mrs. Pope asked.

"I'm so sorry," Nikki said. "She was killed in a car accident earlier this afternoon."

"No. She can't be dead." Mrs. Pope turned to her husband, his anger evident on his face.

"It was his fault, wasn't it?" the older man said. "Brian found out she was going to testify against him and put him in prison."

"We believe her car was pushed over the edge of a ravine," Nikki said. "I really am sorry."

Tears welled in Mrs. Pope's eyes. "I told Frank there was a reason we didn't hear from her. I kept trying to convince myself that she couldn't get through to us, but I think I always knew. Always knew this wasn't going to turn out good for her."

"What are the roads out of here?" Jack asked.

"There's only one main road out of here," Mr. Pope said, "but there are also miles and miles of dirt roads and trails with deer stands, lakes."

"The sheriff and his men have been watching the airstrip," Jack said, "but so far there hasn't been any sign of Russell."

"That's not the only way out. There's a second airstrip on the property." Mr. Pope moved off the couch and pulled out a map from a drawer next to the dining room table.

"Frank, you shouldn't be up."

"Forget about me right now."

"Wait a minute," Nikki said. "There was only one airstrip on the map."

"Doesn't surprise me," Mr. Pope said, showing her on the map. "This one isn't used very often because it's a bit remote and not kept up well. In fact, I'd guess most people don't even know about it. But those of us who are always looking for the best spots to hunt . . . we know this place."

"The sheriff thinks Russell hired a local guy to help," the deputy said. "If their plane wasn't at the main airstrip, it makes sense they'd head to the one most people don't know about."

Jack put a call in to the sheriff, then turned on the speaker. "We just found out about a second airstrip. Looks like we can be there in about five minutes."

"You need to wait for backup," the sheriff said. "We're no more than ten minutes behind you."

"No way," Nikki said. "Russell could be gone in ten minutes. We'll be careful."

"He's going to be expecting you—"

"Then we'll make sure we're as ready as he is."

With no moon out, the cloudy sky was black. The only light was the beam of the headlights from the deputy's car as he drove down the dirt road flanked by rows of thick trees.

"Are you sure we're headed in the right direction?" Brinkley asked, holding up the map Pope had given him. "I'm not convinced this map is accurate—"

The sound of a gunshot ripped through the darkness. The windshield of the car shattered and the vehicle veered toward the side of the road.

"They've got snipers out there," Jack said.

"I think our boy here's been shot." Brinkley tried to grab the wheel from the deputy, but the front tires hit a stump, jerking the wheel from the agent's hands.

Nikki fought to catch her breath as the car flipped, yanking her seat belt tight against her chest. Seconds later the vehicle skidded to a stop. A shooting pain ripped through Nikki's shoulder as she fought to orient herself. Someone groaned. She glanced outside at the beam of headlights that shot out into the darkness as she hung upside down, dangling from her seat belt.

27

Nikki pushed the release button of her seat belt, then used her arms and legs to brace herself as she fell against the roof of the car. Her elbow smashed against something hard, bringing out a sharp cry of pain.

"Nikki?"

"I'm okay," she said, rubbing her elbow where she hit it. She looked up at Jack in the darkness, where she could just barely see him hanging from his seat belt. "What about you?"

"I'll be okay once I get this contraption undone."

A second later he slammed against the roof of the car next to her.

"Brinkley?" Nikki called up to the front seat. "What about you?"

"I'm pretty sure my leg's broken. Which is going to make it hard for me to get out of here."

259

She let out a low groan. If the shooter decided to come back and finish the job, Brinkley was going to be a sitting duck.

"What about you, Deputy Banks? Are you okay?"

There was no answer.

Nikki looked at the driver. "Brinkley . . . you're sure Banks was shot?"

"Yeah, and he's not moving."

She felt for the door handle in the dark. She needed to get out and check on the young deputy.

"Stay low," Jack said, shoving against the door with his shoulder. "We've got a sniper out there."

"Which means if they decide to finish the job, we need to be ready."

Nikki tried the handle of her door, but it wouldn't budge. If Russell's men were out there, they were going to arrive before any backup made it to the rescue. They needed to get out of the car, inform the sheriff what had just happened, and make a plan.

"Turn your head," Jack said, brushing up against her as he turned toward his door. "I'm going to kick out the window."

His third attempt shattered the window.

"Come on," he said, after he'd crawled out through the open space. "But be careful of the glass."

"Wait a minute. We need the radio."

Nikki pulled her phone from her back pocket, surprised the screen wasn't shattered, then turned on the flashlight app in order to search for the radio. She found it wedged next to her door and snatched it up before letting Jack grab her hand and help her out of the car.

She clicked on the call button. "Sheriff Adamson, this is Agent Boyd." The signal was filled with static. "Can you hear me?"

"I hear you. Go ahead."

"A sniper hit our vehicle. We need backup immediately. Repeat. We need immediate backup."

"Copy that. I'm sending everyone we've got your way. Can you give us an exact location?"

"Give me a second, but I think I can," Brinkley said from the front seat. His breathing was heavy, but he'd managed to find his phone and was studying the map Pope had given him.

"Is anyone hurt?" the sheriff asked.

Nikki watched Jack in the darkness as he tried to open the deputy's door.

"Agent Brinkley's leg is broken," she said. "And we're trying to get to your deputy now, but he's been hit."

"I've got our location," Brinkley said.

"I'm handing the radio to Agent Brinkley," Nikki said. "He'll tell you where we are."

She hurried to the driver's side where Jack had managed to partially open the door, hoping Brinkley's assessment was off.

Jack stood up and shook his head. "He's gone."

She leaned in and caught Banks's blank expression. A single bullet hole to the head had taken him. A trickle of blood ran down the side of his face, pooling on the collar of his uniform. He wouldn't have even known what struck him. She stepped away, wondering if he had a wife and kids. A girlfriend. She grabbed the keys out of the ignition. Someone was going to be hurting tonight.

Brinkley handed her the radio. "So what's our plan?"

"Give us a second," Nikki said.

She stepped away from the car to where Jack stood. "What do you think the odds are that they'll come back for us?"

"I don't know, but neither do I think we should sit around and wait," Jack said. "More than likely, Russell's already heading for the plane and his men are with him. He just needed a distraction."

"I think you're right, but if we go after Russell, Brinkley's going to be in trouble if one of them comes back."

Jack glanced back at the car. "Then we need to get him out of the car and hide him until backup gets here."

"And then what? Go take down our sniper?"

"Yes, but Russell and Lily have to be our first priority. We need to locate that plane."

Nikki frowned. How in the world were they supposed to stop a plane from taking off, on foot, in the dark, with a sniper after them? Of course, considering how the last couple days had gone, how hard could that be?

They stepped around the car to Brinkley's side where, between the two of them, they managed to open the door. "We need to get you out."

"I can't move my leg."

Jack motioned to Deputy Banks. "That's better than a bullet through your head."

Brinkley groaned. "Then get me out of here."

"This is going to hurt."

Nikki's shoulder throbbed as they carried Brinkley out of the car and into a small thicket of trees.

"Not that you're going anywhere," Jack said, "but wait for us here."

"Funny. You're both leaving?"

"We'll be back for you, Brinkley," Nikki said. "I promise."

"You'll need this map," Brinkley said, pulling the folded-up paper from his pocket. "Pope circled the landing strip, and if I'm not mistaken"—he pointed to one of the marks on the map—"I believe these markings are the deer blinds."

Nikki quickly oriented herself to where they were and the nearest blind. "That has to be where our sniper took his shot."

"From there, it wouldn't have been that hard to hit a moving car if the shooter knew his business," Jack said. "I guess killing Banks was a bonus."

"Knowing the kind of people Russell associates with, I doubt it was an accident." The thought made her gut ache. "How far away do you think that is?"

"Two, three hundred yards maybe. And if the map is accurate, it's another half a mile or so beyond that to the second airstrip."

"Which means if they were going to come after us, they'd already be here." She quickly switched her cell phone to vibrate only, then stared into the darkness. The cloudy skies might help hide them from the Russell's men, but it was also going to make navigating harder.

"You ready to go?"

"Give me a second." Nikki popped the trunk of the deputy's car with the keys she'd snatched from the ignition.

She pulled out a flashlight, a pair of binoculars, and a first-aid kit, and shoved them into a backpack, along with a couple bottles of water. Hesitating for a brief second, she grabbed a twelve-gauge shotgun for Jack along with some extra shells, then took the AR-15 for herself. They both knew they were going into battle. The extra firepower could quickly become essential, knowing how far Brian Russell was willing to go to get what he wanted.

Taking one last look at the deputy's lifeless body, she gave Brinkley one of the waters and a couple Tylenol, then slung the backpack over her shoulder.

Heading out to catch a sniper on the loose seemed almost as crazy as staying with the vehicle and waiting for him to come to them. She shivered in the darkness, despite the warm humidity in the air. Her thoughts shifted to her mom and dad . . . her brothers . . . to Tyler . . .

He was worrying about her tonight. And probably wishing she'd said no to this assignment. All she knew was that no matter what might happen between them in the future, she wanted a chance to work things out with him. Wanted a chance to see if they could make a relationship work no matter what life threw at them.

Darkness closed in around them. Trees creaked and groaned, while the sounds of insects vibrated in the night air. She reached up to touch her shoulder where it ached as the fatigue of the day threatened to take over.

God, I've beaten the odds too many times lately, and today . . . I don't want this one to be my last.

She mentally shook off the heaviness of despair. Now wasn't the time. She needed to call Gwen. And then they needed to find Lily.

"What's going on?" Gwen asked as soon as she picked up.

"They just hit our vehicle with a sniper shot."

"What?"

Nikki caught the panic in Gwen's voice. And the matter-of-fact report in her own. "The deputy who was driving us is dead, and Brinkley's got a broken leg. Jack and I are heading by foot to a second airstrip."

"Hold on. You need to wait for backup—"

"We don't have time to wait for backup. If the sniper decides to come finish the job, they'll be here before backup can get here. We're on our own."

"Okay, what can I do?"

"I need you to find that plane and get on the radio with the pilot."

"I don't know . . . Even if I can find him, he's in Russell's pocket, Nikki. He's not going to listen to me."

"Then do whatever it takes. The guy might not know that he's about to go down for conspiracy to commit murder. I need you to find a way to stop that plane from taking off. Once it's gone, we'll have no way of stopping him. This is our last chance."

There was a short pause on the line while Gwen weighed Nikki's request. But if anyone could do what she'd just asked, Gwen could.

"I'll call you as soon as I've got something."

Nikki hung up the call and picked up her pace. If they were going to have any chance of getting to Lily before the plane took off, they were going to have to hurry. But in order to avoid being picked off by the sniper, they also had to stay on the edges of the open field, where the ground was uneven and made moving ahead quickly difficult. Brambles scraped against her legs and arms, but despite the hedge of surrounding trees and brush, she still felt vulnerable.

"There's the blind," Jack said. "It's up ahead and to your left."

Nikki spotted the structure, then turned back to where the car was parked, ensuring she was hidden by the tree cover. There was a perfect line of sight, just visible in the moonlight.

She picked up a rock and threw it at the blind, expecting a reaction if someone was there.

Nothing.

She quickly scaled the wooden ladder behind Jack.

"No one's here, but this is definitely where they made the shot." He picked up a bullet casing. "And we would have seen them if they'd headed to our vehicle."

"Which means they're headed for the plane," Nikki said.

She stepped back down onto the ground, searching for movement in the still night. The breeze had dropped off, while the moon had risen halfway up from the horizon as it played cat and mouse with the overhead clouds. Insects buzzed in the woods next to them. But there was no sign of the man who'd killed Deputy Banks.

Nikki hurried back into the relative safety along the edge of the woods, then stopped a hundred yards from the blind. The low rumble of an engine competed with the night sounds.

"It's Russell's plane," she said.

"Looks like Pope's map was correct," Jack said. "They're just northeast of us."

"But if they've started the engine . . ." Nikki felt a burst of renewed energy sweep through her as she picked up the pace to a slow jog, maneuvering carefully through the wooded terrain. Her radio buzzed as she was avoiding a tree limb that had fallen across the path.

"Where are you?" Sheriff Adamson asked.

"We're headed to the location of the second airstrip by foot. We can hear the sound of an engine. They're getting ready to take off."

"I've got three cars headed to your location now."

"How far are you behind us?" she asked.

"Four . . . maybe five minutes."

"Roger that, but we don't have time to wait. We're going in."

Because unless Gwen had been able to find a way to stall the pilot, there was a good chance they'd be gone by then.

The sound of the plane grew louder as they neared the edge of the open space where the airstrip sat. Above them, the clouds had begun to disperse, leaving a trail of moonlight to partially illuminate the night sky.

It's still going to take a miracle, Jesus, but we've almost got him.

She glanced at Jack as he ducked under the low branches of a tree. They didn't have a plan, just a goal. Stop the plane, take down Russell, and save Lily.

She slowed down as they stepped into the edge of the clearing, all her senses alert. They didn't have to guess whether or not Russell had brought his own personal army. They'd already attacked twice. And while he might be in over his head, he was going to want to guarantee he was able to walk out of this situation with Lily.

And it was their job to guarantee he didn't.

Nikki caught movement in her peripheral vision a fraction of a second before she felt the impact of a fist against her ribs from behind. The attack knocked the air out of her lungs and sent her radio flying. She'd barely had time to catch her breath when he came at her again, but this time she managed to shift her body out of the way. She swung around and slammed the barrel of the deputy's gun against her attacker's head.

There were two of them. Sent, no doubt, to ambush them and ensure they didn't make it to the plane. Both over six feet and at least two hundred pounds each, they'd clearly been trained to fight. Her mind switched gears instantly as Jack took on the other man and she managed to block another punch. She'd been trained in hand-to-hand combat, but there were other factors that were going to determine how this ended. Stamina. Momentum. Speed.

God, I don't know if my exhausted body can do this.

She felt another fist slam into her ribs and groaned at the sharp pain that shot through her body.

"Nikki . . ."

But Jack couldn't help her now. He had his own battle to fight. And she was no match for the heavyweight Russell had sent to stop her. The only way she was going to win this was by using his own force to pull him to the ground. And even that was a long shot.

Her attacker proved her doubts real as he slammed her onto the ground, straddled his legs on either side of her, then aimed his weapon at her head. Nikki looked up into the barrel of the gun, caught the gleam in his eye as he got ready to pull the trigger.

Not today, God . . . not today . . .

She heard the gunfire as his body collapsed on top of her.

"Nikki?" Jack grabbed the loaded gun, then shoved her attacker's body off her.

But she couldn't move. Couldn't breathe. She looked down. Blood was smeared across her chest. Thick and warm. She sucked in a lungful of air, but couldn't feel any pain from the bullet.

"Nikki?" Jack was hovering beside her. "You're okay."

"I don't understand." Fear wrapped around her along with confusion over what had just happened. He'd stood over her with a loaded weapon and pulled the trigger. She should be dead.

"I shot him. You're fine."

Her mind struggled with the facts. Jack had shot him. She was okay.

"That means a second later . . ." She looked up at him, still lying on her back, her heart racing with adrenaline, as what happened started to come into focus.

A second later . . .

A second later she would have been dead.

"Don't even go there," Jack said.

He grabbed her wrists and slowly helped her stand up. Her legs were shaking, and she couldn't catch her breath.

"Are you okay?"

"I . . . I can't breathe."

"Bend over and breathe in slowly."

She did what he said, then looked at where the man was lying with bloodstains across his chest. His blood. Not hers. He was dead. She wasn't.

"He's dead, Nikki. He can't hurt you anymore."

"And the other one?"

"Alive, but he won't be walking out of here."

"We still need to get Russell." A sharp pain shot through her rib cage as she stood up.

"You almost got killed just now," Jack said. "Which proves just how determined Russell is at stopping us. We should wait for backup."

"We can't." Nikki started toward the plane. "Backup could be too late."

28

Nikki ignored the sharp spike of pain that rippled across her rib cage. Tomorrow she'd deal with the physical consequences of the past couple days, but not now. Instead she kept her focus on the uneven ground in front of her. The moon was now only partially hidden behind the clouds, giving them some light to see where they were going, yet hopefully enough cover to keep them safe. Frank Pope had told them there had been two men with Russell when he grabbed Lily. But they couldn't be certain there hadn't been others waiting with the plane.

Her phone vibrated in her jacket pocket. She pulled it out and answered it.

"What have you got, Gwen?" she asked, still managing to keep up with Jack.

"I got through to the pilot on his radio," Gwen said. "His name's Captain Hammond, and he does charter flying for private jets."

"And?" Nikki prodded, ducking under the low branch of a tree.

"I convinced him he had two choices. Spend the next twenty to thirty years in prison, or do what I said. He suddenly decided there was a mechanical problem he'd overlooked during his preflight inspection. He's running a diagnostic now, but let me warn you. Russell isn't happy about the delay."

"That's no surprise," Nikki said, stepping over a large rock lying across her path as they approached the southwest corner of the airstrip. "We're almost to the plane now."

"Be careful, Nikki. This guy's ruthless and isn't going to let anything stop him."

Nikki's hand went automatically to her rib cage. *Tell me about it.* "We'll be careful. I promise."

"What did she say?" Jack asked as soon as she'd hung up.

Nikki dropped her phone back into her pocket. "Our pilot's cooperating. He delayed the flight due to a mechanical issue."

"Is Russell buying it?"

"I don't know, but all we need is enough time to get there and arrest him."

The sound of the engine grew louder as they approached the landing strip through the cover of trees. Seconds later she caught sight of the plane's silhouette as they stepped onto the edge of a long strip. She pulled out her weapon, quickly assessing the scene. A strip of solar lights lit the airstrip. Russell stood next to the plane yelling at the pilot to get back in and take off. Apparently he had no plans of waiting for the hit men he'd just sent out.

"Brian Russell . . . TBI," Nikki shouted above the roar of the engines, aiming at his chest as she walked toward him.

Russell hesitated, then pulled a Glock from a hip holster and pointed it at her.

"Put your weapon down and your hands in the air," Jack said.

"Captain Hammond," Nikki said, addressing the pilot. "I want you to go shut down the engines. This plane isn't going anywhere right now."

"Don't listen to her, *Captain* Hammond," Russell said, shifting his weapon toward the pilot. "We're going back to our original plan. You and I are going to get on that plane right now and take off."

The pilot wiped his forehead with the back of his hand. "I-I told you there was a problem. I need to run a diagnostic—"

"What did they threaten you with, Hammond?" Russell asked. "Ten . . . twenty years in prison?"

Hammond hesitated. Clearly Russell was used to being the boss. Even with the white handkerchief wrapped tightly around his arm where he'd been clipped, he looked the part in his black jeans, button-down dress shirt, and vest. Casual and yet completely in control. He was the kind of man who was used to giving out orders and who paid people to do his dirty work, ensuring he never got his own hands dirty in the process. But there was one problem. His control over the situation was beginning to crumble. She could see it in the deep crease in his brow and the tension in his jaw. He wasn't going to be able to charm himself out of this situation.

Russell's gaze swung back at her and Jack. "Let us go, or I will shoot him," Russell said.

"Not going to happen," Jack said. "We've got two weapons pointed at you. You can't take all three of us down, which means you'll go down no matter what you choose. It's over."

"Where's Lily?" Nikki asked.

"Forget it. You're not going to take her."

"It's too late for that," Nikki said. "You're under arrest for the murders of Kim Parks, Justin Peters, Erika Hamilton, and Deputy Banks, and that doesn't include money laundering and a long list of other crimes that will soon be added by the FBI."

"You can't prove I was involved in any of that." Russell glanced behind them, as if he was still convinced that his henchmen were coming. "And this isn't over. Not yet."

"Your men aren't coming." Nikki said. "We took them down."

"No." He tugged at his collar with his free hand. "I have it all arranged. I have a plane . . . passports. It's the only way to raise my daughter. You have to let me go."

"You know we can't do that," Nikki said.

"You don't understand." She caught the desperation in his voice as his Glock—still pointing at the pilot—shook in his hands. "Erika was trying to take Lily away from me."

"Erika was her mother."

"And I'm Lily's father. When Erika came to me and told me she was pregnant, I promised to take care of them. But now . . . she wouldn't even let me see Lily."

"Is that why you killed Erika?"

"No. You're . . . you're not listening to me. She was trying to get me put in jail so they'd take Lily away from me. She didn't want me to see her, and I don't even know why. Erika loved me."

"If that's true, then why did she tell the Feds she would testify against you?" Jack asked.

"Because someone has been spreading lies about me. They scared her and made her decide she needed to get full custody. She knew if I ended up in jail I couldn't fight her. But I couldn't let that happen. Lily is my daughter. I know what it's like to grow up without a father. I couldn't let that happen to her."

"And so you did everything you could to stop Erika, including killing Kim and Justin to stop them from talking."

"Of course not."

"We have evidence, Mr. Russell, of your involvement with Petran," Nikki said, stretching the truth. If they didn't have what the Feds needed yet, they'd have it soon. "Erika found out what you were involved in and decided to turn over the evidence to the FBI."

"They told me she was going to be the principal witness at my trial. How could she do that to me? I would have married her—"

"But instead you had her killed."

"I didn't have a choice," Russell shouted.

She watched the realization of what he'd confessed register on his face. The cocky playboy look vanished, replaced by pure fear.

"Mr. Russell, put the gun down now," Jack said. "You're under arrest for the murder of Erika—"

"No! I'm not going to end up spending the rest of my life in prison while Lily gets raised by strangers." He hesitated, then turned his gun and pressed it against his temple. "All I wanted was to be able to raise Lily as her father. And then Erika . . . she tried to take all of that away from me."

Nikki felt her heart rate rise as she realized what he was about to do. "Don't do it."

"Why not?"

"The DA is going to want your testimony against Petran, and if you cooperate—"

"They'll what? Drop my sentence from life to thirty years? Will that really make a difference? If I lose Lily . . . I've already lost everything."

"Brian, don't—"

The gunshot ripped across the windblown airstrip.

Nikki turned away as his lifeless body slumped to the ground. Brian Russell was dead, but his decision wasn't only going to affect the FBI's case. It was going to affect Lily.

She started for the plane as three backup vehicles finally showed up on the scene.

"Get his body off the airstrip," she shouted at Jack. "I'm going to see if Lily's here."

Nikki stepped onto the plane, praying that Lily was on board, but praying just as hard that if she was there, she hadn't seen what just happened. The little girl had already gone through so much. And now to see her father kill himself . . .

God, Lily needs your protection right now.

She glanced into the cockpit, then started down the row of leather seats. Movement from the back of the plane caught her attention. Big brown eyes stared back at her as Lily peeked her head around the edge of one of the aisle seats. Nikki walked to the back of the plane to where Lily sat, her seat belt fastened tightly across her lap. Brown hair pulled up into pigtails, a pair of jeans, a T-shirt with a cat and a pink sweater . . . Four years old was too young to have to deal with what had just happened on that airstrip.

"You must be Lily," Nikki said, crouching down next to her seat.

The little girl nodded.

"I'm Special Agent Nikki Boyd. Which is just a fancy name that means I'm a police officer. I help take care of people."

"How do you know my name?"

"I've been looking for you. I wanted to make sure you were safe."

Lily's brow wrinkled as if she wasn't sure what she should do. "My daddy told me to stay here. No matter what happened."

Nikki let out a short sigh of relief. If she'd been sitting here the entire time, she wouldn't have seen anything. "I'm sure your daddy was wanting to make sure you were safe."

"He said we were going on an adventure and that Mommy would come later. But then he started shouting at the pilot . . ." Lily pressed her hands against her ears as if she could suppress the memory by blocking out the noise.

Nikki tried to swallow the lump in her throat. How do you tell a little girl that her father and mother were dead? That there was no adventure ahead? And that her entire life had just changed forever?

"Lily?" She waited a few seconds until Lily dropped her hands back into her lap. "How would you like to go see the Popes? Maybe stay with them for a while."

"Instead of Daddy?"

"Yes."

The little girl's brows puckered into a frown. "Is he mad at me?"

"Your daddy?" Nikki asked. "No. Of course not. Why?"

"Mommy sent me to stay with Nana and Pappy, but then one of Daddy's friends took me to the car while he yelled at them. I don't know why he was so mad."

Nikki hesitated. "No one is mad at you, sweetie. Not your mommy. Not your daddy. And not your aunt or uncle."

"Everything's clear," Jack shouted up the open stairway.

"Does that mean we can leave?" Lily asked.

"Yes, it does."

"And Daddy?"

Nikki started to unfasten Lily's seat belt, then hesitated. Lily deserved to find out about her mother and father from someone she knew. Not from a complete stranger. "I'm sorry, Lily, but you can't see him right now. And there is one other thing. There are some police officers outside the airplane, but I don't want you to be afraid, okay? They're just there to make sure everyone is safe."

Lily nodded, then reached up and grabbed Nikki's hand. "Will you go with me to Nana's?"

"Of course. If that's what you want."

A minute later, Jack opened the back door to one of the deputy's cars. "Have you ever ridden in a police car before?" he asked Lily.

Lily shook her head and yawned.

"I'll sit back here with you, while one of the sheriff's deputies drives us to your aunt and uncle's," Nikki said.

"Like a chauffeur?" Lily asked, climbing into the car.

"How do you know about chauffeurs?" Nikki asked, scooting in beside her.

"Daddy has one back in Houston," Lily said matter-of-factly. "He drives me to the park sometimes."

"Then yes. Just like a chauffeur," Nikki said, then addressed the deputy who'd just slipped into the driver's seat. "I need you to take me and Lady Lily to the Pope cabin."

"Yes, ma'am," the deputy said.

Lily giggled, then snuggled up against Nikki with a big yawn. By the time they arrived ten minutes later, she was sound asleep.

Nikki carried the sleeping girl out of the vehicle and up the steps to the Popes' cabin.

Mr. and Mrs. Pope met them at the door.

"You found her," Mr. Pope said.

"Yes, and she's fine," Nikki said. "Just exhausted. She fell asleep on the way here."

"That's fine. Let her keep sleeping," Mrs. Pope said, her voice catching as Nikki laid Lily on the couch. "I can't believe you found her. Poor girl's been through such an ordeal."

"I'm surprised that the two of you are still here and not at the hospital," Jack said.

"Told you Frank was stubborn. He refused to go see a doctor until we knew Lily was safe." She gave her husband a warm smile, then sat down next to Lily. "Though I don't blame him. I've 'bout worn a hole in the carpet here wondering what was happening out there."

"She's safe now, Mrs. Pope," Nikki said.

"Please . . . call us Frank and Helen."

"Where'd you find her?" Frank asked.

"At the second airstrip you told us about. Russell was about to leave for Venezuela with her," Jack said. "Sheriff's department found forged passports and IDs on the plane."

"And Brian? Please tell me you arrested him."

Nikki glanced at Jack. "When faced with life in prison, he . . . he shot himself."

Helen covered her mouth. "And Lily?"

"I'm fairly certain she didn't see anything, though she knows her father was upset about something."

Helen dropped her hand to her lap. "Does she know he's gone?"

Nikki shook her head. "I didn't feel like we should be the ones to tell her."

"We'll find a way." Helen bit her lip. "She's young and will eventually bounce back, but I just wish none of this had ever happened. Erika's gone, Lily's an orphan . . . The whole situation just breaks my heart."

"We're still waiting for the go-ahead," Nikki said, "but we're working on getting special permission for Lily to stay with you until things are worked out officially."

"We'd like that," Frank said. "Erika told us that she named us as Lily's guardians in her will, in case anything ever happened to her."

"I just never , . . I never thought anything would happen. It still seems so surreal." Helen wiped her cheek with the back of her hand. "Frank and I weren't able to have children, and while I wouldn't wish these circumstances on anyone, we're happy to follow Erika's wishes."

One of the sheriff's deputies stepped into the cabin. "Excuse me, but if you're ready to go, the sheriff asked me to take you back to his office where there's a helicopter on its way. He says our people can finish wrapping things up so you can get back to Nashville."

Nikki felt the need to stay, but exhaustion had already begun to settle in as the rush of adrenaline wore off. Her body ached, her head hurt, and she needed a good night's sleep—

"Don't even think about arguing with him," Jack said as he turned to the Popes to say goodbye.

"I wasn't planning on it," she said.

He caught her gaze and nodded. "Right."

Nikki stepped into the sheriff's department at half past one.

"Helo should be ready for takeoff in about ten minutes," the sheriff said, stepping out from behind his desk. "It's been a tough night, though from what I hear, the two of you have had an even rougher couple of days."

"We have, but tonight you lost one of your own," Nikki said, taking the Styrofoam cup of coffee one of the deputies handed her. "We're sorry about Deputy Banks. If there had been anything we could have done to stop what happened—"

"I know you would have. He was a good deputy. He'd been married less than six months. It's something you don't expect out here, and to be honest, we're all still in shock. As soon as I get the two of you on that bird, I'm going to have to drive out to his house and tell his wife what happened, though I'm still not sure how I'm going to do that."

"It's never easy," Jack said.

"I can tell you what will be easy," the sheriff said, hooking his thumbs through his belt loops. "Making sure that sniper Russell sent pays for what he did."

"Where is he?" Jack asked.

"In my interrogation room for now, but the FBI's already called dibs on him, so I'm waiting for them to show up."

"Speaking of the FBI, what about Agent Brinkley?" Nikki asked. "We hated leaving him but didn't have a choice."

"He was a bit grumpy when we found him, but an ambulance

took him to our local hospital, where they're patching him up. He'll be fine."

"You're going to want to see this, boss." A second uniformed deputy walked up to the sheriff's desk carrying a piece of paper in a clear evidence bag.

"Just got this sent over from the morgue. They found it in Russell's pants pocket. It's some kind of letter they thought you should see."

Sheriff Adamson nodded at Jack. "Why don't you let our friends from Nashville here see if it's something worth keeping."

Jack took the paper and studied it.

"What is it?" Nikki said, moving next to him.

"What's the one thing the FBI's missing in this case?" Jack said.

"I don't know . . . Concrete evidence against Petran?"

"Exactly. Take a look."

She set down her coffee, held up the paper, and started reading through the handwritten note. "Wait a minute . . . You've got to be kidding me. It looks like a full confession signed by Russell. Why would he do that?"

"I don't know, but the FBI is going to have a field day with this."

"That's an understatement." She flipped the paper over to where Brian Russell had signed it. "There are names, account numbers, and access codes, and they're all pointing to Petran."

"So if all this checks out," Jack said, "Russell found a way to help take Petran down. But why would he write this?"

Nikki tapped her finger against the letter. Only one answer stood out in her mind. "I don't think he ever planned to go to prison. I think in his mind his only option was leaving the country with Lily. He had no intention of being taken alive."

She picked up her coffee again and took a sip. Their role in the investigation might be over, but she still had a lot of questions. If she couldn't talk to Russell, she wanted to talk to the hit man Jack had managed to take down.

"You know we need to stay and wrap this up. There are still answers I want to find out, not to mention making sure everything is settled with Lily—"

Jack shook his head. "Forget it."

"Jack . . ."

He stepped in front of her, his fatigue mirroring her own. "When's the last time you slept? When's the last time either of us ate, for that matter?"

Nikki shook her head, knowing it was impossible to argue with his logic. "I have no idea."

"I know this case hit home for you in more ways than one, but our job here is over. Lily's safe and you—both of us—need to go home."

"Which is why we've got strict orders from your boss to get you back to Nashville," the sheriff said. "And he told me not to take no for an answer. We'll send you everything we come up with."

"Chopper's just arrived, boss," the deputy said, setting down his phone. "That should put the two of you back in Nashville in just under an hour."

29

Nikki stared at the coffeepot in her condo, willing it to hurry up. But instead, it just continued dripping in slow motion. She finally pulled out the pot and shoved her mug beneath the sluggish drip, hoping to speed up the process of getting the coffee from the filter and into her system.

Stifling a yawn, she glanced at the time on the microwave. The helicopter had dropped them off around three this morning. She'd been asleep by four. Which meant she'd just slept for over twelve hours. And if she were honest with herself, she could probably sleep for another twelve.

She watched the mug fill, then quickly swapped it out for the carafe again as soon as it reached the top. She took a sip, not caring what it tasted like. All she needed was something strong enough to jump-start her system.

Jade rubbed against her leg, begging for some attention.

"Poor girl," Nikki said, reaching down and scratching her

behind the ears. "You probably thought I'd completely forgotten about you."

Jade started purring as Nikki took another sip of her coffee. If only everything could be made better with tuna-flavored kibble and a scratch behind the ears. Instead, in real life the bad guy sometimes won, and things didn't always end the way she hoped.

Her phone beeped on the island behind her as a new message came in. She turned around to check it. There were four text messages.

Mom
Nikki, thanks for the update. I know you're exhausted, so I'm hoping you're getting some needed sleep. Call us when you're awake and if you're up to it, we'll plan on dinner at the restaurant tonight.

Tyler
Hey Nikki. I'm so glad you're done with the case. I know it's been a tough one for you. Let me know when you feel like some company. I miss you. we have so much to catch up on.

Agent Brinkley—FBI
Nikki this is agent brinkley. Just wanted you to know that you hit the jackpot. We might have to miss watching Russell rot in jail, but we've got enough to take Petran and his entire organization down.

Jamie
Nikki, Mom told me about the case you've been working on. Sounds like you've had a rough couple days. with all that's been going on, I'm sure you forgot we were supposed to have lunch today. In case you do happen to remem-

ber, don't worry about it. Seriously. because
I'm hoping you're spending the day sleeping.
we'll catch up soon, though, okay? Little Sarah
misses you.

Nikki smiled at the last message. Her brother Matt and his
wife Jamie's little girl, Sarah, had been their miracle baby. They'd
struggled for years before Jamie finally got pregnant, then ended
up naming their daughter after their missing sister.

Was infertility the same struggle she was about to face?

She glanced at the trash can where she'd crumpled up the
doctor's appointment reminder. She was used to dealing with
cases and solving other people's problems. But this was entirely
new territory. She stared at her phone, wondering what she
should do. At some point, she was going to have to respond to
all of the messages, but she wasn't ready to deal with work yet.
She'd see her mother soon. And as for Tyler . . .

She missed him to the point of that achy physical feeling of
being far away from someone you loved. Which was why she
hated the fact that he was here in Nashville, and after three
months of being apart, they'd barely had time to reconnect.

But there was someone she needed to call first before she saw
Tyler. She punched in Jamie's number.

"Jamie? Hey . . . it's Nikki," she said once her sister-in-law
answered.

"Please don't tell me you're already up. You should still be
asleep, and I'm sure I've only heard a fraction of what's been
going on over the past couple days from your mom. We've all
been worried."

"I just got up, actually. And I am so sorry about lunch. You
were right. I completely forgot."

"I meant it when I said forget it. Seriously. I was just concerned about how you're doing and wanted you to know I was
thinking about you. So how are you?"

"I'm . . ." Nikki hesitated. To say she was fine would be a lie. The last couple of days had shaken her up and left her feeling drained both physically and mentally. "You're right. It's been really tough, but it's over, and for the moment, that's all that really matters."

"Well, good, because if you ask me, being on that plane that crashed would have been enough to knock my nerves senseless."

"That already seems like forever ago." She could hear Sarah cooing in the background and smiled. "Listen . . . I was wondering if you'd mind if I came by for a few minutes."

"Are you sure you're up to it?"

"Yeah. I-I need to ask your advice about something."

Twenty minutes later Jamie was pulling her into a big hug. "I have been so worried about you."

"I'm okay. Really." Nikki took a step back and smiled. "What's that incredible smell?"

"Pumpkin scones. Staying home with Sarah has been wonderful, but I've turned into a bit of a Pinterest addict with all of their DIY projects." Jamie waved Nikki into the kitchen. "Matt's going to stay with Sarah tonight while I go to my book club. Sometimes I feel a bit lost not teaching, so I'm making a bunch of desserts and giving them away. It keeps me busy and not going stir crazy being at home so much and hopefully makes a few people happy in the process."

Jamie slid a scone onto a small plate and handed it to Nikki.

"What do you think?" she asked. "I added a spiced pumpkin glaze."

Nikki took a bite, realizing she'd slept through both breakfast and lunch. Her mouth watered. "Wow . . . ," she said, taking another bite. "These are incredible."

"After you called, I put on some coffee. Do you want some?"

"I don't think I can get enough caffeine at this point," Nikki said, sliding a second scone onto her plate. "You don't mind, do you?"

Jamie laughed. "Of course not. Go on and sit down in the living room and I'll bring your coffee. Sarah will be excited to see you."

"She's so beautiful," Nikki said to Jamie as she set her plate on the coffee table, then picked up Sarah from her bouncy chair. Her niece nestled her face against Nikki's neck, then pulled back and grabbed a strand of Nikki's hair. Nikki felt the familiar stir that both excited and terrified her as Sarah squealed. "I can't believe she's almost five months old."

She sat down with Sarah on the indigo-colored couch, breathing in the smell of baby powder and shampoo. She'd always wanted kids. It was why she'd chosen to be a teacher. Joining the police force had simply given her a different way to stand up for them.

"I can't either." Jamie plopped down across from Nikki on a matching cushioned armchair. "She's outgrowing all her clothes, which is no wonder, because she's eating all the time. I just want her to slow down so I don't miss anything."

Nikki tugged on the bottom of Sarah's pink onesie. "Before you know it, she'll be graduating from high school—"

"Stop. Don't even go there."

Nikki laughed. "I'm sorry. Enjoy every moment with her. I know you do."

Sarah lay on her back on Nikki's lap and looked up at her with big brown eyes while her legs kicked in the air. Nikki's heart melted. What if she couldn't have children? Not that she wouldn't consider Liam as her own son if she and Tyler married, and adoption was always an option. Still, there was something about carrying the child of someone you loved. She'd always known that her career would have to be figured into the mix, but motherhood had always been a given in the back of her mind.

"I've watched the news on and off the past couple days with all the coverage of the plane crash," Jamie said, breaking through Nikki's turbulent thoughts. "I can't imagine how terrifying that had to have been. And then this missing persons case you were working on. I saw a short segment about it on the news that said Brian Russell was dead, but they didn't really give any details."

"You know who he was?" Nikki asked, trying not to seem distracted.

"Some wealthy playboy-slash-philanthropist from Texas."

"He's dead and so is the mother of their little girl." Nikki smiled. "The most adorable four-year-old. Her name is Lily."

"That's so sad."

"I know. There's a couple she's with right now who's like family. I'm hoping things will work out for her to stay with them. When cases go bad like this one . . . sometimes it's just hard to accept. She'll never know her mother."

"Like Liam?"

"Yeah." Sarah started squirming and Nikki slid her back into her bouncy chair, where she immediately grabbed for a missed Cheerio. "Maybe that's part of the reason this case hit so close to home."

"Sounds very personal," Jamie said, handing Sarah another handful of Cheerios. "But despite the tragedy that has happened, that doesn't mean Lily won't grow up to be a well-adjusted teacher, or scientist, or president of the United States, or whatever she wants to be."

Nikki reached for her plate of scones and took another bite. "I know."

Jamie was right. Nikki had seen God bring beauty out of tragedy over and over. And while it didn't erase the pain of the trial, God continued to redeem what was broken. Because as her mom had always told her, God was far more interested in shaping her character than fixing all her problems.

"Something tells me you didn't come over here to discuss your case," Jamie said, taking a sip of her coffee. "Is everything else okay?"

Nikki took another bite of her scone and searched for how to begin. "It's Tyler."

"Have you seen him since he's been back?"

Nikki glanced down at Sarah, who'd fallen asleep next to her pile of Cheerios. She looked content. Happy. Perfect.

"He was at the airport waiting for me when the plane crashed," Nikki said.

"I can't even imagine what he went through. At least I didn't see the footage of the crash until after I knew you were okay, but to have been there when it happened . . ." Jamie paused. "Is everything okay between the two of you? You don't exactly look excited. I mean, there's always been that blush on your cheek when you talk about him, but now . . ."

"Everything's fine right now. I'm happy he's back. Anxious and expectant about the future. Maybe a bit terrified of what happens next. You know how this whole thing between Tyler and me has been so . . . unexpected. I want this to work, Jamie. More than I've ever wanted anything to work."

"So what's the problem? Because trust me, everything you're feeling is normal. The excitement, the nerves, the elation, and sometimes plain terror. All normal."

Nikki laughed. "I'm not sure if that relieves me or makes me even more nervous."

"My advice is to simply enjoy exploring this road together. There's something wonderful about a relationship when everything is new and exciting. You can't stop thinking about him when you're apart and your heart flutters when he enters the room. And besides that, what could be better than falling for your best friend?"

"There is something else. The main reason I wanted to talk with you." Nikki set down her plate of scones. "I haven't told anyone this yet, but long story short, I got some test results back the other day after experiencing a string of weird symptoms. It was something I tried to ignore for a long time, because I never had time to go see my doctor. And I guess I just didn't think it mattered, but now I'm afraid everything might have changed."

"What do you mean?" Jamie asked.

"They think I might have ovarian failure, which basically means they're shutting down, and I probably won't be able to have children."

"Oh Nikki . . . I'm so sorry."

"It's ironic in a way," she rushed on, not wanting a huge show of sympathy. "I mean, I've always worried about how I'd juggle motherhood and my job. I think part of me had given up on finding the man I wanted to spend the rest of my life with. Until everything changed between Tyler and me."

She drew in a deep breath, knowing Jamie wouldn't hit her with a bunch of cliché answers.

"You struggled with infertility," she continued, glancing at Sarah. "I know it had to have affected your relationship with Matt, and I just . . . I'm scared of what this is going to mean for Tyler and me."

"Have you told Tyler?"

"No."

"You need to. Tell him the truth about how you feel. And let him tell you how he feels."

"But I'm scared, Jamie." She hugged one of the throw pillows against her chest and let out a humorless chuckle. "I never thought I would be in a place where I cared for someone as deeply as I care for Tyler. And that something like this would absolutely terrify me."

"You know—more than most people—how life throws curveballs. But there are happy endings. Sometimes, like with you and Tyler, God steps in and manages to take your breath away. Focus on that. The relationship you're building with him. And then let God work the rest out. I had to do that with Michael and our relationship. I had to let go of all my preconceived plans and ideas and surrender everything that I had to God."

"I want to be able to do that."

"Then do it, because Tyler's in love with you, Nikki, not what happens in the future. Not whether or not you can have children. He loves *you*. And from everything I've seen between the two of you, I'm sure of that."

"But what if you're wrong? What if it ends up being the wedge that pushes us apart? I'm so afraid I'll lose him."

Jamie pressed her hand against her mouth and chuckled.

"What's so funny?"

"I'm sorry." Jamie shook her head. "It's just that you face death all the time. *That* would terrify me. Tyler loves you, and he's not going to push you away because of this."

"You might be right, but relationships are far scarier in some ways than facing an assailant with a gun."

"Speak for yourself. But seriously, talk to him. If he really loves you, if he's even half the man I think he is, he's going to support you through this."

"I hope so—"

"I know so."

"Sometimes I think God must get tired of my always begging for answers," Nikki said. "About my sister . . . the cases I work on . . . and now this health issue."

"That's the thing about God. I've decided he doesn't mind us asking questions. He already knows the answers."

A wave of unexpected peace swept through Nikki. She wasn't in control. She never had been. And God knew the answers to the questions about what happened to Sarah. What was going to happen to Lily. And what was going to happen between her and Tyler. If she truly believed God was in control, it was time to start living that way. Jamie was right. It was time to talk to Tyler.

30

6:40 p.m.
Tyler's house

Nikki slid out of her Mini Cooper in front of Tyler's house, then grabbed the chocolate tart she'd picked up at a favorite restaurant down the street. Normally, she would have enjoyed making it herself, but tonight all she wanted was to see the man she'd fallen in love with.

Even with fall around the corner, the rows of petunias and impatiens lining the brick walkway of the house still looked beautiful. It was a final reminder of Katie's touch. Nikki paused at the FOR SALE sign stuck in the ground in front of the house. So much had changed over the past year or so. Both for the better and for the worse. And the past twenty-four hours had reminded her—not for the first time—that life was worth grabbing onto with everything she had. Because one never knew when everything could change forever.

She just hoped that what she had to say to Tyler wasn't going to change everything between them.

Liam bounded out the front door of the house and down the porch steps toward her with a wide smile on his face.

"Hey, bud."

"Daddy told me to watch for you. He's on the phone."

"I've missed you these past few days."

"I missed you too," Liam said, throwing his arms around her waist. He took a step back with his hands on his hips and a serious expression on his face. "Daddy said your plane crashed. I thought . . . I was scared something bad happened to you."

Nikki wound her free hand around his fingers. She'd learned that while he might only be six, he'd experienced more loss than some adults had to deal with. He knew what it was like to have his entire world changed overnight. And he was very aware that sometimes bad things happened.

"Something bad like what happened to your mom?"

Liam nodded. "Grandma didn't want me to see it, but I saw the plane on TV before she turned it off."

"I'm okay. The doctor even checked me out to make sure. All I have is this bump on my head and a bruise on my shoulder." She knelt down and let him run his finger across her forehead.

"Was it scary?" he asked.

"Very scary. I prayed a lot."

"It's okay to be scared. That's what my daddy tells me anyway."

"Like going back to school and moving?" she asked, taking his hand and heading toward the front porch.

"Yeah."

"Do you like your new teacher?"

Liam's blond head bobbed. "Her name's Miss Tucker, and she's pretty. Like you are. I think I'll like her, but I miss my old teacher. But I did make some new friends."

"And how does it feel to have your daddy back?"

Liam's smile radiated across his face. "I think he's happier than he used to be. Like he doesn't miss Mama so much."

"He still misses her, but maybe God's giving him things to fill up those empty places."

"Did you know that we're moving?" he asked as they started up the porch steps.

"Yes."

"We're going to get a new house. Just like Daddy has a new job. And I have a new teacher at school."

His smile began to fade as he ran through the list of changes. She and Tyler had talked about the changes Liam had to face. Tyler had been clearly worried about how those changes were going to affect his son, but she'd been amazed at how Liam had managed to adjust.

She set the tart down on the porch rail, then nodded at the top step before sitting down. Liam plopped down beside her. She breathed in the smell of freshly cut grass from the neighbor's yard and listened to the buzz of the lawn mower. It wouldn't be long until the seasons changed again and winter settled in.

"You're right. There are lots of changes happening right now, aren't there?" she said, to herself almost more than to Liam. "And sometimes those changes can be tough to deal with."

Liam sighed. "My best friend Logan's going to a different school now. I miss him. We always traded stuff at lunch. Like the peanut butter sandwiches he hated."

Nikki chuckled. "How do you feel about all of the changes?"

"Sometimes I wish things would just go back to the way they used to be. When Mama was still here. When Daddy smiled more." His frown softened into a thoughtful look. "But I guess there are a few good things too."

"What kind of good things?"

"You come over a lot more now. Especially when Daddy was gone. And he smiles more when he sees you."

Nikki grinned at Liam's observations. "I enjoyed spending time with you as well."

"Are you going to keep coming over now that Daddy's back?"

"I hope so."

Liam looked up at her and caught her gaze. "Except Daddy thinks you're mad at him."

Nikki felt her heart drop. "Mad at him? Why would he think that?"

Liam shrugged. "I don't know. I just . . . I just don't want you to go away. Like Mama. Like Daddy did for a while."

"Hey . . ." She wrapped her arm around his shoulder and pulled him against her. "I'm not planning to go anywhere. I promise."

"Does that mean you're really not mad at Daddy?"

"No, I'm not. But sometimes things get complicated when you grow up."

"Why?"

Why?

She searched for what to say. Wasn't that the question of the century. She understood what Liam had said. Sometimes she wished things could go back to a place where everything was simpler and where matters of the heart didn't leave her feeling torn in two. Where she wasn't afraid of telling Tyler the truth, or of losing him. Afraid of breaking his heart along with hers.

The screen door squeaked open behind them as Tyler stepped onto the porch.

"Hey. Sorry about that. I've been trying to tie up all the loose ends on the house. Looks like we've got a buyer."

"That's great news," Nikki said, scooting over a few inches so he could sit on the step with them. "And Liam was the perfect welcoming committee."

"She brought us dessert."

"A chocolate tart," Nikki said.

"You definitely know my weakness," he said, sitting down beside her. "Liam, the trash still needs to be taken out before dinner."

"Yes, sir." Liam hopped up and headed into the house.

"The pizza should be here in about fifteen minutes." Tyler nudged her with his shoulder. "Care to stay here and watch the sunset with me?"

"I'd like that."

Nikki glanced at Tyler and felt her nerves sweep through her stomach. She shifted her gaze to the colors displayed across the sky. This was the first time they'd really been together since he'd left. Since the crash. It was the moment she'd dreamed about for three months. The moment when he returned and they could continue exploring their feelings for each other.

"So how are you?" he asked, wrapping his arm around her waist.

"My case has taken pretty much everything out of me," she said, beginning to relax for the first time in days. "But it's over. My boss sent me home and told me not to come back until Monday. And for once I didn't argue."

Tyler laughed as the yellows and golds of the sunset spread across the Nashville skyline. "I'll admit, I find that hard to believe—the not arguing part—but I'm glad you're following orders. This was a hard case."

She studied his profile in the fading light: his strong jawline and sympathetic gaze. They'd talked once about complicated grief. How her sister's disappearance could never have resolution until they found her. At least Erika's family had been given closure, even though the hurt and the pain would never completely go away.

"It was hard," she said. "It's my job to find people in time and when I don't . . . ." Nikki worked to blink back the tears.

She could still see Erika dying in front of her at the crash site. It was a memory that would be ingrained in her mind forever.

"I'm sorry," Tyler said. "But at least it's over, and Russell and his men can't hurt anyone else."

"It might be over, but not for Lily." She leaned against him. "I hate the fact that a little girl will never know her mother. And that Erika won't be there to watch Lily grow up."

He looked at her and she knew he was thinking about Katie and the fact that she couldn't watch her son grow up.

Tyler pulled her closer. Warm. Protective. No matter what their future held, she knew he was the perfect fit for her. But she also knew she had to tell him the truth. Even if that future wasn't going to be what she'd once imagined.

"I'm just glad this case is behind you," he said. "And I'm glad you're here. You've got to be exhausted. You didn't have to agree to my invitation for dinner, but I'm glad you came."

"I'm glad I came too."

"I've missed you, Nikki." He stared down at her, making her heart race. "Sometimes so bad it almost hurt. I never expected to feel like this again."

She could see the emotion in his eyes even in the fading daylight and could hear it in his voice.

"And I'm not the only one," he continued. "Liam hasn't stopped talking about you. All the things the two of you did while I was gone. I know I've said it before, but thank you. You don't know how much it meant, knowing you were here for him."

"You know how much I love him."

"I do. I also know that you're going to make a wonderful mother."

Nikki felt her heart break as she pulled away from him and gripped the edge of the porch step. She'd always imagined having two or three children. And now she longed to have his children.

The possibility it wasn't going to happen still felt raw and unreal. Tyler deserved so much more than what she was able to give him.

"Nikki . . . hey. What's wrong?" He lifted her chin with his thumb. "If I learned anything from my marriage with Katie, it's that if you don't communicate, this won't work. Tell me what you're thinking."

She looked up and caught his gaze, wondering when exactly she'd realized she loved him. In so many ways it seemed as if she'd felt this way forever. What she did know was that one day she'd looked at him and everything changed for her. The unexpected way she longed to be near him. How his touch had suddenly felt intimate. The way he made her heart race when he looked at her.

"There's something we need to talk about," she said finally. "Something that might change the way you feel about me. About us."

"I don't understand," he said, the contented look on his face fading.

Nikki took a deep breath and stared out across the lawn that was bathed in the last lingering bits of daylight. Everything had changed since he asked her to wait for him at the airport. Since that first kiss that had made her realize just how much she wanted to be with him. But now . . .

"Nikki . . . tell me what's going on."

She swallowed hard. "The doctor's office called me a couple of days ago. Right after the plane crash. They'd run some tests and discovered . . . the blood work says I have ovarian failure."

"Which means?"

"Basically that my ovaries have stopped working."

"Okay. Is there something they can do? Surgery . . . medicine?"

"There isn't any treatment. The only thing they can help with is the symptoms." She blew out a short breath. "But it means it's going to be very hard, if not impossible, to have children."

He shook his head. "Doctors can be wrong. God can heal. And if not, there are always other options."

She watched his expression. He was searching for answers, just like she had when the doctor first presented his concerns to her. But the bottom line was that this was a reality she was going to have to accept. And if they were going to choose to spend their lives together, it was one he was going to be forced to accept as well.

"But what if God doesn't heal me," she said, lacing their fingers together and trying to shut out the pain that wouldn't stop flooding her heart. "I know you, Tyler. I know how much you love Liam. And I watched you with Katie when she was expecting again and saw how excited you were. I've heard you talk about how many children you want. If we move forward in this relationship, I might not be able to give that to you."

"Nikki—"

"And please don't try and tell me how it won't affect us, because it will," she said, unable to hold back the tears.

"I wasn't going to. Because of course, this makes me sad. Having more children, giving Liam a couple of brothers and sisters . . . yeah, I wanted that. I still want that. And the past few months have made it clear that I want to have that family with you. But this doesn't mean I want to call it quits. I'm not going to walk away, Nikki."

She heard his words but knew things could change once the reality of what she was telling him sank in. And how could she deny him something so important to him?

"Nikki, you get me," he continued. "That's why I love you. When I left, needing time to figure out what to do with my life, you supported me. I didn't want my leaving to change that. And now that I'm back, I don't want that to change either. Because if anything, being away confirmed that I'm in love with you. And I don't want that to change. Ever. I want you to be a part of my life."

Pent-up emotions surfaced, and she fought to stop the tears. "And if you think differently one day? I can't be the one who stands in the way of the family you always wanted."

"Then you didn't hear what I just said."

She felt her breath catch as he continued.

"Nikki, if we decide to move forward in this relationship, then it will mean for the ups and the downs. We'll struggle, but we'll learn to love each other even more. Together. But children or no children—that will never change how I feel about you. I promise you that."

"I just thought—"

"That I'd be disappointed? Of course I am. But never with you." He pulled her against his chest, still looking at her, but close enough to where she could feel his heart beating. "I've thought long and hard over the past few weeks about my life. About us. I can't imagine my life without you. I love you, Nikki Boyd. And nothing—especially a test result—is going to change that. Have I convinced you yet?"

She let out a soft sigh of relief at his response. "Oh, yeah."

"Good. Because everything I just said isn't going to change. No matter what the future holds."

She smiled as the weight of his reaction began to smooth out the raw edges of her fear. She never should have doubted him. Never should have thought that his love for her was conditional. Because it was exactly why she'd fallen for him. She'd known him long enough to realize he wasn't perfect, but his honesty and integrity had been what had drawn her to him in the first place.

She rested her hands against his chest and felt his heart beating beneath her fingertips. "So what's the next step?"

He smiled at her and slowly brushed his lips against hers. "I suppose we should go out on that first date. Something romantic and . . . uneventful."

"Uneventful." Nikki laughed. "I'd like that."

He kissed her again. Gently at first, then with a growing intensity that left her breathless.

"And after that . . . ," he continued, pausing a moment to run his finger across her jawline, "we've got the rest of our lives to figure that out together."

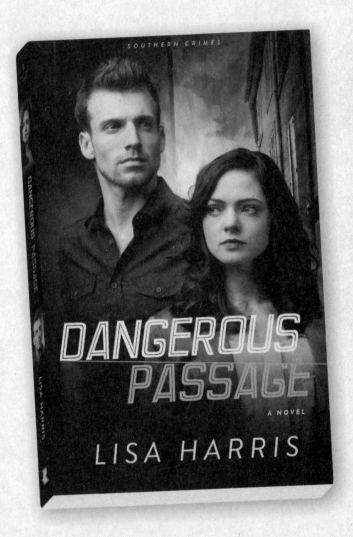

1

After another grueling weekend spent wrapping up a homicide, Detective Avery North was not about to let anything get in the way of her one nonnegotiable indulgence on her first day off in two weeks. She pulled into the parking lot of Glam Day Spa and stepped into the sultry Atlanta morning. The rest of her Monday might end up being a marathon, but she didn't care as long as she had the next hour to look forward to being pampered.

The petite, dark-haired manicurist greeted her at the front counter. "Morning, Miss North. You're right on time."

"Morning, Riza."

"You're off today?"

"Thankfully." Avery finished the rest of her iced tea while following Riza back to an open chair. "I managed not to cancel my appointment a third time. Crazy weekend."

"Then you need to sit down and relax completely. We could add a manicure? I have a new color that would look stunning with your red hair."

Avery melted into the padded chair, kicked off her sandals,

then dipped her feet into the hot, bubbly water, feeling herself relax for the first time in days. "Maybe next time."

Her feet tingled. One whole hour to forget about the leaky kitchen sink, her father's retirement party, and her mother's relentless questions about it. She closed her eyes. One whole hour to completely unwind and indulge her thoughts in something beside caterers, plumbers, and homicide cases.

Something pleasurable like . . . Jackson Bryant. Her first date with Jackson had started off with a severe case of rattled nerves that left her realizing she'd rather confront an armed murder suspect than jump back into the dating scene. By the end of the second date, she'd somehow managed to lose a corner of her heart to the handsome heartthrob, but even that hadn't been enough to lessen her surprise over the fact that there was now a third date planned for tonight.

At thirtysomething, with a somewhat moody tween and a mother whose own emotional stability was currently in question, Avery wasn't exactly Atlanta's perfect catch for a rising professional like the associate medical examiner. She wondered how many dates it would take before he started reconsidering his options—or she got cold feet.

Her shoulders relaxed. Dreaming of Jackson might be dangerous, but it might also prove to be the perfect escape. Gorgeous brown eyes that seemed to peer right through her. Dark hair, solid muscles, and an illegal amount of charm for one person—

Avery's phone rang in her front pocket. She opened her eyes and rubbed the back of her neck. She wasn't going to answer. It was probably her mother again, with more nagging questions about her father's upcoming retirement party.

Or it could be Tess. But she'd just dropped off her daughter at the middle school, so she should already be in her first-hour class.

A glance at the number told her it wasn't either of them. "Detective North speaking."

"This is Simons. 911 just received a call about a homicide. We've got an officer securing the crime scene, but Captain Peterson wants you there ASAP."

Not today, Lord. Please, not today. You know how badly I need a day off . . .

Avery glanced at her watch. She deserved this day off. Having to reschedule the eleven o'clock lunch with her mother was one thing, but missing an hour of pure relaxation was an entirely different story.

Avery pressed her fingers against her now throbbing temple. "It's my day off—"

"There's a tattoo of a small magnolia on the victim's right shoulder."

Avery's chest contracted. The recent crime scene flashed before her. A young girl. Asian. Body discarded next to a Dumpster. And a small magnolia tattooed on her right shoulder.

They'd never found the murderer.

"Where?"

Simons passed on the address.

"I'm on my way." She flipped the phone shut and turned to Riza. "I'm sorry . . . I've got to go."

"Do you want to reschedule?"

Riza patted Avery's feet with a white fluffy towel, but Avery was already reaching for her sandals, ready to slide them on her still damp feet. "Yes . . . no. I'll have to call."

She left a generous tip on the chair, then slipped out the front door, back into the sultry Georgia morning.

2

Avery slowed down as she approached the address Simons had given her over the phone, her gaze scanning the area for anything out of the ordinary. It wouldn't be the first time a killer returned to the scene of the crime.

The tree-lined street, with its brick buildings looming on either side, reminded her of the neighborhoods she'd worked as a rookie police officer. It was a unique mixture of mom-and-pop stores, neighborhood bars, apartment buildings, and charming older homes.

Statistically, crime might be higher in this community situated outside the ritzier golf courses and gated country clubs, but she'd always found the people friendly. More often than not, it turned out to be the combination of too many drinks or the addition of illegal drugs that turned simple disagreements into something ugly.

Like murder.

Of course, it was also the neighborhoods like this one that Mama was convinced would be the downfall of the city. She believed Atlanta's greatest attribute was its lingering pockets of old-fashioned southern charm. And everyone knew that transplants diluted that charm and added to the growing crime rate.

Avery, on the other hand, loved the diversity Atlanta offered with its collection of ethnic neighborhoods. The fact that she and Tess could spend a cultural afternoon in the city or escape to the nearby mountains on her time off was, in her mind, a plus. But someone had just lost any chance to visit Kennesaw Mountain Trail or Amicalola Falls. And it was up to her to find out why.

Especially if they were dealing with a serial killer.

A chill ran through her.

Avery pulled into the open space next to the alleyway, ten feet away from the yellow crime tape blocking off the scene. Detectives Sanders and Martin's unmarked sedan sat next to the medical examiner's vehicle and a couple of patrol cars. Already, a good number of onlookers stood gathered at the edges of the cordoned-off area. Avoiding the press would be impossible.

She grabbed her cell phone from the console, then hesitated. She should call her mother, except she'd never hear the end of missing today's meeting with Aunt Doris, who was catering her father's retirement party. She shoved the phone into her pocket. Mama would have to wait.

She got out of the car and headed for the sidewalk, where she took the clipboard from the uniformed officer standing guard at the front of the alley. She signed in, scribbling her initials and badge number.

Jackson Bryant's name had already been scrawled above hers.

She ignored the unsolicited flutter of her heart and addressed the officer. "Tell me what you've got."

"Asian female. Late teens, early twenties. The scene is secure. The medical examiner and two other officers arrived just before you did."

She nodded toward the growing number of spectators. "Make sure no one steps onto this scene without my permission."

"Yes ma'am."

The alley smelled like cheap liquor and overripe garbage. Cigarette butts lay scattered across the gravel. Green ivy threaded its way up the walls of the brick buildings lining the alley. A white Accord blocked the left side of the alley, its back taillight broken, leaving shards of the red plastic lying scattered on the ground. Determining what was evidence from this crime was going to be long and tedious.

On the other side of the Dumpster lay the body.

Avery's stomach heaved at the familiar smell of death—something she'd never gotten used to—mingling with the coppery taste of blood and the stench of the alcohol. The haunting scene from six weeks ago continued to flash before her. Even at first glance, the similarities were unmistakable. A young Asian victim, no more than seventeen or eighteen. Facedown on the ground, simply dressed in a shirt, short-sleeved sweater, and skirt. No shoes. The only difference was the copper bracelets adorning her left forearm.

Jackson finished covering one of the victim's hands in order to preserve evidence, then looked up. The butterfly-eliciting smile he normally gave Avery was missing.

"Avery." He pulled back the girl's sleeve to reveal the tattooed magnolia. "I knew you'd want to see this."

"What happened to her?"

He leaned forward and pointed to the mass of dried blood on the side of her head. "The autopsy will give us something more conclusive, but for now it looks as if she was killed and then dumped here."

Like the last victim.

Avery tried to push aside the feelings of vulnerability that swept through her. She was supposed to be the strong one who could handle anything. Except it wasn't always like that. "How long ago?"

"Not long. Rigor mortis has already set in, but I still don't think we're looking at more than five or six hours."

She pulled on a pair of latex gloves, then crouched down beside him. "So someone killed her, then dumped her here in the middle of the night, hoping to cover up their crime?"

"That would be my initial guess."

"What about the tattoo?"

Jackson pointed to the edge of the flower. "Healing typically takes anywhere from two to six weeks, so she's had it for some time."

"Any idea who she is?"

Detective Sanders leaned over her, camera in hand. "No ID, wallet, or purse was found on the body or in the car near the Dumpster. Which means, so far, we've got another Jane Doe."

"Signs of sexual assault?"

Jackson shook his head. "I'll let you know for sure after the autopsy, but there are definite signs of struggle. She has scratch marks on her arms and left cheek."

Sanders stepped back and snapped a photo of the wall behind the victim. "I've already taken photos of the body."

"Finish photographing the scene, then I want the area swept in a strip search pattern, with each block numbered individually." Avery signaled to the other detective working on sketches. "Martin, when you're done, talk to Missing Persons and see if anyone has been reported missing in the past seventy-two hours that fits her description. Maybe we'll get lucky. Then find out who owns that car and make sure the Dumpster is searched for evidence."

She stood up. "Who called this in?"

"A guy who works at the bar . . ." Martin flipped open his notebook. "A Jeffery Vine. He was taking out the trash about six forty and found her."

"Let him know I want to talk to him once we've gone over the scene and processed the evidence. For now, we need to canvass the neighborhood to see if anyone saw anything."

Avery strode to the far end of the alley. Anger simmered as she tried to imagine what the girl had gone through the last moments of her life. Tried not to imagine if this had been Tess or one of her friends.

Pushing aside her emotions, she studied the narrow passageway, trying to see it through the eyes of the victim. Windows lined the brick walls. Trash bags and piles of empty boxes lay on the ground next to the overflowing Dumpster. There had been a fight with someone. A boyfriend? A stranger? Then someone had dumped her body here . . .

She turned around and started back toward Jackson. TV shows concentrated on the value of forensics evidence and high-tech computers, but experience had proven over and over again that it was the door-to-door grind and gathering of evidence that usually paid off with the best results. Which was exactly what they were going to do. Because her job was to ensure that whoever did this didn't get away with a senseless murder.

As with all their cases, they'd end up sifting through piles of evidence, most of which had nothing to do with the case. But all they needed was one lead. One tiny clue that would point them in the direction of the killer.

Jackson caught up with her halfway down the alley. "As soon as you're done with the body, I'll bag her and take her back to the morgue."

"Promise you'll call me as soon as you're done with the autopsy."

"Of course."

She didn't want to be there. Some cases hit too close to home.

"Hey, are you going to be okay?"

"I don't know." She shook her head and started back toward

the Dumpster again. "These are the cases that always get to me. Somebody's baby, lying in an alley. Just like the last one."

"Avery."

She glanced back at him and let his sympathetic gaze wash over her.

"This isn't your fault."

Avery stopped midstride. "What if these cases are related? If I'd found the murderer of the last victim, this girl might not be lying in the back of some alley."

"Maybe, but you don't know that."

"Sometimes I can't help but wonder if I'm really cut out for this. I want to make the world a safer place, but the evil around us never stops. What did she do to deserve being murdered? What did my other Jane Doe do?"

"That's what you have to figure out." Jackson's hand brushed the back of her arm. "The reason you do this is because you have this uncanny ability to look inside a person and see why they do what they do. You look at the root cause and motivation behind the crime. In the end, you win more than you lose—and make things safer for Tess and all the other young girls out there."

"What about the next girl he murders?"

"We don't know yet if this is the work of a serial killer."

"But what if it is? What if I can't save his next victim?" The guilt still refused to dissipate, but Jackson didn't deserve to see this side of her. "I'm sorry. It was a long weekend and my mother . . ."

She missed her mother. The strong, supportive woman she used to be. Instead, they'd argued again this morning over the details of Daddy's retirement party. Lately Mama would argue with a fence post if there were no one around.

"You have no reason to be sorry." Jackson's comment pulled her from her thoughts. "I know things have been extra hard for you lately. Any new leads on your brother's case?"

They walked a few silent paces. Michael's unsolved murder had left all of them searching for answers.

"I found a discrepancy in the witness list." For months there had been nothing but dead ends. She didn't expect this latest lead to turn into anything, but like every other piece of information, it was worth following up on. She'd learned firsthand that seeing death through the eyes of a homicide detective was nothing compared to experiencing it through the eyes of the victim's family. Which was one reason she wanted to stop someone else from experiencing the unending grief she still wrestled with.

"Maybe it will turn out to be what you've been looking for."

"I hope so."

"What I said about this case is true, Avery. None of this is your fault—"

"Maybe not." Avery turned back to face him. "But we've got to find out who did this before he strikes again."

Acknowledgments

Every book takes a village to bring a story into the hands of a reader. Nikki's journey has been one of those stories of my heart—as well as being incredibly fun to write—and I'm grateful to everyone who has helped me tell her story.

A huge thanks to my incredible team at Revell who has made Nikki's stories possible. To my agent, Joyce Hart, who found Nikki's story a home and has never stopped encouraging me. For Ellen Tarver's brainstorming edits, and Janet's police expertise. Thank you!

And my family, who continues to give me time to spin yet another adventure. I'm forever grateful.

Lisa Harris is a bestselling author, Christy Award finalist for *Blood Ransom* and *Vendetta*, Christy Award winner for *Dangerous Passage*, and the winner of the Best Inspirational Suspense Novel for 2011 (*Blood Covenant*) and 2015 (*Vendetta*) from Romantic Times. She has written over thirty novels and novella collections. Along with her husband, she and her three children have spent over thirteen years living as missionaries in Africa, where she homeschools and runs a nonprofit organization that works alongside their church-planting ministry. The ECHO Project works in southern Africa promoting Education, Compassion, Health, and Opportunity and is a way for her to "speak up for those who cannot speak for themselves . . . the poor and helpless, and see that they get justice" (Prov. 31:8–9).

When she's not working, she loves hanging out with her family, cooking different ethnic dishes, photography, and heading into the African bush on safari. For more information about her books and life in Africa, visit her website at www.lisaharris writes.com or her blog at http://myblogintheheartofafrica .blogspot.com. For more information about The ECHO Project, please visit www.theECHOproject.org.

meet
LISA HARRIS

lisaharriswrites.com

AuthorLisaHarris

@heartofafrica